TULSA TIME

Oak Tree Press

For information, visit website OakTreeBooks.com, or address Oak Tree Press, 915 W. Foothill Blvd, #411, Claremont, CA 91711-3356.

Oak Tree Press Books may be purchased for educational, business or sales promotional use. Contact Publisher for quantity discounts.

This book is intended for entertainment purposes only, and all the characters and situations are purely the invention of the author. Any similarity to real persons, living or dead, is purely coincidental.

First Edition   10 9 8 7 6 5 4 3 2 1

Cover Design by Yvet ~ Cover Art by Carol Cross

Author Photograph by Deanna Dikeman

The Library of Congress Cataloging In Publication Data

Albright, Letha, 1952—
Tulsa Time / Letha Albright. — 1st ed.
p cm.
ISBN 1-892343-12-6 (alk. Paper)
I.   Women journalists—Fiction. I. Oklahoma—Fiction. I. Title

PS3551.L286 T85 2000
813'.6—dc21   00-040670

To Ken,
who knows all about loyalty
and has been teaching me for more than 25 years.

ACKNOWLEDGEMENTS

They say the life of a writer is solitary, but no book is created by one person. I'd like to thank the following people:

My front-line editors Kevin Fansler and Sandy Watts.

Micah Gilbert, my favorite singer-songwriter, for showing me the spiritual side of musicians and for inspiring me with his music.

Oklahoma musicians George Barton and Mark Sweeney for their insider view of the music industry.

The public information officer at the Tulsa County Jail, for his thorough and illuminating tour.

Susan Witt, who read my manuscript for errors regarding Tulsa. If any remain, they're my fault entirely.

Publisher Billie Johnson, who read and believed.

AUTHOR'S NOTES

The Tulsa County Jail is no longer on the top floors of the county courthouse, and it's not under the control of the Sheriff's Department. Since mid-1999, it has been at First Street and Elgin Avenue and is administered by a private company.

The Middle Path Café, Tulsa's premier health-food restaurant, has been closed for several years, but I still lovingly remember the Hot Toddy Bread.

Download Charley Pack's music, view the medical examiner's report and read more about the events behind the crime at...

www.letha-albright.com

TULSA TIME

Judy: Enjoy this tale of Oklahoma lies and murder.

BY LETHA ALBRIGHT

Letha Albright

Oak Tree Press
Claremont CA

ONE

What some people do for fun.

I huddled against a February wind in a barren break of trees that edged a field outside Vinita, Oklahoma. The uniformed deputy to my right hauled back a lunging German shepherd with one hand and in his other clutched a pump action Remington 870 shotgun.

To my left, Cherokee County deputy sheriff Bobby Martinez wore a stoic look. He was bundled in an army-surplus parka and pac boots, and frost edged his bristly black mustache. He stood his shotgun against a spindly locust tree and beat his gloved hands together to restore circulation.

I held a reporter's notebook and an auto-focus Nikon. At least I think I did. Women are supposed to have an extra layer of insulating fat, but mine wasn't doing its job. My toes registered a deep ache, and my fingers were numb through the Polartec gloves.

"Martinez. I'm dying here."

"Shut up, Powers," he said, without looking at me.

The deputies' and my eyes were trained on the abandoned homestead in the center of the field. One corner of the roof had caved in, and the weathered gray walls of the small house sagged. The blinded sockets of broken windows ushered the arctic wind inside. Two more deputies pressed against the side of the house and crept toward the corner.

In the trees on the far side of the field, the pale winter sun glinted off a rifle barrel, and in the dim shadows more deputies moved into position. The Craig County sheriff, who was directing the operation, stood in the shelter of the open door of his Ford Explorer and motioned to one of the men crouched beside the house. His arms jerked with impatience.

An older model ambulance was parked alongside the sheriff's vehicle. It was running, and a white column of smoke rose behind it. The shapes of two people filled the front seat. They were from the forensic psychology unit at Eastern State Hospital in Vinita, which is a kind way to say "prison for the criminally insane."

Signs warn motorists along the Will Rogers Turnpike outside Vinita, "Caution: hitchhikers may be escaped inmates." The red brick buildings of the mental hospital aren't visible from the four-lane, but the warnings add an air of menace to the quiet countryside.

The facility had reported two men missing after the midnight ward check 16 hours earlier. They were thought to be holed up inside the abandoned house — unarmed but dangerous.

The escapees represented both ends of the spectrum, from petty thief to psychotic murderer. The petty thief, Frank Darman, 23, from Big Cabin, had been hospitalized for evaluation of competency to stand trial for a liquor store robbery. The arresting officer had found him a block from the store moments after the robbery, clutching a fifth of Johnny Walker Black label, now half-empty, and shouting incoherent threats outside a Southern Baptist church.

Tommy Hoffing, 47, from Welling, was a darker story. He illuminated the blackness of our deepest being, the hate and rage that we avoid examining in ourselves but which fascinates us when it appears in others. A nonthreatening trip into our own hearts of darkness. Because of Tommy Hoffing, most of the Craig County Sheriff's Department and various other law enforcement officers, including the stoic Martinez, had converged on this spot to form an impenetrable barrier.

"Did he really cut up those people?" I asked Martinez.

The man with the German shepherd growled, or maybe it was the dog that growled.

"Shut up," Martinez told me again. But he couldn't resist talking about Cherokee County's most brutal murder — even though the events had occurred eight years earlier.

"For one thing," he said, "he carved symbols on their bodies, satanic symbols. He didn't cut them into pieces." He leaned down and picked up his shotgun, as though the thought of the crime made him feel the need for its protective heft.

"Is that why Hoffing's called Oklahoma's Charles Manson?"

Martinez snorted. "You reporters are all alike. You want blood and guts. Well, here's some tabloid for you. He dipped his fingers in the victims' blood and wrote the word 'Pig' on the walls of their laundry room. That's where he did'em, you know."

That was a little too graphic even for the hardened reporter Martinez thought me to be. I turned away and watched the two deputies next to the house. They stopped at the corner and paused as though to gather themselves for the final assault.

My thoughts returned to the man who might be inside. Tommy Hoffing had been found guilty but mentally ill in the murder and robbery of the Tahlequah couple. Although the case had occurred a year before I moved to the northeastern Oklahoma town, I was familiar with the details. After all, it was one of the state's most infamous crimes.

James and Sylvia Blackinwater lived in a seven-bedroom, seven-bath home built in the style of Frank Lloyd Wright. The dramatic wood-and-stone mansion perched on a bluff above Lake Tenkiller, and an underground river emerged next to a wall of glass before cascading over artfully placed stones. The Blackinwater home was a mansion by any standards, but it stood out like a rose in clover among the small and drab homes of Cherokee County. Despite its remote location, it drew a steady stream of onlookers and architectural buffs.

The remote location was, in retrospect, not a wise choice given Mr. Blackinwater's profession. He was a lawyer who defended drug dealers, and it was rumored that not all his fees could be deposited in a bank.

Eight years ago, the couple returned home unexpectedly early on a Saturday night and interrupted a robbery in progress. Forensics later established that Tommy Hoffing, a handyman who occasionally worked for the couple, herded them into the laundry room and murdered them with a weapon determined to be a sledgehammer.

Tommy Hoffing stuffed packets of bills into a gym bag, drove his 1974 Chevy pickup to Combs Bridge a dozen miles up the Illinois River and opened the bag above the fast water. Only a few water-soaked bills were recovered. In the days that followed, Tommy Hoffing was questioned repeatedly by the police, but his words were as senseless and chaotic as his crime.

Of such tragedy ballads are written and treasure buffs thrill to.

The court decreed that Tommy Hoffing would serve the initial part of his sentence in a psychiatric facility until he was sane enough to serve a life prison sentence. Eight years later, he was still in the hospital. Until now.

I felt the man with the dog eyeing me, and I turned to meet his gaze. He looked away contemptuously, as though to say I had no business there.

I could have pulled out my press card and argued First Amendment rights, but my blue lips didn't want to form around the words. Besides, he may have had a point. A small point. Vinita was outside the readership of the Tahlequah Daily Tribune. The small town of Tahlequah, population 10,398 by last count, lay nearly 60 miles south in the claustrophobic hills and hollows of Cherokee County. But Tommy Hoffing was one of ours, born and bred just outside Tahlequah. We owed our readers an eyewitness report.

Furthermore, Martinez, the Cherokee County deputy who had invited himself along and then asked me to accompany him, hoped to be the next county sheriff. A photo and story about his role in the recapture of a notorious killer would be valuable publicity.

The two deputies rounded the end of the house and dropped to their knees to traverse the windowed side. I lost sight of them briefly as they passed between the house and a rusty propane tank. They emerged on the other side, scrambling crab-like along the wall. One stayed in position by the window hole while the other crept forward to the front porch.

The pale sun faded behind a bank of clouds in the west, too bleak to tint their gray edges. The temperature dropped with the sun, and the wind blew steady across the flat land.

The officer on the porch made his move. He kicked in the front door and rushed through it, joined by another officer who appeared from the other side of the house.

We waited in deafening silence. My ears strained for the sound of a struggle, but I couldn't hear anything. The dog beside me pricked his ears forward and whined.

Minutes later, two men emerged with a small, sick-looking man pressed between them. The man had to be Darman. From the newspaper accounts I had read, Tommy Hoffing was tall and husky.

"Shit," said the man with the German shepherd. He and the dog headed for the shelter of a vehicle.

The two deputies hustled Darman across the field, tramping down the skeletal stalks of last fall's snakeweed and goldenrod. Martinez and I scrambled behind, trying to catch up before Darman was whisked beyond camera range.

No one was inclined to linger in the bitter wind. Martinez elbowed his way to the ambulance door; I lifted the Nikon with hands made clumsy by the cold and snapped three frames of film before Darman was bundled inside. Darman was silent until the doors began to close on him. Then his blank face seemed to awaken and he looked at me and the camera.

"Raskolnikov must die," he said.

The ambulance attendants acted like he hadn't spoken, and the sheriff, pushing me aside, ignored him also.

Darman's eyes locked with mine. His were a watery, murky brown, opaque and empty.

Again he said, "Raskolnikov must die."

The doors slammed shut.

TWO

The story was a hit with the 7,000-plus readers of the Tahlequah Daily Tribune. The Raskolnikov quote confirmed what most of them already thought: Mentally ill people were nuts. A literature professor from Northeastern State University called to let us know that Raskolnikov was the tormented character in Dostoevsky's *Crime and Punishment*. I resisted the urge to tell him that I wasn't just an ignorant country reporter: I hold an English degree from the University of Colorado.

However, the real question on the mind of Cherokee County readers was: Where's Tommy Hoffing? And: Will he kill again?

In a community where people are lax about locking their doors, there was a sudden run on dead bolts and ammunition at True Value and Wal-Mart. The sheriff's office was swamped with calls from people whose dogs barked at suspicious noises in their outbuildings.

Tommy Hoffing was a celebrity all over again.

"We've got to make hay out of this while the sun is shining," said Hank Daniels, my editor.

I looked out the office window. "Or snow people while the snow is falling."

He jumped out of his chair and pressed his face to the window. "Snow! We're going to be busier than a one-legged man in a butt-kicking contest."

"You've been eating breakfast at The Shack with the good old boys, haven't you?"

He gave me a sour look, and his woolly eyebrows humped up and down like stampeding bison. "Are you going to follow the sheriff and his deputies around and catch the crumbs that fall from their table, or are you going to act like a reporter and show some initiative?"

"If this is your idea of a pep talk, it sucks," I said. "I froze my butt off yesterday showing initiative." I held out my hands for proof. "See this white spot on my pinkie? I think it's frostbite. I may have to file for workers' comp."

Hank's lips pursed. "I need a fresh story on Tommy Hoffing's escape before you go home. I'll take the snow detail."

I decided later that I had the better deal. I watched the flakes fall in fat, lazy spirals. They formed a gauzy curtain between the newspaper office and the concrete walls of the Cherokee County courthouse across the street.

A snow that promises big things — traffic snarls, material for snowball fights, lazy days in front of the wood stove — is exciting news in this part of the country. It's rare. It's significant. Qualities Tahlequah usually lacks.

Tahlequah has two things going for it: It's the end of the Trail of Tears, the deadly emigration the U.S. government forced on the Cherokees in 1838; and it's the trailhead for the Illinois River, one of Oklahoma's few raftable waterways. When the river turns cold and the Cherokees close down Tsa-La-Gi ampitheater, where they reenact their long march, Tahlequah is just another small midwestern town.

Our only other claim to fame was the brief time when David Letterman called Tahlequah his home office, swelling the city council's pride and making us think we weren't such small frogs in a big pond after all.

Small frogs in a big, snowy pond. It was time to burrow in and sit it out. But first I owed Hank a story.

Aside from the worsening weather, I had no reason to hurry home. My housemate and long-time love, musician Charley Pack, was in Tulsa recording tracks for his band's CD, and he probably wouldn't be home before midnight.

I had declined — as he knew I would — his invitation to join him. These days I seldom followed Charley and Powers That Be to their gigs and recording sessions. I had grown tired of the knowing appraisal of over-muscled bar bouncers when I told them I was with the band. The older I got, the less the term "Charley Pack's old lady" amused me.

Charley said he understood. Charley, with his indigo eyes and his thinning hair and his compact body strong and wiry like a circus acrobat, said that about everything. Just once, I'd like to see his self-assurance evaporate. To see his Buddha-like serenity crumble. Do I sound bitter? I have no right.

I live my own life. Viv Powers, small-town newspaper reporter. A life that includes following law officers to frozen fields while they recapture a cold and frightened escapee from a mental hospital. Taking pictures of deputies as they grin over their prize like hunters over a kill.

But where was the trophy buck?

A few phone calls confirmed that there was nothing new on Tommy Hoffing. He had slid like smoke into a cloudy sky, and none of the reported sightings had panned out.

His wife still lived along the Illinois River in the home they had shared at the time of the killings. She claimed she hadn't heard from him. That information came from a source at the sheriff's office. If Roz Hoffing had a phone, it wasn't listed. The same source speculated that Tommy had left northeast Oklahoma, maybe even the state. The other favored theory, he said, was that Tommy had frozen to death and his body would be found by some farmer come spring.

I filed the story, locked the door of the empty newsroom and headed home while it was still possible to get there. Charley's and my house lay more than a dozen miles of winding highway north of Tahlequah. On a day like this, I didn't want to be on that road after dark.

The snow fell thick and fast, like powdered sugar on the trees and houses, like Crisco on the highway.

Snow is enough of a rarity in Cherokee County that it is cause for panic. Few know how to drive on it, and the traffic on north Muskogee foundered as though the pavement had turned to quicksand. A red sports car skidded into a ditch and the delivery truck in front of me spun to face the other way. My Isuzu Trooper was in four-wheel drive, but I barely managed to avoid a head-on with the truck.

I passed the red brick buildings of the deserted Northeastern State University campus and stopped at Hilltop Grocery to pick up some necessities, but the shelves were already stripped bare by shoppers who acted like the snowfall was their last chance to stock up on Cherokee County's four food groups: caffeine, nicotine, lard and sugar. For many of us, add a fifth: alcohol. I settled for crackers, peanut butter and a six-pack of beer.

The Ozark hills that run like rugged wrinkles across this part of the state are gray and grim in February. The snow softened their abrupt contours and made them luminous as though painted with tiny dots of light.

I guided the Trooper down the steep slope of Long John Hill, across the icy rails of the Spring Creek bridge — nearly home now — and hoped Charley wasn't on the highway. And that even the killer Tommy Hoffing had found shelter from the storm.

Six hours later, my eyes drooped shut, and the book I had been reading slid from my lap and slapped the floor. Mack the gray cat sprang from a lazy curl next to the woodstove and glared at me.

"Sorry," I said. "Faulkner can be pretty heavy." I was reading James M. Cain, but it's no sin to lie to cats.

Mack licked his paw and studied it as though he found something interesting there.

The small room was warm and snug; the space flowed smoothly from office to living area to dining room to kitchen. One room, that's all Charley and I needed, with stairs leading to a sleeping loft.

It pleased me, this house. I liked the exposed red oak beams that lent it solidity. I liked the art that covered the walls: baskets and weavings and paintings, all created by the hands of friends more artistic than I. I liked Charley's guitars and other musical instruments grouped in a corner, reminders of late night jam sessions. I liked the big windows that overlooked Spring Creek, and I liked the rough-hewn furniture and the handsome Vermont Castings woodstove that seemed to draw the room close around it.

Speaking of which, it was time to feed the fire. And then once again try to get a message to Charley. All I wanted to tell him was stay in Tulsa. Don't risk the slippery highways just to spend the night at home. The recording studio where he was working was a soundproof room at the back of High Spirits, the bar owned by Gil Martin and Tapply, Charley's producers. I called the bar's number since there was no phone in the studio. No answer. It probably was closed because of the weather.

I stepped out on the porch to gather an armload of stove wood for the night. The snow tempered the cold, like an airy cotton blanket floating over the earth. I wanted to pull on my boots and walk through the deepening drifts, but first I would call Tulsa once more.

This time I would call Gil Martin's house. Charley sometimes spent the night there when it wasn't practical to drive the 80 miles home from Tulsa. Gil's wife, Mica, would probably be at home or Iris, her daughter.

Many years ago, Charley and Mica had been married, Mica for the second time. Charley's new stepdaughter, Iris, had been a toddler; now she was 13. The divorce had been amicable, and now Mica's husband was Charley's producer. Small world, we often say, not really believing it despite the onslaught of evidence.

My arms were laden with three chunks of seasoned white oak when headlights stabbed through the falling snow. Even from a distance I recognized the wide-apart lights of Charley's Chevy van. I took a deep breath, not realizing until then how worried I had been.

I dropped the wood on the porch and walked out in the snow, coatless and in tennis shoes, to meet him.

But it wasn't Charley who climbed out of the driver's seat.

Instead, Allan Jakes, road manager for Charley and Powers That Be, stretched his long legs to the ground and stood unsteadily in the dim light of the dash. The snow settled on his frizzy red hair like flecks of dandruff, and fatigue glazed his eyes.

Two more weary figures followed him out of the van: Jason Calico, Charley's just-out-of-high-school bass player, and Heather Rusk, Jason's girlfriend, who hugged a two-liter bottle of Coke.

"Where's Charley?" I said in the silence.

"I thought we weren't going to make it." Allan was already walking toward the warm yellow windows.

"Where's Charley?" I said again, louder this time.

Heather stopped and looked at me, her young eyes wide with excitement. "He's been arrested for murder."

THREE

The sun rested on top of the snow-crested oaks by the time the Trooper fought through the drifts to the state highway. The glare burned my eyes. The snowplows hadn't made it to this stretch of Highway 82. Other vehicles had passed this way since the snow ended; their tires had left icy trails, but for now we had the highway to ourselves. Our progress was slow. I drove in silence, and in the passenger seat, Allan Jakes closed his eyes and pretended to sleep. His red hair formed a halo around his head.

My night had been virtually sleepless after Heather's announcement; the news translated into a jangle of nightmares and nerves. I had wanted to set out immediately for Tulsa, but Allan convinced me that nothing could be done until morning.

Morning finally came, and I left Jason and Heather in charge of Mack and the house — with the recording session on hold, they had nowhere else to go anyway — and Allan and I charged off in the snow like the cavalry to the rescue.

A man was dead. Gil Martin was dead, one of Charley's producers and his ex-wife's husband. Charley had been seen leaving the backstage dressing room at High Spirits where the body was discovered soon after. Allan told me patiently and repeatedly that he didn't know what motive Charley would have to murder Gil. The answers to my questions would have to wait.

West of Wagoner, the hills flattened into prairie and the road straightened, and snowplows threw up powdery plumes. I matched the pace of the yellow plow in front of me and watched the sun glitter through the ice crystals.

I wanted to be home with Charley, rolling down the hill in the snow below our house until we were dizzy and breathless. We used to do that in Colorado, in the mountains above Boulder where we first met. His cheeks had reddened in the cold like they were rubbed with rouge and his eyes glowed with life. Not all our years together were tinged with nostalgia or pleasure, but Charley would never commit murder, I told myself.

"Tell me again," I ordered Allan.

He stirred beside me. "Charley and Gil got in a pushing match yesterday afternoon."

Allan's and my eyes met briefly, and he read the disbelief in my face.

"I know it sounds weird," he said, "but I saw it happen. I didn't tell the police, but someone did, because they asked me about it."

"What happened? From the beginning." My mouth felt dry. I had asked Allan the same questions the night before, but the same sense of unreality that held me now had prevented me from listening closely to his answers.

"Yesterday afternoon, after it started snowing, some of us were at the studio. All the band was supposed to be there, along with Gil and Tapply and me to listen to the tracks we had been working on. Mica and Iris even came by." He made a dismissive gesture. "Not everyone was there on time, so we were hanging out. Charley and Gil were talking about something at the soundboard, and the next thing I knew they were pushing each other. I've never seen a look like that on Charley's face."

I forgot the roads were slick and passed the snowplow. The Trooper skidded crazily and I managed to fight it back onto the right side of the road.

"Jesus!" Allan said. "Can we talk about this later?"

I breathed deeply. "What happened then?"

Allan fastened his seat belt. "Tapply got in their faces and pushed them apart. Gil stomped out of the room, and as far as I know, he wasn't seen again. Alive."

"Did you hear what Charley and Gil were talking about?"

He rubbed his gloved hands together. "I was too far away."

Despite Charley's relationship with Gil Martin, I knew little about him. He was a Cherokee County native, a boy from the wrong side of town, who had been smart enough to get a scholarship to Northeastern State University in Tahlequah. He had followed his business schemes to

Tulsa by the time I met him. Charley and Powers That Be had been playing at least once a month at Gil and Tapply's bar for about a year now.

Gil and Charley's friendship was quintessential Tahlequah. Dating from the time that their lives had intersected at Northeastern, they had been friends. Tapply and Allan also had been a part of those days. I remembered hearing that the four of them once had a band. Only Charley still played; the others had fallen into the types of jobs that draw music-lovers with no special musical talent.

When I first met Gil, he had just married Charley's ex-wife. That practically made him family. However, I couldn't like him. The few times I had seen him, he reeked of false enthusiasm and hyperbole. Words tumbled out of his mouth like a hyperactive child's somersaults. Look at me!

I glanced at Allan. "You go back, don't you. The four of you."

Allan knew what I meant. "We formed our own fraternity," he said, staring at the snow through the window. "Rock climbing and rock music — that's what brought us together. We lived in a dump at the edge of town that we called the Farmhouse. It was a place to hang out, get high, make music, have sex — everything a college boy could wish for."

They weren't really boys at that point, I silently contradicted him. I wasn't sure about Gil, Tapply and Allan's ages, but Charley had been a nontraditional student, not even beginning his studies until he was in his mid-20s.

"What happened?"

He looked at me obliquely. "You don't know the story? Charley wasn't around long. He left to play music in Boulder. Not long after, I went to Nashville, thinking I'd break into the big time. Gil and Tapply quit school and opened High Spirits."

"One flew east, one flew west, one flew over the cuckoo's nest."

"Two," he said. "Two flew over the cuckoo's nest."

Tulsa's handful of downtown skyscrapers glowed in the snow; the streets were practically empty of traffic. Along the Broken Arrow Expressway, where cheap motels and fast food joints lined the frontage road, an American flag as big as a bedsheet whipped in the breeze.

With the usual whimsy of February in Oklahoma, winter decided it had sufficiently flayed the thin-skinned inhabitants. Where the sun struck the pavement, the crust of snow left by the snowplows began to melt.

The Trooper splashed through a pool of gray slush onto Riverside Drive along the Arkansas River waterfront.

"I thought we were going to see Charley," Allan said.

"First I have to see where it happened." None of it made any sense;

the world I knew was upside-down, so I was applying my own cockeyed rules of order. Not that it helped.

Allan looked at me skeptically and stuck a cigarette in his mouth. It bobbed in his mouth, unlit, until the 11th Street Bridge rose in the distance, and I pulled into the empty parking lot beside the High Spirits bar. The sprawling, brown brick building looked more like an abandoned warehouse than the movie theater it had once been. A plow had been by, and the parking lot was scraped clean, gravel-crusted snow piled at its edges.

Allan jumped out and lit the cigarette. He drew deeply before turning to me and saying. "It's Charley's best work. The new CD. It'll be a shame if he's not able to promote it."

"I'm more concerned about Charley than his music."

"You know what I meant."

I turned away. "Long night." It was as close to an apology as I could manage.

I led the way to the delivery door, which was locked. Our knocking didn't rouse anyone, but I could hear a thumping bass beat from somewhere inside the building.

"The studio," Allan said.

The studio was located at the back of the bar, and its door was on the far side. We rounded the back of the building and found a silver MG parked beside the studio door.

"Good," Allan said. "Tapply's here. He'll know what's going on."

I had never heard Tapply called anything but Tapply. I asked Charley once if he had a first name, and he just shrugged. I had met Tapply the previous fall when he and Gil Martin threw a party for Charley and Powers That Be. Unlike Gil, who paraded his insecurity, Tapply radiated self-confidence.

Our first meeting stood out in my memory. Charley and I had shown up early for the party at Tapply's request. The October day was warm, and the front door of his modern stone and redwood house stood open, so Charley yelled Tapply's name and we walked in.

Tapply hung from one hand high on a wall of stone in his vaulted living room. The muscles on his shirtless back rippled with tension. When he saw us, he smiled widely, looking like a Patagonia model with his shock of dark hair and gleaming white teeth. He casually released his hold and allowed the rope, anchored from the ceiling, to save him from a 16-foot fall.

After he belayed himself to the floor, he slapped Charley on the back and offered me the rope. "I hear you climb," he said. The statement held a challenge, far from the usual gracious host's offer of a drink.

"Left my Sportivas home," I said. Whatever his game was, I didn't feel like playing.

He shrugged, and the look that flashed across his face was little more than a shadow.

I followed tracks in the snow to the studio door. It wasn't locked. "So. Tapply the Wonder Boy," I said.

The music, suddenly loud, jolted me. It was Charley's voice. "Gotta leave the city. Got to get away," he sang. I started running down the hall and just as suddenly stopped. The song was Canned Heat's "Going Up the Country." Charley was covering it on the new CD, and the voice was recorded. Charley wasn't here. He was in jail.

Through the window of the studio door, I saw Tapply sitting at the controls of the soundboard. His mouth was grim, and he looked deep in thought as the sound of the guitars and wailing harmonica swelled around him.

I figured he was thinking about the money he would lose if Charley wasn't able to finish the recording. I didn't know how much cash Tapply and Gil had put up, but I knew it was more than I had ever seen at one time.

The music business is as chancy as trying your luck at a Las Vegas casino — and the cards are stacked in favor of the producer, not the artist. Charley's deal was the typical tradeoff musicians make in order to be recorded. He wrote the songs, then signed the rights over to the publishing company, in this case Gil and Tapply. In return, they and Charley would split the mechanical royalty, or the fee payable to the copyright holder for each song recorded. In addition, Charley and the Powers that Be would earn an artist royalty for performing each song.

Before any royalties were paid, Gil and Tapply would take off the standard 25 percent fee for packaging deductions. The best the band could hope to earn was a net royalty of 6 to 7 percent, which would be used to pay back the advance.

On the other hand, successful songs can be more valuable than gemstones. A lawyer friend told me about a sound engineer who sued ZZ Top, claiming the band stole his song "Thug" and recorded it on the Eliminator album. The lawyer's percentage of the settlement paid for his house. It was a nice house.

However, most records don't earn out their advance. And most musicians make a living by performing, not by selling records.

Tapply made an abrupt movement at the soundboard, and the studio was suddenly silent.

I broke the silence by walking through the door.

He stared at me, and I imagined what he saw: a tall, tough, weathered woman. Not beautiful and not plain, not young but not yet old, not a genius but smart-looking enough to scare off most men. It was obvious that he didn't have a clue who I was. Not until Allan appeared behind me.

Recognition lit his eyes then, and he walked toward me with outstretched hands. "Viv Powers," he said. "Muse of the Powers That Be."

"What happened here last night?"

His hands squeezed mine and then let go. "It's all a stupid mistake," he said. "Gil could be a little shit, but Charley wouldn't kill him. He wasn't worth killing."

Little shit? "He was your partner, for chrissakes," I said.

He looked at me sharply. "And I'm going to miss the guy. We go back. But he must have done something to get himself killed, and now with Charley in jail, everything is screwed up."

Tapply was more than a pretty face; there was veiled intelligence in his eyes. And something more — a ruthless drive to make things happen. That we were on the same side gave me a small surge of hope.

The studio, like most I had seen, was an electronic abattoir: electric cords were strewn across the floor like the disemboweled remains of plastic animals, a mutilated drum head curled in one corner. Spatters of red, yellow and blue paint defaced a wall.

I looked at Tapply and repeated my question. "What happened?"

"Let's go in the bar and get a beer," he said.

Allan and I followed Tapply through a narrow corridor, dimly lit and decorated with the graffiti of bored musicians who had waited here to go on stage. Near the stage, a metal door was padlocked. The door led to what they called the Green Room, a kind of party room/lounge for bands. Gil Martin's body had been found in there. The padlock's cheap metal was still bright as though it were freshly installed. I paused by the door and tried to remember how the room had looked the one time I had been inside.

The space was small and windowless, thick with smoke in my memory. Shabby furniture lined the walls: a stained and torn sofa; a half dozen rickety, ladder-back chairs; a worn desk, names and obscenities carved in its wooden top; tattered copies of *Billboard*, *Spin*, *Guitar World*; an apartment-size refrigerator with a photo of John Lennon taped to it. Someone had turned the photo into a wanted poster.

The glamour of the road, Charley liked to say.

Allan and Tapply had disappeared through the door leading to the bar. I turned away from the locked room and followed them.

When we were seated at a table with glasses of foamy Budweiser, Tapply returned to the subject that had brought us together.

"Two things to do right away," Tapply said. "We've got to get Charley a lawyer and arrange bail." He wiped the foam from his lips with the back of his hand.

"Charley has a lawyer," I said. "The guy was the Cherokee County DA before he went into private practice. Gary Hanson."

"Call him."

I gave Tapply a look. "I took care of that this morning before I left Tahlequah. Left a message on his machine. Gave him this number."

I had left a message for Hank, too. I didn't tell him why I was taking the day off from the newspaper, just that it was an emergency.

I would have made a third phone call. This one to my sister, Maggie Powers. But she was somewhere in the Caribbean, escaping winter and cavorting on a sandy beach with her latest love, Lonnie Tritt, a podiatrist from Muskogee. Maggie owed me some comfort and concern, but she was out of reach.

Tapply heard the edge in my voice. "I didn't mean to imply that you aren't taking care of things. I'm just worried. That's all."

"Hanson's office hasn't called?"

"Not since I've been here."

"I'll try to reach him again before I go to the jail. But first, tell me what happened yesterday. In detail."

"She's a reporter," Allan said, speaking for the first time. He blushed, as though he realized he should have remained part of the woodwork.

"Ah, a reporter. I had forgotten." Sudden interest gleamed in Tapply's eyes. "You dig up the facts and put them in order."

"Charley's not a violent man."

Tapply's hazel eyes studied the daylight walls of the bar, as though he noticed their dinginess for the first time. The bar's theater origins were evident. The velvet swags that hung over the arched stage were shabby and faded, and the high ceiling sheltered a balcony in the back and box seats along the sides. The bar was located under the balcony. Every surface, except for the rows of gleaming bottles behind the bar, seemed smoke-stained and tarnished.

Tapply said as if to no one, "Each of us is unknowable, even to himself."

"How was Gil murdered?" I asked.

"He was bludgeoned," Tapply said.

Beside me, I heard Allan suck in his breath. He buried his face in his hands.

"Perhaps with a chunk of granite that band from Seattle left in the Green Room months ago," Tapply continued. "The police took it with them."

Tapply confirmed what Allan had already told me. He broke up a fight between Charley and Gil. He didn't know what they were fighting about.

"I don't think it had anything to do with the music or our CD deal," Tapply said, "or Charley would have been talking to me, too."

Gil disappeared, Tapply continued. There was a lot of confusion as people came and went. Allan Jakes, going to the Green Room refrigerator in search of leftover pizza, discovered Gil's body at about 6 p.m.

I turned to Allan. "Why didn't you tell me you were the one who found him?"

His freckled face flushed again. "I didn't want to talk about it."

"Was it you who saw Charley leave the room?"

Charley and I used to joke that Allan Jakes was like the Irish setter Charley had when we first met, with his red hair and his eager, clumsy body and liquid eyes that telegraphed every passing emotion. Mostly they held an injured look. Like now.

"What did Charley tell the police?" I asked.

"Nothing. He wasn't talking."

I felt a sickness in the pit of my stomach. Imagined my lover, manacled and caged like an animal. How could he not be shouting his innocence?

FOUR

The Tulsa County Courthouse, nine ugly stories of alternating stripes of red brick and blank windows, anchored the south side of a concrete plaza on Denver Avenue. Two other buildings completed the complex: the city building and the central library. The cumulative effect was that of a communist-built apartment block in an eastern European industrial city.

A gaggle of smokers blocked the double glass doors that led into the courthouse. A young Navaho woman came through the doors as I approached. Her eyes were glassy and distracted, and she carried a small boy under one arm as though he were a bag of groceries; his black hair was spiked like porcupine needles.

Inside, I emptied my pockets to pass through a metal detector. The courthouse lobby was a vault of cold, slick marble: the walls rosy as sunset, and the floor dark-speckled like a riverbed. A line of well-dressed, cowboy-booted men stood at a shoeshine stand near the elevators. They were laughing — something about a judge's retirement party.

The Tulsa County Sheriff's Department took up the west end of the first floor. The deputy at the sliding glass window dismissed me with a glance after I told him who I was.

"Jail visiting hours are on Saturday," he said. "Unless you're his lawyer or clergy." With a stubby pencil, he filled in a word on the Tulsa paper's crossword puzzle.

"I told you, his lawyer's out of town. I need to tell him so we can make other arrangements."

He didn't even look up. "He has access to a phone at all times. If he wants to talk to you he has to make a collect call."

I swallowed my frustration.

Earlier, before leaving Tapply and Allan at the High Spirits, I had called Gary Hanson's office again. This time I reached his secretary, who told me Gary was in Florida for his father's funeral and wouldn't be back for another week.

"It's an emergency," I had said.

I was told Fay Blackfox was covering for the missing Hanson. So I had called Fay Blackfox's office, but she was in court all day. Her receptionist assured me that everything would be fine.

As if she knew.

I turned my attention back to the deputy. "When's the hearing?"

He blinked in annoyance and pursed his thick lips. "Tomorrow at 2 p.m."

"And it's open to the public." It helped to be a reporter. I knew my access rights.

"Supreme Court says so," he said in a voice that clearly didn't agree with the Supreme Court.

The jail was on the eighth and ninth floors. I went back to the central hallway of the courthouse and took the elevator, but public access ended on the seventh floor. I was alone in the car on the way down. I leaned my head against the cool metal wall of the elevator and felt the electric hum of the cables run through me.

I suddenly felt exhausted. Charley was somewhere in this building, and I couldn't get to him. I needed him to look me in the eyes and tell me it was all a mistake. Tell me everything would be all right.

"For better or for worse," the traditional marriage ceremony says. Charley and I had decided many years ago that we didn't need that ceremony. Our bond didn't require the glue of a priest or minister or justice of the peace.

But now I didn't know how to feel or what to do. As a necessary corollary to our commitment, Charley and I had always held onto our separateness. Both of us strong and complete without the other. This situation called for a new dimension to our relationship, one that might be outside my repertoire.

I was taught two ways to face life. The Saint, as Maggie and I called our mother, said to put it in the hands of a higher power. "Trust ever in Jesus. He will carry you through," were the words of a hymn she sang in the fundamentalist church that she went to every Sunday morning and

Sunday night and Wednesday night.

My father, Randolph Gunter Powers, retired Army sergeant, leaned toward self-reliance. The survival drills The Sergeant prodded my younger sister and me through were relentless and punishing. It may have been his way of showing love, or perhaps he hoped we would crack so he could send us home in disgrace like one of his raw recruits. To this day I don't know his motive.

I graduated from his brutal school the day he and I drove alone into the Appalachians above Helen, Georgia. The autumn day was cold, and a fine mist fell. A steady north wind drove the temperature down as The Sergeant and I bumped along in his pickup. We had the narrow dirt road to ourselves. Deer season hadn't yet begun, and the backpackers had disappeared after the golden days of Indian summer.

Farther and farther up the mountain we followed the road until it came to an end along a high ridge top. The mountains around us were shouldering ghosts in the mist.

We were to drop below the ridge, The Sergeant ordered, he on one side and I on the other, and meet in an hour on a spur of the Appalachian trail. It was pointless to ask why. The Sergeant never explained; it was enough that he said to do it.

I watched him fade into the forest, limping slightly on his bad leg, and then made my way through the rain-blackened trees to our rendezvous point. My boots and wool jacket were soon soggy in the wetness. I waited an hour for The Sergeant to appear before it occurred to me to look for him. Eventually I made it back to the place we had parked and found the pickup was gone. Water filled the indentations left by the tires. The Sergeant had left long before.

I spent the night on the mountain, shivering in my makeshift shelter of damp leaves under a rock overhang. My dinner was bitter hickory nuts whose shells I smashed with rocks. The next day, hurting from hunger and cold, I followed a beacon of smoke to a cabin in the woods, and a bearded, rough-looking man drove me to the highway where I hitched a ride back to the army base. I was fifteen.

I never fully forgave my father. All he said when I walked through the door that day and flew at him, throwing punches, was that when the time came, I would understand. Now it was The Sergeant's lessons that led me. There is no god above that of self-reliance.

Think the unthinkable. What if Charley was convicted? I couldn't be one of those pitiful women who wait faithfully while their lover grows old in jail. Somehow they're diminished, both man and woman. I was more the type to cut my losses and get out while I still had dignity.

It wasn't an admirable trait.

The elevator shuddered to a stop on the first floor of the courthouse, and I stepped out carefully, as though the elevator had transported me through time and the door had opened on the unknown.

I had to make my way through this unfamiliar terrain and find my way home.

FIVE

The phone jerked me out of an unpleasant dream of torture and chains.

My boss's voice was gravel in my ear. "There's been a Tommy spotting," he said, without preamble.

Dawn's feeble light hadn't penetrated the windows, and I fumbled the lamp on beside my bed.

"Where?"

"Pharmacy in Tulsa. He broke in last night and took some drugs."

"How do they know it was him?" I squinted in the pool of golden light until the clock came into focus. Seven a.m.

"Apparently the night watchman he killed had a tale to tell."

"Jesus." I thought a minute. "Was it like the Blackinwater murders? Carved symbols? Words written in blood?"

"Don't know," Hank said. "I do know that he was interrupted. There was a silent alarm. The police showed up shortly after, but they couldn't catch him."

By now I was awake enough to guess what was coming next.

"You want me to go to Tulsa."

"I want a picture of the inside of the pharmacy, interviews with locals, the latest from the police."

From habit I looked at the clock again. "I'll be by to pick up a camera in about an hour."

* * *

The newspaper office lies across from the Cherokee County Courthouse on West Delaware, wedged in the center of a shabby line of shops. Other than Hank Daniels and me, three other people work full-time to put out the five-day-a-week paper: LaRue Bunch, office secretary, classified ad salesperson, proofreader and de facto mother; Dale Moss, head pressman; and Terri Mouse, a reporter whose beat is The Nation and the small communities around Tahlequah.

The Nation, of course, is the Cherokee Nation; ever since the Cherokees were forced across the Trail of Tears from Georgia to Oklahoma, their capital has been Tahlequah. Terri covers the squabbles over water rights, bingo earnings, sovereignty, health care, nepotism and federal entitlements that dominate the Nation's politics. Terri has the instincts of a martyr and the doggedness of a trainspotter. She's not popular at The Nation, but our readers love her.

In addition, the Tahlequah Daily Tribune underpays a slew of part-timers who take care of display ad sales, sports reporting, community calendar and newspaper distribution. A half-time photographer covers sporting events, but it's up to Terri and me to shoot the grip-and-grins, car crashes and ribbon cuttings that make up the bulk of small-town news photography.

I report on crime, the university, and on whatever else Hank assigns.

The AP wire takes care of filling the rest of the paper.

It was a long step down from my days as a reporter for the Boulder Daily Camera — in both influence and pay — but I had chosen to follow Charley here. "Tahlequah is different from any place in the world," he had warned me beforehand. "You love it and you hate it, but it gets under your skin and doesn't let go."

When I first saw the town, I stayed only because Charley was here. It was so small, with a population of less than 12,000, and so poor. Cherokee County, along with neighboring Adair County, with their large populations of Cherokees and other Native Americans, was similar to the Pine Ridge Reservation in South Dakota and the Navaho Reservation in Arizona, impoverished through decades of racism and neglect.

Yet there was something about the place that began to grow on me. It's not an ordinary small midwestern town. Unexpected things happen. On Sparrow Hawk mountain, just to the east of Tahlequah, the Sancta Sophia Seminary joins New Agers with ancient religions; recent guests included nine Tibetan lamas who performed some kind of cleansing ceremony. Cherokee County is home to a talented colony of musicians, artists and writers. The Cherokee language is taught in the public schools.

The town is a resting place for underachieving dreamers and drunks, with a surprising percentage of college graduates. Bar conversations veer from Buckminster Fuller to Leonard Peltier to Nietzsche to Deepak Chopra.

Yes, Tahlequah grew on me, and before I knew it, I was an old-timer of seven years. And if the newspaper was a step down from Boulder's, at least it paid me to do what I was trained to do: nose into other people's lives and write about what I found.

The newspaper office's small gravel parking lot was empty except for the dirty piles of slush that remained from the storm two days earlier.

Hank was hunched over his computer when I swung through the door. His glasses were on top of his head, and he sipped coffee from a styrofoam cup.

"Save any for me?"

"You wouldn't want this recycled battery acid."

Our eyes met and held a little too long.

Shit, I thought.

"You think I don't have any contacts in Tulsa?" Hank said.

I had nothing to say. Just an image of Charley in a gray prison cell. What was he wearing? What did jailers feed a vegetarian? Did they care? But most important, most unimaginable, what was he thinking? Was the cool, unruffled Charley Pack afraid?

"Terri's covering the story. It's coming out today with a file photo. He's one of Tahlequah's up-and-coming." Hank looked at me as though seeking my approval.

"The voice of the people is the voice of God," I said, quoting some long-dead journalist as though the whole mess had nothing to do with me. I shouldered the camera and slammed the door on the way out.

The Fort Gibson Lake bridge, nearly halfway to Tulsa, loomed before I became aware of my surroundings. I had been lost in thought, remembering the chaos of the day before.

After my failed attempt to visit Charley, I had returned home to find Heather and Jason trying to coax the fire in the woodstove to life. The temperature inside the house was only barely warmer than outside. Now that the sun was gone, the cold would creep across the house like the slow revelation of a lover's lie. I treated Jason and Heather to a quick lesson in fire building ("give it some air") and showed them where to find the dry wood.

They were proving to be good houseguests. Earlier in the day, they had driven Charley's van to Tahlequah to replenish the Coca-Cola supply and restock the pantry. "Here's when we knew we had to drive on those icy roads," Heather said. "I looked in the cupboards, and you had crackers and peanut butter and some gross pancake mix. That was it. We would have starved."

"Buckwheat pancakes," I said. "Charley's favorite." Once I had seen him polish off a stack of twelve. He was skinny as a rail and ate like a ranch hand. "Real butter, maple syrup and buckwheat pancakes," Charley had said. "Better than sex."

I think he was daring me to prove him wrong, so I took the challenge.

Dangerous territory. I forced my thoughts away from the memory. "Anyway," I said to Jason and Heather, "I'm glad you didn't starve to death."

Once the fire began crackling, Jason picked out a tune on Charley's Gibson guitar. His long black hair fell across his face. His shoes were off, and a toe peeked through his dingy socks.

Compared to Jason, Heather seemed out of place with her sleek page-boy cut and carefully applied makeup, a high school cheerleader for a losing team who was putting on a happy face for her boys. Heather smiled at Jason while she cooked supper. The faithless Mack rubbed against her legs.

The telephone rang continuously until I finally disconnected it. Charley had many friends and fans. They all wanted to express their shock and to ask how they could help. I had no answers. Earlier, Heather had handed me a sheaf of similar phone messages. I shoved the papers into a bag to deliver to Charley.

There had been no collect calls from the Tulsa County Jail. And when I tried to call the jail, the phone rang and rang.

Only one message had interested me. Fay Blackfox, Charley's erstwhile lawyer, had called. Bring a suit for Charley to wear tomorrow, the message said.

That was last night. A small island of calm between battles.

Now, as I once more followed the road to Tulsa, the dark cloth swung from a hanger in the back of the Trooper. Charley hadn't even owned a suit until his mother died a year earlier.

Its color matched the silhouetted hawks that perched like sentries on electrical poles and atop slender trees along the highway.

The placid water of Fort Gibson Lake reflected the brilliant blue of the sky. Seagulls wheeled above a lone sailboat. The low outlines of Brushy Hill and Bald Knob, barren and gray in their winter coats, framed the east side of the lake. The snow was a memory.

Certainty was a memory. My mind was tired from wrestling with the same questions. Had Charley killed Gil? What had they been fighting about? If Charley was innocent, why wasn't he talking?

Tommy Hoffing though. The thought of Tommy didn't wear out my mind. The concept was simple. An escaped, insane killer. Killing again.

***

The pharmacy was on a street off Greenwood on the north side of downtown. Once known as "The Black Wall Street of America," the Greenwood neighborhood had never completely recovered from a race riot in 1921 that left scores of people dead and 40 city blocks leveled. Despite decades of rebuilding, many of the commercial properties were empty, and in the background sounded the constant clamor of the low-rent neighborhood — the freeway.

The pharmacist was agitated. Her hands stayed busy while she talked, pushing back her springy black hair, smoothing her white smock, twisting and plucking.

"This has been the third break-in in the past 12 months," she said. "Just because our neighborhood doesn't front the country club doesn't mean we're not entitled to police protection. We've installed burglar-proof locks, silent alarm systems and recently, several of the businesses on this block joined to hire a night watchman."

"Derrick Johnson." I had been listening to the radio.

"Poor man," she said. "We expected junkies to be our greatest threat, not an escaped killer."

"What makes the police think it was Tommy Hoffing?" I had already asked the officer in charge of the investigation that same question, but he said the information couldn't be released yet.

The dark eyes of the pharmacist were drawn to a stain on the white tile floor behind the counter where blood had congealed. The area was taped off by yellow crime scene tape, commanding us to stay out. The signs of a life-and-death struggle filled the space. Broken bottles and crushed pills were strewn across the floor as though thrown by an angry child. Papers had been swept from the drawers. Shards of broken glass from a framed diploma lay in a pool of pink liquid. But most chilling was a bloody hand print on the white wall next to the phone. I raised the camera and tried to capture the scene.

My mouth held the iron taste of blood, as though an invisible mist from Derrick Johnson's death remained in the air of the pharmacy.

By the time I finished the camera work, the pharmacist and I were on a first-name basis. The words poured out of her like a spring flood as she described the night's events. "I got here about 4 a.m., after the alarm woke me. The place was swarming with cops. I overheard some of them say something about a piece of a shirt Derrick tore from the killer. Something connected it to Eastern State Hospital."

I had a sudden picture in my mind of a T-shirt with the slogan, "I survived electroshock." I mentally kicked myself and turned back to the woman.

"What did he take?"

She frowned. "I won't know until the inventory is complete. It's hard to tell with this mess. And the cops won't let me touch anything unless they're here."

"What was the cause of death?"

"As far as I know, he was beaten to death." Her hands, finally still, covered her heart. "Oh, the poor man."

SIX

My next stop was the Tulsa Dispatch. Hank had an ongoing arrangement with Augustus "Gus" Fernandez, the managing editor, who once worked for Hank.

"You could be me someday," Gus said, sneering at me after our perfunctory greetings were completed.

I looked at his looming belly and stained tie and said, "I don't think so."

"What you working on, hot shot?"

"Tommy Hoffing."

He grimaced. "It creeps me out to think he's running loose around here. And how the hell did he get here from Vinita? That must be a hundred miles."

"Sixty. I checked the map."

"Well, it's still too far for someone to walk in — what is it? — four days?"

"Three if he was here last night."

I borrowed a word processor and modem and sent the story to Hank. Then I sorted through the scanned AP photos of the murder scene and decided they were better than anything I had.

The efficiency of the Associated Press is a marvel to behold. Apparently a photographer had arrived on the scene about the time the police got there. One photo showed Derrick Johnson's body face down in a pool of blood. I rejected it as being too graphic for our readers and selected one of the body in its zipped, black body bag being loaded into a police van. I attached the digital image to an e-mail and sent it to Hank. That, along with my photos of the trashed pharmacy, should please him.

Fay Blackfox wasn't pleased; she twitched with frustration. A pencil snapped in her carefully manicured hands, and she hurled the broken ends into a trash can. "Gary Hanson owes me big time," she said.

It was just before 2 p.m. We were in a barren room designated for defense attorneys and their clients on the fifth floor of the Tulsa County Courthouse, where Charley Pack had a date with the judge.

The wooden table where Blackfox's leather briefcase rested was scarred; someone had carved "Jesus saves" in one corner. Dust gathered like dead mice in the corners of the room.

Blackfox was a petite, raven-haired beauty, fresh out of law school. A black wool suit held her in a curvy embrace. She stamped a spike-heeled foot and scowled at me.

"He wouldn't say anything to me except to thank me for coming. What am I supposed to say to the judge? 'Your honor, my client wishes to continue the pleasure of your hospitality.' My ass!"

"If I could talk to him . . ."

"There's no time to arrange that now," Blackfox snapped. "Your boyfriend's on in five. They won't even let him wear the clothes you brought."

Blackfox was one of a rising tide of Cherokee women who, inspired by former tribal chief Wilma Mankiller, had abandoned the reed baskets and ribbon shirts of their mothers and grandmothers and went into law, medicine and government. Then they came face-to-face with reality. Blackfox had taken one look at me when I arrived — late — and figured we'd be paying her on a monthly basis for the rest of our lives. That, on top of Charley's refusal to talk to her, had pushed her over the edge.

I was feeling a little edgy myself. "What are you going to do?"

"I'll tell the judge what a fine, upstanding citizen he is. Pillar of the community. Plays guitar in a rock band. No steady job. No money. I'll ask that he set a reasonable bond. The judge will laugh — discreetly of course. Charley Pack will be led back to his jail cell where he'll stay until the preliminary hearing."

"Which will be when?"

"A week or two, depending on the docket. Plenty of time for Gary Hanson to take over."

I breathed a sigh of relief that Hanson would be back, a sigh that didn't go unnoticed by Blackfox.

"I may be new at this," she said, glaring at me, "but I've been around long enough to know that this isn't the way it works. You talk to your attorney. That's the only way I can help."

She was trying to free my lover. The least I could do was support her. "We're really fortunate that you were available at such short notice. I'm sorry Charley is making it so difficult for you." I meant it, but the words sounded insincere.

And I'm sorry Charley was so careless as to get himself arrested for murder. That thought had to go unsaid. But it dominated my thoughts these days.

Blackfox's face softened. "Wish me luck."

"Luck," I said.

She turned to go.

"Fay?" She looked back at me over her shoulder.

"Can you arrange for me to visit him?"

"I don't know the jail rules in Tulsa County. I'll do what I can."

"Can you at least give him these notes from his friends?"

She took the packet. I didn't mention that I had written my own note to Charley — two false starts — and torn up both.

Then she was gone, and I was left again with my uncertainty.

The sun streamed in through the high west windows of the courtroom and bathed the dark wood in golden light. The room filled slowly: a court clerk who expertly threaded a new roll of paper in her transcription machine; the bailiff standing guard at the oversize double doors; Fay Blackfox, carefully smoothing the back of her skirt before sitting at a table in front of the judge's dais; a young man in the back I tagged as a reporter; the prosecutor; and me. No sign yet of the two major players, Charley and the judge.

I sat a few rows back from the railing that separated the common folk from the representatives of law and order and held an imaginary conversation with Charley. In my mind's eye, we were perched on an outcrop of limestone that overlooks the clear water of Spring Creek. The creek cuts a deep valley below our house, and the stone is more than a favorite seat — on one occasion long ago Charley had teasingly dubbed it Honesty Rock. When I asked why, he said because that's where I went when I was searching for answers. As though its smooth cold surface might hide the door to some alternate realm. He was right, though. Something drew me to the rock when I was troubled.

For what that's worth, I now said to the imaginary Charley.

Charley looked at me with his deep indigo eyes.

I'm trying to believe in you, but you're not helping me, I told him.

Faith always was your shortfall, Charley said. He winked at me, leaned over and plunged from the rock into the icy water below.

A sudden commotion snapped me out of my reverie. A uniformed guard ushered Charley in through a side door. Charley wore orange prison garb and plastic shower sandals, and his hands were cuffed in front of him. A chain connected the handcuffs to ankle cuffs and forced him to take short, shuffling steps.

His eyes sought out mine, and he smiled. The smile wasn't much, but it made me take a sudden, deep breath.

He took his place beside Fay Blackfox and stood at rigid attention while the judge entered in her black robes.

I watched Charley as though through the eyes of a stranger.

In the pajama-like clothing, his slender frame seemed frail. Charley had charisma on stage, an energy and intensity that flowed to his audience. Today, though, the energy was absent. His short hair, thinning on top, made him look more like a career criminal than a rising rock musician. I had a feeling I wouldn't be taking him home.

The judge apparently agreed with me. Her questions to the prosecutor and Blackfox were perfunctory, and she hardly seemed to listen to their answers.

"Bail denied," she finally said, after the attorneys had completed their statements.

"But, your honor . . ." Blackfox began.

Charley put a hand on her arm and shook his head.

Blackfox looked in his eyes and fell silent.

The judge nodded to the bailiff to take Charley out.

I felt a sudden panic that I wouldn't see him again. Rising from the hard wooden bench, I rapidly stepped forward to where he stood beside Blackfox.

"Charley," I said.

He turned toward me, and the sudden look of compassion on his face made me forget what I was going to say. Our eyes locked for a long moment, and he reached toward me as though to stroke my face. The forgotten cuffs jerked his hands back down.

"I'm glad you're here, Viv."

"Charley, what happened?"

The bailiff grabbed his arm, and Charley shuffled away from me like a condemned man to the gallows.

"Check on Mica and Iris," he said. And then he was gone.

SEVEN

Gil and Mica Martin and Mica's daughter, Iris, lived in a remodeled Victorian complete with fish-scale slate on its mansard roof. The broad lawn fronted fashionable Riverside Drive. Beyond the street lay the ribbon-like River Parks with its miles of jogging trail alongside the sluggish brown water of the Arkansas River.

A thin layer of clouds grayed the fading light and dirtied the ice floes that bobbed down the Arkansas. The gloominess added to my reluctance to visit Mica. What could I say to her? Would she even want to see me? What would Miss Manners advise about visiting the woman your lover was accused of widowing?

I pulled the Trooper into the narrow driveway and then backed out and parked on the street when I saw that the driveway was already taken by a familiar car. The car was a dark blue Honda, similar in color to Mica's Volvo. I felt a frustrating tickle of memory. I should know the car. However, the events of the past few days had left me scattered and uncertain.

I slowly crossed the yellowed grass and climbed the steps to the wide porch. A light glowed though the leaded windows, casting a golden haze on my clothes. As always, when I came to this house, I wondered how Gil and Mica could afford such a showcase. I knew Mica had a small income from her family, but it wouldn't support more than a double-wide trailer.

Either Gil had done very well with High Spirits and the production company he and Tapply shared, or he had another source of income.

I lifted my hand to ring the bell. Paused. Thought about turning around and going home. Remembered the look on Charley's face. I couldn't let him down over a small thing like this. Not when he was under so much pressure.

The bell rang like a service station signal, out of keeping with the genteel surroundings. The sound of heavy footsteps coming to the door startled me. Mica, small and waif-like, usually moved like a wisp of fog.

The door flew open and I stood face-to-face with Allan Jakes. His surprise matched mine.

"Viv, what are you doing here?"

"I came to pay my respects." The words sounded stiff and old-fashioned; I stifled an impulse to giggle.

Allan's face flushed nearly as red as his hair. His tall body blocked the door.

"May I come in?"

"I'll tell Mica you're here."

Allan closed the door and disappeared inside. I felt as welcome as a Jehovah's Witness. The pungent fragrance of herbs, fanned by the door, wafted around me.

A slow burn of anger suffused me. Allan had been a friend of Gil's and was Charley's manager. Suddenly he was giving me the snotty maitre d' treatment.

My anger evaporated, though, when Mica opened the door and ran into my arms. I was vaguely aware of Allan standing behind her, his arms folded in disapproval.

"Viv! I knew you'd come!" Mica stepped back to look up into my face. Her eyes were swollen, and she dabbed at her face with a crumpled tissue. Other than that she was gorgeous. Her long blond hair was swept back with baroque silver barrettes, and her gypsy-like garb, flowing skirt and a patchwork velvet vest over a black silk shirt, gave her an exotic appearance. She looked far too young and fragile to have a 13-year-old daughter.

She made me feel awkward and dowdy, an effect that can only be explained by some unspoken competition. The ex-wife syndrome. I sometimes wondered how Charley could have fallen in love with two women who were so different from one another. Mica the mystic and Viv the practical.

Mica took my hand and pulled me inside, across the inlaid parquet floor in the entry, past the handsome oak staircase with its carved newel post, down a short hallway and into the kitchen.

"Allan was making tea," she said, indicating the Celestial Seasonings tags hanging from two delicate china cups. "Want a cup?"

"I don't want to intrude, Mica. I just wanted to let you know how sorry I am about Gil, and if there's anything I can do . . ." I trailed off when I heard myself making meaningless babble. I couldn't bring her husband back.

"I'm leaving," Allan said abruptly.

Our eyes bounced off each other, and he looked away. Strange vibes, I thought, lapsing into '70s-speak.

"But . . . your tea." Mica clutched his arm, and he brushed it away.

"Just remember what I said."

Mica glanced at me guiltily.

She was silent for a moment after he left. She dipped the tea bags in and out of the water as though she wasn't aware of it.

I sat at the kitchen bar and put my hand over one of hers to stay its motion.

"Mica? How are you really?"

She held up the tea bag. "Chamomile. It has a calming effect."

"Iris?"

Her eyes involuntarily looked up in the direction of Iris's room. "She's with friends."

"Is she taking this okay?"

"She's 13. When I was that age, I had fantasies about my parents dying. Everyone would feel sorry for me and I would be free to do what I wanted."

I remembered the feeling, and I interpreted that to mean Iris wasn't devastated.

"I just came from the courthouse."

She looked at me expectantly.

"The judge wouldn't set bail. Charley's going to have to stay in jail until the preliminary hearing. Or longer."

Her face crumpled. "It's all my fault!"

"What do you mean?"

Mica hid her face in her hands and cried. After awhile, the tears subsided and she excused herself, heading in the direction of the main-floor bathroom.

I waited in the kitchen, taking an occasional sip of tea, too lost in thought to remember that I didn't like herbal tea.

Mica came back after what seemed like a long time, still dabbing at her face. She sat opposite me and looked as resolute as a child confessing a lie.

"It's my fault Charley killed Gil," she said.

Up to now, I had told myself that Charley's arrest was all some horrible mistake that would soon be corrected. Charley and I would go home; life would go on. But Mica's bald statement shook my confidence.

She read the look on my face and pushed back the sleeves of her silk shirt. Her forearms were stained with ugly black bruises that were beginning to yellow at the edges.

"Charley saw these," she said in a matter-of-fact voice. "He asked me, and I was tired of lying. I told him."

"You told him . . ."

Mica turned away from me, and her voice was so low I had to strain to hear it. "It wasn't like that at first. Gil showered me with gifts. He said he'd die of love for me. He said Iris and I were his precious gems."

She was silent for a minute as she remembered.

"The first time," she said, her voice harder now, "he'd been drinking, and he came home late with the smell of another woman on him. We fought, and he slapped me. The next day he cried and begged me to stay with him.

"It became a ritual. He drank, we fought, he hit me, we made up. I thought I could change him." Mica's laugh held a note of self-hatred.

"I didn't know."

She turned toward me, anger and grief distorting her face. "We hid it well."

We sat in uncomfortable silence for a moment. I could hear the grandfather clock ticking in the next room.

"What changed?" I asked. "What made you decide to tell Charley?"

Mica stood, her slight body swaying as though blown by the wind. "Come with me," she said.

I followed her into the living room with its high ceiling and ornate fireplace. A polished baby grand piano took up a corner of the room. Mica stopped in front of the fireplace and sat on the stone hearth. A partly burned log lay in a pile of cold ashes.

"I don't ask for much," she said. "Maybe that's why I don't get much. But there are a few things in this life I can't compromise. My study group is one."

I looked at her blankly. Study group? Russian? Calculus? Women's studies?

"Each month on the night of the full moon we meet," she said. "Our shaman helps us invoke the spirits of the earth to give us insight and renewal. This month we were to meet here."

She reached for a beaded bowl on the mantle. "See? My offerings."

A small crystal, a bright red cardinal feather and a silver medallion lay in the bowl.

"I offer them to my spirit guide, the jaguar, through the flames of the fire." She chanted in an other-worldly tone: "Earth my body, water my blood, air my breath, fire my spirit."

Mica's eyes glittered with a fervor that I hadn't seen since the days my mother had dragged me to her church, where prayers were dredged aloud from the depths of suffering and guilt. I felt the same distaste I had felt then, and Mica read it in my face.

"You're like Gil," she said. "He made fun of me, and I tried to stop him. He grabbed my arms, and he hurt me. He said no shaman was coming to this house."

I mentally slapped myself. Who was I to criticize anyone's path to peace? Let them eat lotus leaves or pray to sequoias or flagellate themselves with thorny branches. Whatever worked. I reached toward Mica, hoping somehow to communicate that to her, but she wasn't paying attention.

"He was worse than usual last week," she said. "As though his world was crumbling around him, and he was going to take me down with him. I was so afraid."

"So you told Charley?"

"I had to get out I thought." Her voice broke. "Now that Gil's gone, I miss him. Isn't that crazy?"

EIGHT

I awoke the next morning to a memory of Iris and Charley. In the twilight of half-sleep, the night's dreams and the past twisted together like bindweed on a bush so that later, in the solid ground of wakefulness, it was impossible to sort out what was dream and what was memory.

We had sweltered through the summer day. The leaves drooped on the trees and the humid air didn't hold a breath of breeze. Iris was spending the weekend with us, and the three of us languidly complained about the heat and drank iced tea by the gallon.

At dusk the cicadas began their hoarse, saw-like singing as though they were the acolytes of hell.

We fled to the Boy Scout hole on Spring Creek, which even in August was clear and cool and inviting. Iris was 12 that summer, and already her breasts were budding and her body taking on the curves of womanhood. She wore her sun-bleached hair long and free. Always self-assured, she was graceful in her Speedo as, barefoot, she picked her way among the rocks.

Spring Creek is fed from a thousand hidden, bubbling springs, its winding stream bed lined with deep-rooted sycamores, cottonwood and scaly-bark hickory. In the fading light, the creek held secret depths. It gurgled faintly where the water left the pool and scraped over the rocks.

"Last one in's a rotten egg," Charley shouted. Wearing ragged tennis shoes and cut-off blue jeans, he raced past Iris, who said, "Hey!" and plunged headfirst into the water.

Iris was an otter in the water. She dived after Charley, and when he emerged sputtering from the cold, she pushed him back under. They wrestled like children for a minute, Charley letting Iris have the upper hand, and then they collapsed, laughing, in each other's arms.

As I watched from the rocky bank, I felt jealous. Jealous of their innocent play; jealous of their affection.

All this time later, the feeling lingered. Jealousy. It was a cancer in my heart. I pulled the covers tighter around me and thought about what Mica had said the day before.

She had sounded so certain that Charley murdered Gil. I imagined Mica on the witness stand at Charley's trial, telling the jury what she had told me. Charley wouldn't have a chance.

But would Charley kill to avenge his ex-wife? I had seen them together. Had heard Charley talk about her. "Air head," was his most common epithet. But he said it fondly. After all these years he was still protective of her. He treated all his friends, male and female, with a kind of dogged loyalty. I could imagine him warning Gil to leave Mica alone, but murder?

Besides, I liked to think that Charley worshipped the ground I walked on. The thought that he might still love Mica pricked my ego like a needle probing for a splinter. Worship. Ha. When was the last time a man truly worshipped a woman? Antony and Cleopatra? Sampson and Delilah? John Hinckley and Jodie Foster? Lovers, take warning.

I pushed my feet out from under the covers on the theory that the rest of me would follow. The air in the house was cold, and I shivered into a robe and moccasins.

Jason and Heather were camped in the living room by the woodstove, but they hadn't bothered to throw another log on the fire in the night. What are house guests for if they don't make themselves useful?

I felt my usual reaction to stress taking hold. Anger. Resentment. If I had a dog, I would have kicked him. Had Charley been here, I would have snarled.

The only victims awaiting me downstairs were a laid-back cat and two sleeping kids barely out of school. Luckily for them and for me, they stayed out of my way while I showered and made coffee. Under their sleeping bags, Jason and Heather were shapeless lumps, with Mack the cat curled atop them. He watched me with one eye when I stomped past.

I wondered if I had inherited Jason and Heather as Charley's legacy. Drawn to Charley like a moth to a porch light, Jason had quit his roofing job and devoted himself to the band. Now there was no Charley to play music with, and Jason, with his tousled black hair and large, dark eyes, had taken on the pathos of an orphan even though his parents lived only 10 miles southeast in Pumpkin Hollow. Heather, Jason's shadow, was the bonus.

They had plied me with questions about Charley when I arrived home the night before, but I had been too numbed from Charley's bail hearing and my visit with Mica to utter more than monosyllabic replies.

Heather had presented me with a fresh sheaf of telephone messages. Apparently she liked playing the part of secretary. As she handed them to me, she rattled off the highlights: "The phone rang off the hook today — again. Friends and fans expressing concern and support. A Tulsa reporter wanting to know how we felt about the charges and what kind of person Charley is. John called to let you know he has Charley's Takamine. His favorite guitar. He says to keep your chin up." Heather looked at me anxiously, and her sculpted eyebrows rose beneath her blunt-cut bangs. "You look like you haven't slept for days. And when was the last time you ate?"

"She's going to make some poor kid a hell of a mother," I said to Jason.

Jason looked up from Charley's Gibson. "Huh?" he said.

But nothing from Charley. The sheriff's deputy had told me Charley had access to a phone and could make collect calls. I wondered why he chose to remain silent.

Now, in the blunt morning light, it was too early to face Jason and Heather's chatter; I poured a cup of coffee and slipped out the door, carrying the cup in one hand and a bag containing a black dress, hose and pumps in the other.

The clothing was for Gil's funeral. I had promised Mica that I would be there even though the thought of it left a bitter taste in my mouth — as though I were responsible for his death. The funeral was in Tahlequah at 4, so I planned go through the motions of my reporting job then change into my black dress at the office.

The sun was already high when I nosed the Trooper onto the county road. The February day hinted at spring, and the musty odor of warming earth floated in the air. From the top of Long John Hill, knobby hilltops stretched in every direction, raggedly outlined with bare, gray trees. In a few weeks the green haze of unfurling leaves would overlay the Ozarks like a neon cloud. But for now, the blustery wind pushed dust and trash into whirling dervishes, and spring was just beyond reach.

LaRue Bunch was on the phone when I walked through the door of the Tahlequah Daily Tribune. Terri Mouse was on her way out. She lifted the camera case off my shoulder. Her hand lingered there as though to comfort me, and then she saw the look on my face.

"Okay," she said. "Any film?"

"Camera's empty, but there's a roll of TMax in the case."

"The Nation's marshal's office is confiscating some of the tribal records from the chief's office." Terri winked at me. "With any luck I'll record the scuffle on film."

I was too dispirited to ask for details. "Have fun," I said.

Terri nodded and left, and I went in search of Hank.

When I entered his office, Hank's eyes met mine then skittered away.

"Viv!" He grabbed for the newspaper on his desk.

I beat him to it. Charley's face stared at me like a wanted poster at the post office. Page one, above the fold. "Local musician suspect in murder," the headline screamed in 72-point Helvetica.

I took a deep breath and told my heart to grow up.

"I should have brought you a better photo," I said, dropping the paper back on Hank's desk.

"How is he?" Hank said. "How are you?"

"Wonderful. Terrible." I let numbness settle over me. Much better than feeling.

"You look like hell," Hank said, peering at me over his reading glasses.

"Did you leave any space on page one for my Tommy Hoffing story?"

Hank picked up the paper again and pointed to the AP photo of the pharmacy and the body in its black bag. "Good work," he said.

"I'm leaving early today for Gil Martin's funeral." The numb spot that used to be my heart throbbed briefly.

Hank looked at me a long minute. "We need a new angle on the Tommy story today."

"Raskolnikov is dead," I said. Without knowing why, I had parroted Frank Darman's non sequitur. Maybe they'd lock us up together.

Hank went on as though he hadn't heard me. "I want you to go out to Roz Hoffing's house and interview her. Find out if she's heard from Tommy. If she's afraid he might come home."

"Now that's newsworthy."

"Our readers care even if you don't," Hank said. His deliberate tone indicated he was at the end of his patience.

I tried to decide if that mattered to me. I remembered Charley's face as he spotted me in the courtroom the day before, Mica's face as she begged me to attend Gil's funeral. Tommy Hoffing and his wife belonged in someone else's soap opera.

"So far she's refused to talk to the media," Hank said. His face shimmered with suppressed excitement. That meant one of two things: He was setting me up, or he saw an opportunity to sell a lot of newspapers. Or both.

"So why waste my time?"

There was a significant pause while Hank's black eyebrows humped up and down. "She asked for you."

"Bullshit."

"She called this morning," he said. "Said she wouldn't talk to anyone but you. 'Viv Powers,' she said."

"That doesn't make any sense. I don't even know her. She doesn't know me." I realized I was pushing my hair back nervously. I made my hands be still.

"I don't care if you were lovers in a past life," Hank said. "Go talk to her. Now."

NINE

The Trooper crossed the bridge past Cherokee Landing where the Illinois River widened into Lake Tenkiller, and twenty square miles of dazzling blue water spread out like a ragged tablecloth. Here, the Cookson Hills rise above the surrounding terrain; the hollows are deep, and the trees grow as thick as grass.

Summer homes line much of the lake, but the developers hadn't made it to this end. On the dirt road that led to Roz Hoffing's home, the few houses were uniformly small and poorly made, as though the same careless carpenter had built them all. I topped a hill to find a blue tick hound lying in the middle of the road. He raised his head then slowly stood and shuffled stiff-legged into the brush that walled the narrow track.

The next turnoff was marked by a dusty gray mailbox with the number 144 in faded paint. According to Hank's directions, this lane led to Roz Hoffing's house. The sense of unease that had settled on me when Hank dropped his bombshell now increased.

The driveway was deeply rutted, and I drove the Trooper slowly over the rocks. A thin thread of smoke rose above the scraggly oaks. I slowed even more, reluctant to talk to Tommy Hoffing's wife. What was ironic, I reflected, was that had it been my idea instead of hers, I would have been eager for this interview. I would have been plotting my approach like a coyote reconnoiters a hen house. Now I felt more like the hen than the coyote.

The road opened onto a clearing above the lake. Roz Hoffing's small frame house was flanked by a shed and a chicken coop. The house needed paint, and the front porch sagged. The house was the source of the smoke I had seen earlier. It threaded out the top of a stovepipe that emerged from a window pane.

Smoke didn't mean anyone was home. If you heat with wood, you keep the fire going when it's cold. Build it up, bank it, damp it, shovel out the ashes, start over again.

A small flock of game hens scratched the bare earth at the side of the house, and a hound that could have been brother to the one I saw on the road thumped its tail from its position under the porch. It made no effort to alert its owners to company.

A battered pickup stood in front of the house alongside a rusty tractor and an old sedan with flat tires. I honked my horn in the universal country warning that a visitor had come and waited for a minute before climbing out of the Trooper.

No one responded, but now that I was here, I had no intention of leaving before I found out why Roz Hoffing had summoned me. I knocked on the door and strained to hear the sound of footsteps within while trying not to stare in the dirty window beside the door.

In the distance, a chainsaw growled.

A narrow track barely wide enough for a vehicle traced a line through the oak forest. Since no one seemed to be home, I followed the track toward the sound of the chainsaw. The hound dragged himself from under the porch and joined me, wagging a stumpy tail.

The day had been sunny and pleasant, but it abruptly withdrew its promise. A sharp wind pinned last year's leaves against a stand of shortleaf pines. Gray clouds scudded across the sky like cruising sharks and covered the sun. Through the winter-bare trees, a slice of lake gleamed, and I cut through the brush toward it.

After a few minutes, I emerged at the top of a rocky cliff, and the lake spread below like gray sludge under the cloudy sky. The pale light glinted off a pair of mallards that paddled along the shoreline; above them wheeled gray gulls. Their shrill cries sounded like wounded puppies.

A light rain began to fall, blurring the hills across the lake.

The sound of the chainsaw stopped, and a profound silence held the lake for a minute. The stillness was broken by the rhythmic chunk of an ax. Then the ax fell silent, and I realized the dog had disappeared.

Without the dog's companionship, I suddenly felt exposed and vulnerable. What lurked in these woods? What if Tommy had come home? Was it he who wielded the ax?

I felt someone watching me.

I turned slowly, casually and made my way back to the track. Once there, I knelt and retied my shoelace, scanning the forest with head down while I fiddled with the string. I couldn't see anyone. But I still felt eyes on me.

Ahead of me the brush rustled, and the hound appeared briefly before disappearing again.

The chainsaw suddenly roared to life. The sound was closer than before, and I jumped as though it had growled my name.

I looked around wildly, no longer caring whether the person watching me knew I was aware of his or her presence. All I wanted at the moment was to emerge from the solitary, stifling forest and find a place where I felt safe.

I forced myself to walk, not run, toward the sound of the chainsaw. The sound represented safety on the theory that cutting wood was hard work, and no one who worked so hard could be all bad.

The trail turned and opened onto a view of the woodcutter. It was a woman who hefted the chainsaw, and beside her a small boy threw branches on a brush pile.

I had found Roz Hoffing.

Her back was to me, but something alerted her to my presence. The chainsaw made a choking sound and died. She turned toward me, the saw raised in her hands like a weapon. The boy darted to a tree and snatched a rifle that leaned against it. He pointed it in my general direction.

We looked at one another in silence for a minute. Roz Hoffing was tall and big-boned. She wore dirty jeans and a flannel shirt, and her mouse-gray hair was pulled back in a tangled ponytail. She looked rough, with a weathered face and a broad slash of a mouth. She looked like a woman who was used to making do and taking care of herself.

She surprised me. I had expected the wife of Tommy Hoffing to be timid and beaten down, that perhaps he had terrorized her before killing the Blackinwaters.

The boy didn't look like his mother. He was slight and tow-headed. But he held the rifle like he knew how to use it.

I wasn't inclined to test him.

Mother and son had one trait in common. Their eyes were fearless. They both regarded me silently. With contempt.

"I'm Viv Powers," I said.

Roz Hoffing turned her head, and I thought she was going to spit, but instead she wiped her face on her sleeve. "I know who you are," she said. Her voice was low and gritty like sandpaper.

She lay the chainsaw on the ground, which made her look slightly less threatening.

"Matthew," she said, nodding at the boy.

He lowered the rifle but held it ready.

"Junior!" This in a louder voice.

Another tow-headed boy emerged from the trees behind me, this one larger than Matthew. Junior seemed softer than the other two; his eyes stayed on the ground, and he walked hunched over like an old man. However, he, too, carried a rifle, and the hound followed him.

Standing in the light rain, we were a cozy gathering.

"Why the guns?" I said finally.

Another silence grew before Roz answered. "Someone's been messin' around here," she said.

"Tommy?"

She turned to the children with the guns. "You boys go on back to the house and git the truck."

They disappeared down the track without a word, the dog following.

Roz Hoffing watched me while she dug in her shirt pocket with thick fingers and fished out a cigarette. Lighting it, she coolly and deliberately blew a stream of smoke toward me. Then she sat on one of the chunks of wood she had cut.

I remained standing. I thought I might need the advantage of a head start.

"You wrote some shit about my husband," she said.

"I'm a reporter. That's my job." I tried to sound matter-of-fact.

"Ain't it your job to get the story straight?"

"Is there something you want to tell me?" I pulled out my notebook and pen.

Roz Hoffing's face darkened. "How about you're full of shit. Tommy wasn't nowhere near that place in Tulsa. He couldn'ta killed that man."

"How can you be sure of that?"

She looked me in the eyes, challenging me. "He was here."

Over the lake, the gulls cried again. Like lost puppies. Like someone was hurting them.

"Have you told the police?"

There was a look of disgust on her face. "Would that be the same police I talked to eight years ago? They was real eager to help. 'Look at him,' I told 'em. 'He can't even feed his family. I have to roust him outta bed in the mornin' — that's how much gumption he's got. He ain't gonna go out and kill no one.'" She mashed the cigarette into the damp earth. "They didn't listen then and they didn't listen now."

He was here that night. Of course he was. And Elvis lives in South America; Lee Harvey Oswald didn't fire the fatal shot; behind the comet lies a spaceship coming to carry us home. A sudden despair welled inside me, pity for all the believers, for all the innocent dupes in this world.

"Can you show me any proof that he was here?"

"Proof. There's somethin' higher than proof. There's truth." The rain had wet her face, and the reflected light polished her skin like carved wood.

"In the newspaper business, we prefer proof."

Roz Hoffing stood and moved closer to me, and for a minute, I considered running. I'm tall and I'm tough, but this woman could crush me if she wanted to. And besides, she had a good 50 pounds on me.

"You got your own problems, don't you?" she said.

"I'm not here to talk about me."

She stopped, an ax length away. "You gonna settle for proof?" she broke in. "Or you want to know the truth about your man?"

Her teeth were uneven and stained like stones in a creek bed. She was so close I could smell chainsaw oil and the fresh wood chips that clung to her shirt.

"We're in the same pile of shit, ain't we." she said. "I never believed Tommy did all that stuff by himself. He wasn't that smart. But your man — he's another story."

"You don't know anything about him."

A crooked smile creased her face. "You'd be surprised," she said.

I didn't want to talk to this woman about Charley. I grabbed the first thought that popped in my mind. "How long did Tommy know Frank Darman? The man he escaped with."

Her eyes narrowed. "I never heard of him before your rag wrote him up."

I pictured Darman's face as he was bundled into the ambulance. Raskolnikov must die, he had said.

"Do you own a copy of *Crime and Punishment*?" I asked.

Roz Hoffing's mouth twisted. "Crime and punishment," she said. "That's what we live ever day."

"I mean the book by Dostoevsky."

"I ain't got time to read," she said.

Her eyes looked beyond me, and I turned, too, when I heard the low, grinding gears of a truck.

The boys had returned, Junior's eyes peeking over the dash. He drove past us and backed the pickup to the wood pile. Before Junior cut the engine, the smaller boy jumped out and started heaving wood into the bed.

Roz motioned Junior to her. He stood in front of her, eyes trained on his feet, as though he expected to be punished.

"Take this lady back to her car and make sure she gets gone," Roz said. Her words were harsh, but there was a softness to her voice when she spoke to her eldest son.

"Yes, ma'am," Junior said. His eyes darted to me and away again, like a barn swallow fleeing a hawk.

It began raining in earnest now, a hard, slanting rain. I followed Junior's hunched figure in silence through the woods and back to the clearing, where the game hens scratched in the puddles.

His thin jacket was soaked, and his hair plastered against his head. He stopped on the front steps of the house and half-heartedly waved toward the Trooper as though to remind me to leave.

Roz Hoffing's dismissal rankled, though, and I wasn't ready to be dismissed. I sat on the wet wooden steps. Junior sucked in his breath.

"How old are you, Junior?"

"Eleven," he mumbled. He scratched the back of his neck, unsure what to do next.

I had often seen Iris make the same gesture, and I suddenly realized that what was between Charley and Iris was forever changed by Gil's murder. Changed in what way was impossible to know; the interior life of children is complex and unknowable. When we cross the threshold to adulthood, the knowledge is stripped from us, and only a residue remains, like the whisper of a lost lover's touch.

"Eleven," I said. "I would have guessed twelve at least."

For the first time, he looked like a child rather than an old man in a child's body. His hunched back straightened and he said, "I just had my birthday."

"Really?" I sounded too interested.

No one has a sharper ear for false notes than children.

He looked at me suspiciously and said, "Mom said you had to go."

I stood. "I'm leaving, but can I get a drink of water first?"

He hesitated then went inside, leaving the door open.

I started to follow him.

"You wait there," he said.

I stood on the porch, peering through the door. Inside, the light was dim, but there was enough to illuminate a torn and dirty sofa, greasy shag carpet, and a television as large as the one in The Stadium, Tahlequah's newest sports bar. In the shabby room, the expensive television stood out like a manicured poodle at the dog pound. I wondered how Roz had found the money to buy it.

Junior brought me water in a plastic cup that wore the faded logo of a fast-food restaurant, and I gulped it down while he watched.

"Thanks," I said, handing the cup back. "Nice TV."

He glanced at the television and then at me, a worried look on his face. "You git now," he said.

I drove away with more questions than answers. But the one that ate at me as I guided the Trooper back to town was the one Roz Hoffing had asked: "You gonna settle for proof, or you want to know the truth about your man?"

There was no way around it. I had to know whether Charley had murdered Gil Martin.

TEN

I function best with lists. Do this, do that. With a list, stay out of my way, I have a purpose. At the head of my list, was Charley's innocence. Or his lack of. I had been foundering since his arrest, closing my eyes to what had to be done. Roz Hoffing's question had forced my eyes open.

Just having an answer would suffice for now. What would I do with that knowledge? Well, that was an item for a different list.

With my new task dominating my thoughts, I returned to the newspaper office. A story fresh off the AP wire lay on my desk.

Hank had scribbled a possible headline across the top: "Search for escaped killer shifts east." The story said that the house of a Spavinaw couple who were visiting their daughter in Texas had been broken into the night before, and a neighbor had seen a man fitting Tommy's description fleeing into the nearby woods. I checked my map. Spavinaw was about 60 miles north of Tahlequah and less than 20 miles south of Vinita, where the state mental hospital was located.

Investigators found that someone had forced a door, entered the house, taken a couple of hamburger patties from the freezer and cooked them on the gas range.

The Mayes County Sheriff's Department was cooperating with the Craig County Sheriff's Department in setting up roadblocks and searching vacant buildings in the area, the story went on to say. An FBI tracking expert was joining the manhunt.

I've always been a sucker for underdogs, and I was beginning to admire the elusive Tommy Hoffing. There's something mythic about a man who can evade so many searchers at such a harsh time of the year.

I wrote and filed the story about my interview with Roz Hoffing and her claim that Tommy was with her the night the watchman on Greenwood was killed.

I wasn't happy with the story, and I knew Hank wouldn't be, either. I kicked myself for not asking Roz Hoffing the obvious questions: Where did Tommy say he was going after his nocturnal visit? How did he get there? Was he alone? Did he have a vehicle? Just because I doubted her story was no excuse for not asking.

I still didn't have a phone number for Roz — didn't even know if she had a phone — and the closing deadline for the day's edition was too near to return to her house to ask follow-up questions. Anyway, I had other business to take care of. I had my list. Charley came first.

The AP story complicated matters. If the burglar was indeed Tommy, what was he doing near Vinita?

And then there was the issue of the guns the Hoffing sons carried. Someone's been messing around here, Roz Hoffing had said. That someone apparently wasn't Tommy. She seemed to have no fear of him. Who then? And why?

Across the office, then, I saw Hank, with a book in one hand and heading toward the bathroom. Time for me to disappear.

As I turned the Trooper north, I pulled my notebook open on the seat beside me and with one hand on the steering wheel and the other clutching a pen, I added to the list of people I needed to talk to and questions that must be answered.

I had told Tapply and Allan Jakes that Charley was not a violent man, that he was incapable of murder, and for the most part, I believed that to be true. However, in my heart, I felt anyone was capable of murder under certain circumstances. Everyone has a secret combination of events that will shove us over the edge to savagery. It might be love or hate or greed or insanity. It might be the wrong perfume in a crowded room. I had to know for myself what the circumstances had been in the High Spirits bar the day Gil Martin died. I had to know if my lover was a killer.

I would start with Jason and Heather.

A gentle rain fell as I drove. It bathed the hills in a ghostly stillness. At the Spring Creek bridge, the water fluttered below me, a kaleidoscope of fractured light. I stopped at the mailbox and picked up the mail, not bothering to look through the sheaf of envelopes and magazines.

In the gloomy day, the house looked dark and uninviting. I walked up the steps slowly, not wanting to be there, but not wanting to be anywhere else, either.

Like a true musician and his consort, Jason and Heather were still in their bed on the living room floor at midday. I opened the door to a flash of humping buttocks and bare breasts, and closed it just as rapidly.

I was an intruder in my own house. With everything that had happened the past few days, this was the last straw. A thoughtful hostess might retreat to her vehicle to read her mail while her guests completed their sexual games, but I wasn't feeling like a good hostess. I wanted to be alone in my house. Now.

A clay pot that held the blackened stems of last summer's basil sat on the porch. I kicked it off, and it shattered on the rocks below.

My anger evaporated as quickly as it had exploded. I waited a discreet minute or two then entered the house. Jason had disappeared, probably into the bathroom, and Heather was buttoning her shirt.

"I'm going to heat some soup, Viv," she said. "Want some?"

So while Heather busied herself in my kitchen, we made small talk, and when Heather called to Jason that lunch was ready, he joined us, and we ate canned soup and whole wheat crackers.

Mack jumped into Heather's lap, and she absently slipped him a chunk of chicken.

I pushed aside my barely touched soup and asked Jason to recall the night of the murder. The comings and goings. For instance, were Mica and Iris still there when Gil's body was discovered?

"You're asking the wrong guy," Heather said, rolling her eyes. "Mr. Short-term Memory."

"Twice around a toothpick," Jason said cheerfully. He knitted his eyebrows in concentration. "Iris was with you at one point," he said to Heather.

She nodded.

Jason continued, "Gil and Charley had that little go 'round and Gil left. I came over to where you and Iris were sitting on the floor against the wall. Iris got up, said she had to take a leak, didn't come back. A few minutes later, Mica comes by, asks Heather if she's seen Iris. Mica leaves in search of her. Didn't see either of them again. I guess they left."

"Where was Allan during that time? Tapply? Who else was there?"

Jason shrugged. "You already got more out of me than I know."

Heather couldn't add much to Jason's account. John, drummer for the Powers That Be, had left early. The engineer that ran the mixing board was in and out, as were Tapply and Allan Jakes. It had been a night like many others until Allan had emerged pale and shaken from the Green

Room and blurted that Gil Martin was dead.

"Did Gil have any enemies?" I asked.

Heather and Jason looked at each other, and then Jason said, as though reluctant to speak ill of the dead, "Did he have any friends?"

I was upstairs in Charley's and my loft bedroom, peeling off my damp clothes, when I saw what was on top of the stack of mail I had brought in. A plain white envelope with my name printed in blue ink. There was no return address, but it had a Tulsa postmark.

I turned it over, and my heart started thumping painfully. I quickly pulled my clothes back on and walked downstairs past Heather and Jason and out the front door, the envelope hidden in my waist band. Hidden as though it were jail contraband. As I brushed by Heather, she must have seen something in my face because she started to say something then put her hand over her mouth.

I hurried down the sharp-rocked path past the barren dogwood trees to Honesty Rock. The day's rain had muddied Spring Creek, and the water ran fast and loud into the deep pool below me.

I tore the envelope flap from the cheap paper and pulled out Charley's letter.

"Viv," it began. "There are so many things I wish I could say to you. But it's impossible. Not only for the obvious reasons: that I'm in a 16 by 20 cell with nine other men, 10 narrow bunks and an open toilet. No secrets here. Not because the guards who will post this note for me will read it. But for other reasons I'm not yet free to tell. All I can ask now is that you read between the lines. Remember what you know to be true of me. Remember that I love you. Have faith, Charley"

Faith. The word was bitter in my mouth. Why couldn't he tell me something helpful?

I realized to my surprise that I was crying. The unfamiliar wetness burned my cheeks; I scrubbed it away. I was crying and cursing Charley, and my heart was breaking with love for him. I remembered making love with him the last time he was home. Charley hovered above me in the dim light. We moved in almost perfect silence. In the moment of his orgasm, he let out a low moan as though something precious had been taken from him, and I looked on his face. His eyes were closed and his face turned upward; a penitent gazing at something holy. The look of rapture lengthened and lined his thin face and transformed it into one of El Greco's gaunt saints. As though Charley were worshipping.

ELEVEN

The funeral was an ordeal to be endured. I had a purpose, and the funeral was a roadblock along the way. My heart demanded to know the truth about Charley, but it wasn't the proper time to approach Mica and ask questions. I had to wait. I wasn't good at waiting.

The rain had stopped, but the afternoon was gray and the wind cold. At the front of the church an elderly couple sat beside Mica. They were hunched and shrunken in black. Gil's parents, I thought, since I knew Mica's father was in a rest home and her mother was dead.

The ceremony at the Hilltop Holiness Church was a traditional one as was the burial at the small cemetery beside it. It seemed out of keeping with what I knew of Gil and Mica. I would have expected a memorial service sans conventional trappings. Cremation, perhaps, with the remains disposed of in whatever way was acceptable to Mica's study group — a few hip words said over the ashes while someone thumped a drum.

Instead the heavy odor of lilies saturated the close air of the church, and an organist played "Shall we gather at the river." A stiff preacher in a shiny black suit and hair combed over the top of his balding head invited us to open our Bibles and follow as he read a passage from Isaiah about mounting up with wings as eagles.

Perhaps it is when we face death that our true yearnings become known. Our hipness and cynicism are stripped away, and we return to our earliest teachings, back to the days when parents were our only gods.

Mica sat with her head bowed and a black scarf hid her hair. Behind her were arrayed those who knew Gil best: Tapply, Allan Jakes, Heather and Jason, the other members of Charley's band.

In the back of the church sat Terri Mouse, discreetly taking notes for another sensational story in the Tahlequah Daily Tribune. The headline would say something like, "Tulsa celebrity laid to rest while local musician awaits trial." Ah, Hank. I hoped to repay his attention some day.

But where was Iris? I hadn't noticed her absence until now.

Perhaps she, like me, avoided funerals. And Iris was young enough to ignore the pull of social and moral obligations that drew me there.

I followed Mica's lead and bowed my head. I practiced endurance. I concentrated on breathing. In and out. In and out until it was over.

Past Wagoner, the road to Tulsa was as straight and narrow as the preacher's backbone, and I drove fast with the window down, letting the cold rush of air scrub away the odor of lilies and candle smoke that still clung to me even after a change of clothes.

Tapply was hosting a memorial for Gil at High Spirits, and I hoped it would be an opportunity for me to talk to others who had been there the night of the murder.

The fallow fields along the highway rushed by, and I wondered why the tourism council called this part of the state Green Country. This time of the year, it is Gray Country, and brown and tan and taupe country and all the coppers, siennas and umbers from the crayon pack. In a cornfield, the stubble was a bed of golden nails.

The only green was the wreaths of mistletoe high in the barren oaks, and a growth of shortleaf pine that stood on a ridge top like flags flying from a fortress wall.

As soon as I had that thought, Oklahoma, like a fickle friend, proved me a liar and provided a riot of color. A red-earth ribbon of road curled over a distant hill, and an emerald field of winter wheat spilled into the ditch along the highway. And in the western sky, the sun burst through the smoky gray clouds and burned their edges scarlet, as though a celestial fire raged.

By the time I reached High Spirits it was dark, and a cold wind blew. I locked the Trooper — a foreign act that I seldom bothered with in Tahlequah — and zipped my jacket. From outside the bar I could hear a bass guitar's beating heart. A thin man, amulet tattoo on his upper arm and a nose ring, perched on a barstool inside the door. He wore a denim jacket with the sleeves torn out.

"Private party," he said. Then he did a double take. "Jesus! You're Charley Pack's old lady. Go on in."

I didn't know him. Just another hanger on that all bars seem to attract.

In the dim light of the stage, a band played. I recognized it as one of the groups Gil had produced. Above the musicians gossamer wraiths of smoke materialized then wafted away. The lead singer's hair was long and stringy, and he humped his guitar and screamed, "Oh baby, oh baby." The feedback from the bass and lead guitars crashed into one another and spiked in a wall of sound that was as incoherent as a tornado scooping up houses and trees.

Tapply stood in a pool of light behind the bar, and he watched me as I worked my way through the crowd. Based on this turnout, Gil had many friends, and most of them were young and drunk.

I leaned against the bar and raised my eyebrows at Tapply. His dark hair was slicked down, and with his open-necked white shirt, he looked like a handsome Cuban mobster.

Tapply let his eyes slide over my body. "You wear your illusions well," he said over the music, as though he had been saving that line just for me.

"Give me a break," I said. I had reached the age where men no longer automatically made passes, and my skill at gentle deflection — the art women learn young to salve the fragile male ego — had atrophied. I didn't miss it.

He smiled like a boy caught with his hand in the cookie jar. "What's your poison?" he asked.

"Beer. Whatever's on tap." The noise level of the music rose again, and I had to shout.

He drew two beers and said something to the bartender. The bartender looked at me as Tapply balanced the full glasses in one of his large hands and with the other took my arm and propelled me to his office.

Tapply shut the door and the music receded into the distance.

"Gil was grooming that group for obscurity," he said. Then he fell silent.

I took the beer he handed me and sipped it while I looked around the office Gil and Tapply had shared. I'd never been in the inner sanctum before. The room was Zen-like in its simplicity. A pair of seafoam fiberglass Eames chairs were placed near a low, black surfboard-shaped table. The table held only a vase of budding gladioluses and a clean ashtray. The soft, green walls were bare, and the lighting indirect. The floor was dark, polished hardwood. If any work took place in this office, it was behind the accordion-fold doors that covered the far wall.

While I looked around his office, Tapply fiddled with a remote control, and piano music filled the room. It was slow and quiet at first, but it grew progressively faster and less disciplined until there was something disturbing about it.

"My composition," Tapply said. He looked like he didn't need any praise, but I figured he wouldn't put it on if he weren't looking for something. His fingers jerked, as though they played an invisible piano.

"Interesting," I said.

Tapply lowered the sound, and I sat in one of the chairs. It was more comfortable than it looked.

I had come here to talk, and it was obvious Tapply had something on his mind, but we both were reluctant to begin. My reluctance was calculated. I may not be a reporter of the Woodward and Bernstein caliber, but I do know you learn more by listening than by talking, and I wanted to know what Tapply thought was important.

He finally began.

"Chuck Berry's one of the greatest songwriters in rock-and-roll," he said. "He spent three years in the Algoa reform school before he first hit the charts in the '50s with Maybelline. Even then he wasn't widely known. Then in El Paso he picked up a little 14-year-old Spanish-speaking Apache prostitute to work in his St. Louis nightclub. He was indicted under the Mann Act . . ."

Tapply paused in his lesson and looked at me.

"Transporting a minor across the state line for immoral purposes," I said like a good student.

Tapply continued. "Berry went to prison for two years. While he was in jail, Chess Records issued "Chuck Berry on Stage," which reached 29, his first charted album. In the years since, he served two more stints in prison." He leaned toward me to emphasize his point. "Is there any rock-and-roll fan alive who doesn't know who Chuck Berry is?"

"Are you saying I should feel fortunate that Charley's in jail?"

"I know it sounds cold, but getting arrested doesn't kill a career. It might even help. Look at Jerry Lee Lewis. Look at Steve Earle. Look at the gangsta rappers."

The recording of Tapply's wild piano music ended, and I watched his long fingers grow still in the silence.

"Did Charley kill Gil?" I asked.

Tapply's face was somber. "It's a terrible mistake, and it's up to us to help the police sort it out."

"That's not exactly a 'no'."

His eyebrows shot up. "No! God, no! Charley wouldn't kill anyone."

I felt a sudden stab of guilt that I couldn't proclaim Charley's innocence with Tapply's fervor. "But you saw them fighting the day Gil was killed."

"They were in each other's faces. Gil shoved Charley, and I pushed them apart."

"Why were they fighting?"

Tapply's face was shadowed. "I told you the other day. I have no idea."

"How long after that was Gil's body discovered?"

Tapply thought awhile before he answered. "I told the police 30 minutes, but now that I think about it, it must have been more like 45."

"Where was Charley in the meantime?"

He shrugged. "That's where it all breaks down. People were moving around. In and out. Who knows?"

I attacked it from another direction. "Can you think of anyone else who might have a reason to murder Gil?"

"Gil owns — owned — a bar. Businessmen always make a few enemies. But they were the type to sue, not to kill." Again there was a long pause while he thought. "I didn't tell the police this, but Gil had something on his mind the last few days before he was killed. He was short-tempered; his mind wasn't on his work."

"Any idea what?"

He gave me a slanting look. "Mica didn't say?"

I was frustrated. "She said he was edgy, dammit! She didn't seem to know why."

Tapply's fingers played the invisible piano again. "Tommy Hoffing escaped."

I was missing something. "So?"

"They were cousins. Gil thought Tommy was coming for him."

TWELVE

Hope surged through me like a burst dam. Tommy Hoffing had killed Gil. Charley could come home.

"Do the police know?"

Annoyance flashed across Tapply's face. "I had assumed so. But I overestimated Mica's intelligence."

"Perhaps you overestimated Mica's knowledge of her husband." My mind wasn't on defending Mica, though, it was on the growing tentacles of this revelation. I had missed something important when I talked to Roz Hoffing. Her husband and one of Charley's college roommates had been cousins.

I turned to Tapply with sudden intensity. "When the four of you lived together at the Farmhouse — you and Charley and Allan and Gil — did he visit you? Tommy Hoffing?"

Tapply's hazel eyes looked black in the shadows. "He may have come by when I was there. I didn't take much notice of him. Who could have known he was a time bomb waiting to go off?"

"Why was Gil frightened?"

Tapply shrugged. "He never said. Maybe for the same reason we fear tornadoes and hurricanes. Their destruction has no logic."

It wasn't much to go on. And, yet so much to hope for.

I imagined Charley and me at home. We would crack peanuts still hot from roasting on top of the woodstove, talk about music and books, banish the memory of the Tulsa County Jail. Then I thought of Roz Hoffing. Had she been lying about Tommy being with her the night the pharmacy's watchman was murdered? Could he have tucked his sons in bed and still made it to Tulsa in time to kill the man? Was that murder related to Gil's in any way?

"We've got to tell the police."

"You do," Tapply said.

"Me?"

"They've already talked to me. How would it look if I suddenly come forward with more information? You know how paranoid the police can be."

Interviewing the guests at Gil's memorial party suddenly seemed irrelevant. I needed to find Mica; she was the best person to tell the police about Gil and Tommy Hoffing's relationship. It meant nothing coming from me.

It was 9:30, not too late to go by Mica's house. I drove faster than the speed limit allowed. The window was cranked down, and the cold night air blew in my face. I felt as though something inside me were swelling, and my ribs tightened with each breath until I couldn't suck in enough oxygen. I wondered what Charley was doing. He seemed to have a connection with things unseen. Could he sense the change in the air?

Ten minutes after leaving the High Spirits, I was in front of Mica's huge house. The windows were shrouded in darkness, and the street was quiet, with only a few cars parked along it. A car in front of the house two doors down from Mica's was familiar. A dark Honda.

I cursed as I guided the Trooper into the steep driveway. Allan Jakes was the last person I wanted to see right now. If he blocked the entrance to Mica's house tonight, someone would get hurt.

As I cut the engine, I caught a glimpse of a dark figure. It scurried out the kitchen door at the side of the house and disappeared into the shadows of the yard.

My first thought was for Mica's safety. Had Tommy Hoffing shown up to finish his grisly work? Even now Mica and Allan might be lying in a pool of blood. And what about Iris? I hesitated a moment, unsure whether to summon help or to find out first if help was needed.

The man ran away, I told myself. Go inside.

So I ran up the steps to the front door, and grabbed the handle. Something — or someone — held it from the other side, preventing me from turning it.

I released the handle and pounded on the door.

"Mica!"

The door opened with such force I almost fell into the foyer. On the other side stood Mica, wearing a long, silk robe and an enigmatic expression.

"I was afraid something had happened to you."

She brushed by me to close the door. "I'm here," she said. Her voice, cool and noncommittal, was a 180-degree turnaround from the emotional Mica I had last talked to.

She smelled of soap as though she had just showered, and it struck me with a sudden certainty that on the day of her husband's burial Mica had bedded another man.

And that man just happened to be the redheaded Allan Jakes — the man who found her husband's body.

I needed a moment to regain my composure.

"Could I get a glass of water?" I asked Mica.

She looked as though she were seriously considering my question, then turned and went to the kitchen.

I stayed by the door and reappraised the situation. My trip to Tulsa had been linear, with one goal, to establish Charley's innocence — or guilt. Now the options were multiplying like sprouts from an oak stump. Tommy Hoffing, Allan Jakes, even Mica. Any one of them had reason to kill Gil Martin. Each had opportunity.

I watched Mica glide across the floor as she returned with a glass of water. She handed it to me and shook her blond hair back. It was a sultry motion that had once made me feel graceless, as though Charley had settled for less when he chose me.

Mica watched me gulp the water.

"Why did you come? The house was full after the funeral, but everyone left hours ago." Her voice challenged me to contradict her.

Plausible deniability has entered our national idiom. Do whatever you want, but leave no tracks. Deny it as often as necessary and with conviction. Then sit back with arms folded and dare anyone to prove you a liar.

For now, I would play Mica's game. I would say nothing about Allan Jakes fleeing in the darkness.

"I just now came from High Spirits," I said. "Tapply told me something interesting."

A look of alarm crossed Mica's face. She recovered quickly. "Shall we sit down?"

I followed her into the living room, and we sat carefully on the brocaded side chairs as though they, like our fragile relationship, were in danger.

"Have you told the police Gil and Tommy Hoffing were cousins?"

"Tommy Hoffing? The killer!"

To judge from Mica's shocked expression, she hadn't known.

"Are they? Cousins?"

Her mouth opened and closed several times before anything came out. "Gil never said his name, but it suddenly makes sense."

I leaned toward her. "What, Mica?"

Her hands fluttered like rising birds. "The last few days. The fear. The anger. The phone calls behind closed doors. It was like some bad karma was catching up with him."

She stood and motioned me to follow her. "Come see."

She opened the door to Gil's office and from the bottom drawer of a heavy wooden desk drew out a manila folder. "He kept this office locked."

So, Gil's body was hardly cold, and Mica had already searched his office. I wondered what she had been looking for. Money? Legal documents? Or something else?

Stop it, I scolded myself. Her husband — the jerk who cheated on her and beat her — is dead. What was his is now hers. She has the right to dig through it, burn it, throw it out with the trash.

I took the folder she handed me and looked inside. Newspaper clippings described Tommy Hoffing's escape from Eastern State Hospital, including the story I had written about Frank Darman's capture.

As I thumbed through them, the clippings jumped back in time to eight years earlier when Tommy Hoffing was on trial for the murders of James and Sylvia Blackinwater. The papers were yellow with age and smelled as though they'd been dipped in urine and dried.

"If Tommy Hoffing was Gil's cousin, then it makes sense that he would have these, doesn't it?" Mica said, looking at me for confirmation.

"Mmmm," I said. I was reading headlines: "Portion of Blackinwater money recovered," "DA aims for death penalty," "Jury buys insanity defense."

I closed the folder and looked at Mica. "He ever say anything about Tommy Hoffing?"

She hesitated. "I don't remember hearing his name. But Gil used to say things like, 'I come from a long line of crazies.' I thought he was trying to scare me."

I thought aloud. "The question remains, why would Tommy Hoffing come after Gil?"

Mica took the folder from me and replaced it in the desk. "He had nightmares the night before he was killed. He was kicking and thrashing in his sleep like he did sometimes when he drank too much. But he was muttering something, too, something about a rash. I wanted to wake him, but I was afraid to."

"Did he have nightmares often?"

"He was in Beirut, you know. When the Marine barracks was bombed in '83. He had to help dig out the dead. Two hundred thirty seven of them. He talked to me about it one time. Then he started crying. That was in the early days of our marriage. When I still thought I could help him. Maybe that's what drew me to him. He was a man who needed healing, and I thought I had some special power." Mica's voice caught with unshed tears. She lifted her shoulders as though to shake off the memories, and then she added, "He was treated for post-traumatic stress syndrome. When he said 'rash,' the other night, I thought of Agent Orange."

"That was Vietnam."

"What?"

"Agent Orange."

"Whatever." Mica shrugged with a movement clearly picked up from her daughter.

We returned to the living room and discussed the possibilities, but we didn't have enough information to cobble together a scenario that made any sense. Mica was more relaxed now that the spotlight had turned and was no longer shining in her eyes.

"Call the police," I finally said.

Mica's conversation with one of the detectives investigating Gil's murder turned out to be a long one, and I wandered into the kitchen. The refrigerator was crammed with food: pies and cakes, casseroles and sliced meats, remainders of the feast of the dead. Two bottles remained of a six-pack of Moosehead, and I helped myself to one. The beer slid down my throat like molten ice.

From the other room, I could hear Mica saying, "I see. Uh-huh," and so on. She seemed to be listening more than talking. I decided to check in on Iris while I waited.

Her room was at the top of the stairs and down a long hall. The stair runner was thick and the color of crisp paper money; the balustrade walnut. At the end of the dark hallway, a light shone from the open door of her room.

"Iris?" I said.

There was no answer, so I knocked on the door and looked in the room.

Iris wasn't inside, but the large room wasn't empty in any other sense. Clothing, both dirty and clean, was strewn across the floor. A stereo system and television unit filled half a wall; another wall held bookcases. Books and CDs were jumbled among the discarded clothing and hid the tops of the desk and dresser. From a school bag near the door spilled papers and more books. A soccer ball sat in the center of her un-made bed, and a small net goal blocked the open closet doors. The deep blue walls were covered with posters; most were underwater ocean scenes featuring whales. It was a room to drown in.

On the night stand beside Iris's bed was a framed picture I had taken the previous summer. I took a few steps into the room and picked it up. Iris and Charley stood ankle deep in the fast-flowing current of Spring Creek, holding up a water-filled mason jar to the light of the sun. The jar's contents were too small to read in the photo, but I remembered the unex-pected flush of pride I felt in Charley that day as, father-like, he explained to Iris the mayfly life cycle.

"The adult mayflies can't feed — they don't have the equipment for it — so they only live a day or so. Their scientific name is Ephemeroptera, that's from the Greek for 'living a day.' They metamorphose into their adult form, mate and die. All in a day."

"Carpe diem," Iris said, having recently watched Dead Poet's Society.

Charley kicked over another rock in the creek, and Iris scooped may-fly naiads with a small net.

"These critters, on the other hand," Charley said, "live for up to four years before becoming adult mayflies. But they're sensitive to pollution. So if their numbers are down, we have problems."

Iris had stopped listening. "They look gross," she said, examining the miniature, crawdad-like creatures. "I'd rather be a dragonfly." She spread her arms out and lifted her face to the sun as though she would fly away.

Charley had tucked away that passing comment, and on Iris's thir-teenth birthday a few weeks ago, he had presented her with a dragonfly pendant of silver and abalone shell.

The jewelry case for the pendant stood open next to the photo, but it was empty. Iris, wherever she was, must be wearing her dragonfly.

THIRTEEN

A sudden noise from behind made me jump.

"You shouldn't be in here," Mica said. She stood in the open doorway, arms crossed in disapproval.

"I was looking for Iris," I placed the photo back on the night stand.

"Iris isn't here."

"Where is she?"

"She's not here," Mica repeated. She seemed to shrink, her presence diminished by a sudden loss of focus.

"Is she all right?" I allowed Mica to lead me away from Iris's room and back down the stairs.

"She just needs some time to sort things out."

"What things?"

"She's not your business."

Mica was ahead of me on the stairs, and her back was to me.

"I care about Iris. That makes me her business."

She turned, her face twisted with anger or anguish; it was hard to tell. "Drop it," she said.

The subject of the police was just as unsatisfying. Mica told me that they already knew that Gil and Tommy Hoffing were cousins; Gil's parents had told them. But there was no evidence that Tommy Hoffing had been in Tulsa the night of Gil's murder, much less in High Spirits. The two had been boyhood friends, Gil's parents had said, but they hadn't seen each other for years.

"So as far as the police are concerned, they have their man," I said. The series of ups and downs I had experienced in the past twelve hours, beginning with the visit to Roz Hoffing's house, had left me with a dull headache.

"It might help if Charley would talk," Mica said.

Charley's silence. I pondered the problem while I began the long drive home. Allan Jakes could have murdered Gil so he could have Mica. Mica could have murdered Gil in retaliation for his abuse. Even Tapply could have murdered Gil for financial gain. And Tommy? Who knew why a man like that would murder?

But no matter who I trotted out on the stage as a likely suspect, Charley's silence stood between us, obscuring motive and opportunity and creating a cloud of doubt that had momentarily lifted when Tapply had told me about Tommy Hoffing and Gil's relationship.

Was it possible that Tapply had convinced Charley that a little jail time would be good publicity? Or was something darker forcing his silence?

Despite the anxiety churning in my stomach like a trapped animal, I began to relax as the miles melted away. The hypnotic slap of the tires on the highway, the deserted road, the starless sky, all conspired to lower my guard. I had picked up a public access station out of Tulsa, turned down low, and John Lee Hooker was singing the blues. I was wrapped in a warm cocoon, and I hadn't been sleeping well.

East of Coweta, where the road narrows to two lanes and the trees push close to the highway, I nodded off. The rough scrape of tires on gravel and the wrench of the steering wheel when the Trooper left the pavement jerked me awake.

I cursed and fought the vehicle back on the road. It fishtailed across both lanes like a Saturday night drunk. Luckily no other cars were coming from the other direction. When the Trooper was under control, I drew in a shaky breath and rolled down the window so the unpleasantly cold air would force my attention.

The miles slipped by. The highest object on the horizon was the wavy line of electric poles next to the highway. A group of shuttered fireworks stands beside the road looked like derailed train cars. Far behind me in the rearview mirror, I saw the headlights of another vehicle. Other than that, the night was quiet, and the highway almost deserted. Thursday night after 10, most Oklahomans were watching TV or were in bed, resting for the last work day of the week and the big Friday night ahead.

The other vehicle caught up with me at the Verdigris River. It's not called a river here; it's the McClellan-Kerr Arkansas Navigation System. The channels on this river and the nearby Arkansas have been deepened by the U.S. Corps of Engineers so that tugboats can push barges half the size of football fields from the Gulf of Mexico to the Port of Muskogee and the Port of Catoosa — as though these landlocked towns could smell the sea breeze. Outside the dredged channel, the river sometimes floods and spreads across the flat land to form a shallow lake. The highway arches like the back of a cat over the lake, and the narrow two-lane road requires drivers to be alert.

The other vehicle was riding my tail, high beams on. I squinted into the mirror. It was a pickup, with an over-sized cowcatcher on the front. The grill looked like it was inches from my back bumper. Had I been on a wider road, I would have pulled over to let the jerk past, but here there was nothing but water on either side. I thought he would pass me — I thought of the driver as a he because of the truck and because of the aggressive driving — but he came even closer.

I sped up, angry now. He matched my speed. Then the pickup's bumper nudged mine. The wheel jumped in my hands. I gripped it hard and yelled, "Son of a bitch."

The pressure from behind made the Trooper hard to handle. I stomped the gas pedal and pulled away. For a moment I was free of him. My speedometer read 75, then 80, and the water on either side of the road glittered in the headlights like the eyes of a malevolent creature.

Then the pickup was on me again, his front bumper against my back. He made some kind of side-to-side rocking movement, and the steering wheel bucked again. This time the Trooper skidded to the right, into the gravel shoulder. Had I been calm, perhaps I could have steered into the skid and regained control. Instead, I panicked and jerked the wheel to the left. The Trooper, never the most stable of vehicles, slued sickeningly, bounced a couple of times then rolled over the embankment and into the water.

It may have been seconds, it may have been minutes later. The Trooper lay on its side, and the rattling and banging noises it had made as it left the road echoed in my head as though they had just now caught up. The air crackled with the odors of gasoline and swampy water.

I was suspended in air, the seat belt harness holding me in place. The radio still played. "I want to come back home, baby. Baby, I won't roam no more," John Lee sang.

I didn't know if I was hurt, or how badly. My mind was frozen, unable to take it in. But slowly the knowledge sunk in that someone had run me off the road.

I could see in the dim light of the dash that water was filling the passenger side. A fresh wave of panic swept me. I didn't want to drown.

I struggled out of the seat belt, bracing my legs against the dash and my back against the seat. The driver's window was still open, and I emerged from it to stand in knee-deep water. The deadly contest between the pickup and Trooper had taken us to the east side of the river, where the shallow water is punctured by the skeletons of drowned trees.

The Trooper seemed to be stable. It lay on its side, wheels in the air, like a dying insect. The front fender that stood above water was caved in as though a giant's club had struck it. I reached in the window, switched off the lights and removed the keys. The engine was off; I didn't know whether I or the wreck had shut it down.

I seemed to be in one piece. My left shoulder throbbed, and the knuckles on my right hand were scraped and bleeding. Other than a feeling that my brain was still turning cartwheels with the Trooper, I was okay.

I struggled to the water's edge, slipping in the mud once and falling. The water smelled of fish and decayed vegetation. A crust of ice lined its edge, and the cold February night gripped me like a vise. If I didn't find shelter soon, I would die of exposure.

The highway was deserted. The pickup was gone. I clumsily scrambled up the slope to the roadway and began walking.

I alternately walked and jogged for about a mile. Two cars passed me, but the drivers looked at me as though I were Tommy Hoffing and sped past. My hands were numb, and my ears ached with the deep burn of frostbite by the time I came to a house. Its windows were dark, but a car and a pickup were parked beside the small dwelling. I took a look at the front of the pickup to make sure it didn't have an over-sized grill before I knocked on the door.

It seemed like an eternity passed before a bare bulb lit the porch, and a deep voice asked what I wanted.

When I said I had been in a wreck, the door opened and a young man stood aside to let me in. A woman in a robe, black hair mussed with sleep, peeked from behind him. Their brown faces were angular and handsome. Cherokees. I used their phone to call the highway patrol, and then they sat side by side on a worn sofa and watched me without meeting my eyes while I stood by the woodstove and thawed out. In the corner of the room, a baby slept in a wooden cradle.

The two patrolmen who answered my call took me back to the scene of the accident. In the glare of their headlights, they pulled out a tape measure and noted the distance from the skid marks to the place where the Trooper left the road. They told me I was lucky to be alive. After picking up shards of broken glass off the highway, they arranged to have the Trooper pulled out of the water and towed. Finally they took me back to Wagoner where I signed a statement. My sketchy description of the assailant was useless. "Probably a DUI," said one of the men.

"Do you have anyone you can call?" the other asked. He was young, and he sounded like he cared.

I suddenly wanted to cry. The person I wanted to call was in jail. I couldn't tell the patrolman that, though. Instead, I tried to call home. I would ask Heather and Jason to come get me in Charley's van. They owed me that, at least. But no one answered the phone.

Before I had left High Spirits earlier that evening, Tapply had pressed his card in my hand. "Anything you need. . . anything at all . . ." he had said. That had been after I declined his offer to spend the night at the bar. Apparently one of the doors in the antiseptic office led to a room with a bed. Tapply had reissued the invitation just before I headed home when I had called him to report my conversation with Mica. There had been a long silence after I told him the police already knew Gil and Tommy were cousins.

"What's Charley's game?" he finally had said, as though to himself.

At the highway patrol office, I pulled Tapply's card out of my pocket. It was studded with options. Business phone, bar phone, home phone, car phone, e-mail, fax, pager. I would find out how sincere Tapply had been in his offer. The clock on the wall said it was just past midnight. I tried the business number first, and Tapply answered on the second ring.

After he expressed the proper shock and concern, he offered to come get me.

While I waited, I leaned my head against the wall and tried to rest, but a disturbing realization was growing. Someone had tried to commit vehicular homicide — with me as the victim.

FOURTEEN

"We call this the Clinton Bedroom," Tapply said.

I looked at the small room, dominated by a double bed with a lime-green chenille bedspread and sagging mattress and managed a short laugh. "Skip the details," I said.

The High Spirits was quiet now, closed for the night; only the stale odor of beer and cigarette smoke lingered.

Tapply looked rough around the edges. His eyes were rimmed with weariness, and he didn't bother to remove his fleece jacket. He had to look better than me, though. My boots and jeans were crusted with mud from the McClellan-Kerr Arkansas Navigation System. A quick glance in the mirror revealed a streak of mud across my forehead, and hair mashed by the wool watch cap, borrowed from Tapply, that I now stuffed in my coat pocket.

Tapply ignored my comment and went on. "Gil spent a lot of time here when he was in trouble with Mica. Sometimes before he got in trouble. If you know what I mean."

I didn't want to talk about it.

"You've been a stand-up guy," I said. "I don't know what I would have done." A fleeting impression rushed by of the Trooper on its side in the water.

Tapply brushed off my gratitude. "You're a survivor," he said. "I knew the first time I saw you."

"I didn't know the scars were visible." I laughed lightly as though we were joking. Uncomfortable territory that I didn't want to enter.

I sat on the bed and changed the subject. "We've got to prove that Charley didn't kill Gil."

Tapply pulled a ladder-back chair close to the bed and sat facing me. "What's your plan?"

"How do you like Allan Jakes for a suspect?"

A startled look crossed his face, and his fingers began playing an invisible piano. "Allan?" he said.

"Someone tried to kill me tonight. Allan could have borrowed a pickup . . ."

Even as I said the words, I realized how lame they sounded. What reason could he have to kill me? I started over.

"You're an observant guy. You know about Allan and Mica." I made it a statement.

"Eliminate the competition? That's a common motive for murder." A slow smile curved his lips.

"He beat her. Gil beat Mica."

"He wasn't a nice guy," Tapply said. "But he knew how to make money."

"Other than nipping at Allan's heels, my only strategy at this point is to dig up everything I can about Gil and Tommy Hoffing. Create some reasonable doubt for our lawyer's use."

"That's it. That's exactly what you should be doing," Tapply said. From the excitement in his voice, you'd have thought I had just discovered a cache of early Beatles bootleg tapes.

"You do believe Charley's innocent, don't you?" I sounded accusatory as though I myself weren't grappling with the same question.

Tapply looked thoughtful. "Charley's too smart to commit a dumb crime," he finally said. "If he decided to murder someone, he'd plan it. He wouldn't get caught."

"I hope you're right," I said.

Tapply excused himself and returned a few minutes later with a steaming cup of whiskey-laced coffee.

I grimaced at its bitter taste but drank it down, as though it were medicine.

"You're going to hurt tomorrow in places you didn't know could hurt," Tapply said. "You're lucky to be alive after a wreck like that."

He promised to arrange a ride back to Tahlequah for me the next day, and we sat in companionable silence.

I yawned hugely. The whiskey had calmed my after-wreck jitters; I was exhausted.

Tapply stood to leave. In the small room, he was so close I could have reached out to touch him. "Anything else I can do for you?" His hazel eyes locked onto mine.

The question was suddenly charged with meaning, as though I, the damsel in distress, were supposed to lay down with the hero. Lots of women probably had in this room. But I wasn't into role-playing.

"You've done more than enough," I said.

Tapply's smile didn't reach his eyes.

After he left, I removed my boots, scraped the crusted mud from my jeans into a trash can and lay down fully clothed on the bed. I felt uneasy in this place. I felt the need to be ready to move quickly if necessary, from what I wasn't sure, but the readiness comforted me.

I thought I would fall asleep immediately. Instead, as I lay in the darkened room, my mind roamed restlessly over the day's events. My thoughts darted from the morning visit to Roz Hoffing to Gil's funeral to Mica and Allan to Tapply. And always the wrecked Trooper was in the back of my mind along with a sense of wonder that I had survived to wrestle these demons for another night.

I tried to construct a timeline of Tommy's escape and the events that had occurred since then. Suppose Roz Hoffing had lied to me, and Tommy hadn't been with her the night the pharmacy guard was murdered? Isn't it Occam's razor that says the most likely explanation of an event is the simplest? Go with the percentages: figure a 10 percent chance that Tommy had gone home, and figure a 90 percent chance — supported by the evidence — that he had gone to the pharmacy.

What had Tommy been seeking at the pharmacy? Was he hooked on some kind of drug? Was he looking for money? Could Frank Darman, the guy he escaped with, shed any light on Tommy's movements or his motives? What about Roz? Perhaps I could persuade her to tell me more about Tommy's past, especially as it related to Gil.

After awhile, I gave up on sleep and turned the light back on. The room seemed unutterably dreary. A headache was working its way up my neck, and I remembered that a bottle of Tylenol was in the glove compartment of the Trooper. A fresh wave of anger washed over me at the person who had forced me off the road.

I went in search of painkiller, but most of the doors were locked, including the panels in Gil and Tapply's office. Only the office, bathrooms and hallway were open to me, the latter glowing with a neon exit sign. The pale light reflected off the yellow crime scene tape that still barred the door to the room where Gil was murdered. I hadn't realized until then that the Clinton Bedroom was next door to the murder scene.

Some people believe that the spirits of the dead linger in the place where they die. That they can't find eternal rest until their business on earth is finished. Comforting thought, that we have power beyond the grave. But I didn't believe it for a minute. When we die, we are no more. Dust to dust. Yet, staying in a room next to one where murder had occurred made me uneasy. The feeling was akin to a radio test of the emergency broadcast signal turned to the bare level of sensation. A noise scratching at your ears, diverting your attention.

I returned to my cell and sank back on the bed, wishing I were home. The lamp next to the bed cast a jaundiced light on the yellow water stains on the ceiling. The stains continued down the wall to where a framed photo hung. I rose to my knees to examine it more closely.

Two men and two women stood on a dock alongside a small bass boat. They were dressed in shorts and T-shirts and smiling as though they had nothing more on their minds than a day of sun and water. One of the men was Gil, and I recognized Roz, younger and smiling, but still looking leathery tough. The man with his arm around Roz was surely Tommy Hoffing.

I studied him. He was a large man with a full beard and long, dark hair. There was a hint of pleading in his expression, as though he wanted the photographer to like him. He slouched alongside his wife. It was hard to imagine him killing anyone.

The other woman I couldn't identify. She had classically beautiful features: high cheekbones, wide-set eyes, a sensual mouth and long, greyhound-like limbs. Gil held her arm possessively.

Behind them, the boat rose on a gentle swell. It could have been floating on almost any lake in Oklahoma, although the hills in the background made me think of Lake Tenkiller. I made a mental note to ask Tapply about the picture, then turned the light off and willed sleep to come.

When I finally fell asleep, I was thinking of trust. Or my lack of it. I felt guilty for letting Charley down, for being unable to believe in him completely.

Faithfulness. Loyalty. Trust. Each a part of the whole. All bound up like some snake eating its tail.

I drifted into sleep, and the dream came. It always came when I was most vulnerable.

I dreamed I was rock climbing with The Sergeant. He chose the route, finding the ledges and crimpers in the red sandstone, pulling himself up by sheer will when the holds faded into the rock. His leg was whole again; in my dreams he was always whole and strong. He stopped at a ledge and belayed while I climbed, the umbilical cord of rope and hardware unfurling above me.

The rock was gritty and warm to the touch. My toes through the Sportivas gripped the rock; my fingers cramped from holding too long. I tried not to look down in my dream, but I always did. The ground was far below, falling away in a dizzying kaleidoscope of jumbled stone and swaying pine tops, and a sudden fear clutched my heart. I knew I was going to die.

Above me, The Sergeant watched as I worked my way upward. My breath came in shallow gasps.

"Come on, kid," The Sergeant said. "Just a little more. Take my hand."

The rope was gone. At some point it had disappeared, and I hadn't noticed.

The Sergeant always reached his hand down in the dream, and I always reached for it, never remembering that behind trust lay treachery.

"Come on," he said, softly, seductively.

I committed myself to his hand, and he jerked away. I hurtled down. Down into nothingness.

FIFTEEN

"I'll bet a dime to a doughnut you've already run this cockamamie story by the Tulsa guys." Martinez scowled at me and spooned more gravy over his biscuits. He showered the gravy with black pepper.

Martinez had been easy to find. The Bull Pen Cafe, on the lower end of Muskogee, attracts the tractor-hat and cop crowd. The breakfast special runs from 6 a.m. to midnight. The small room was thick with cigarette smoke and echoed with the clatter of sturdy china and cutlery from the kitchen. I nursed a cup of coffee and watched Martinez across the table while he ate his late-morning breakfast.

I hadn't seen Bobby Martinez since the day we'd watched the cops storm the abandoned house outside Vinita where they had thought Tommy Hoffing was holed up. I'd known him a long time. He'd been a city cop before joining the sheriff's department, and we had some history. Or more accurately, my sister, Maggie, and he had some history. He still had a thing for her even though she currently was sunning in the Caribbean with her new golden boy. So for the moment he gave me more slack than he ordinarily would. In addition, he still had some idea that I was the publicity machine that would help him win the sheriff's election next fall. Martinez was ambitious but not too bright.

I returned his scowl, and his black mustache bristled.

"Pretend you don't know Charley for a minute," he said. "It don't matter that Tommy Hoffing and Gil Martin are cousins and that Gil was scared Tommy was comin' for him. The fact remains that Charley ain't talkin.' I can't get past that one." He shoveled a load of biscuit and gravy into his mouth.

"You know Charley. You know he wouldn't kill anyone."

"I've seen him around," Martinez said. "We talked some. That's not the same as knowin' a person."

I tried a different angle. "Gil Martin was afraid of Tommy Hoffing. I think they had a falling out before Tommy was put away at Vinita. I want to find out what it was about."

Martinez pushed his plate aside and regarded me with an air of superiority. "Who do you think you are? Tommy Hoffing's shrink?"

I didn't tell Martinez that I had already run into that roadblock this morning. After Tapply drove me home — a home unexpectedly empty of Jason and Heather, only the grumpy Mack holding down the fort, and he meowing and carrying on as though he had been alone for days — I called the Northeast Oklahoma Correctional Center. It was the prison facility at Eastern State Hospital in Vinita. I hoped to set an appointment with the psychiatrist who had been treating Tommy Hoffing.

Instead, the receptionist transferred me to the public affairs office, where a man who identified himself as the information officer said it was against hospital policy to talk about inmates. As a member of the press, he added, I was welcome to attend the daily briefing on the progress of the manhunt for Tommy Hoffing.

After I hung up the phone, I studied again the photo that had been on the wall of the Clinton Bedroom. When Tapply had picked me up at High Spirits after my nearly sleepless night, I asked if I could take it with me. Unfortunately, he couldn't tell me anything about when it was taken or who the unidentified girl was in the photo. Some chick Gil used to date, he said.

The girl, along with Roz, Tommy and Gil, smiled enigmatically, as though they had stories to tell.

I pushed the morning from my mind and leaned in closer to Martinez. "Help me here, Martinez. Who can I talk to?"

A flicker of sympathy showed in Martinez' eyes. "About Tommy? How about his wife?"

"We've talked," I said dryly. "I thought she was going to cut me up for firewood."

"She's a pistol, isn't she?" Martinez chewed his lower lip and came to a decision. "There is someone. But I wouldn't want you to let on that I sicked you onto him."

"I swear."

"Pete Terrapin. He's retired OSBI. Was in charge of the Blackinwater investigation."

Great. The Oklahoma State Bureau of Investigation wasn't exactly famous for talking to reporters. Or for talking to anyone but themselves, for that matter.

Martinez, the bastard, went on as though he didn't know he was setting me up for failure. "Lives out past Chewey. There's a little axle-buster of a road heads out toward the river. His is the house by the cemetery."

The ever-present Oklahoma wind buffeted Charley's Chevy van as I nosed it into the north-bound Muskogee Avenue traffic. At least I had something to drive. The broken shell of the Trooper was at a salvage yard in Wagoner being evaluated by a claims adjuster for damages. I had a feeling it would stay there.

I had awakened early with shoulders stiff from the wreck, and a spasm of pain occasionally shot up my back. Whiplash, probably. Bruises like smashed plums covered my body, but I felt lucky nothing was broken.

Now, hours later, the morning sun was bright, but it didn't hold much warmth. In someone's yard, crocuses were blooming. The cheerful gold and purple blossoms lifted my spirits for a minute. Spring was just around the corner. The feeling faded as quickly as it had come. I was on my way to the newspaper office, and I dreaded facing Hank.

I needed more time off; I needed to follow-up on Martinez' tip. Hank wouldn't be happy about that. A fool's errand, he would say. How many inches will it get me for the paper, he would say. And I would reply, this is personal business, not for the public to drool over with their after-work beer. Maybe someday ... when it's over ...

No, Hank, wouldn't be happy.

I also needed access to the newspaper morgue. Before I faced Pete Terrapin, I wanted to look again at the Blackinwater clippings that described the capture of Tommy Hoffing. Terrapin's name rang a bell, and I wanted to find out why before I tackled him.

I turned onto West Delaware and drove past the Tribune office and around back. Hank's car wasn't there. Maybe my luck was changing. I could get points for putting in an appearance, maybe even pick up an assignment, but not have to face the beast himself.

I parked in front of the office and breezed through the door as though I hadn't been AWOL all morning.

LaRue Bunch looked up from the classifieds she was proofreading. "Hank's looking for you," she said.

"I'm looking for him, too." The lie was brazen, but Hank wasn't around to hear it. "Where is he, anyway?"

"Chamber luncheon." LaRue felt for a strand of white hair that had fallen from the bun on top of her head and pushed it back in place with a hairpin. "He'll be back in an hour or so."

I breathed a sigh of relief and headed for the morgue, which was nothing more than a bank of file cabinets in a closet. LaRue's voice arrested me. "He left a note on your desk."

"Yes, mother," I said.

The note was terse and to the point. Interview the new college wrestling coach. Copy due today. Today was underlined. I cursed and glanced at my watch. The coach's name and phone number was at the bottom of the note. I called the number and arranged an interview for 1 p.m. That gave me time to scan the eight-year-old stories about the capture of Tommy Hoffing.

There was nothing I hadn't read before about the case. James Blackinwater, 61, was an attorney who had clients in Tulsa and Little Rock. On the night of the murder, he and his wife had dined out with friends. They had tickets for the Trail of Tears drama out at the Cherokee Heritage Center, but Sylvia Blackinwater became ill at dinner, and the couple went home early.

Tommy Hoffing had been hired to do odd jobs at the house: cleaning windows, painting the exterior, clearing brush. On the night of the murders, Tommy returned to the house after dark and broke into the wall safe. When the Blackinwaters surprised him with their early return, he panicked and used his safe-cracking tools on them.

Tommy was discovered at daybreak on Combs Bridge, in blood-soaked clothing. He lay on the dusty, wooden planks in a fetal position. A gym bag, money spilling out, contained Mr. Blackinwater's business card. The police went to the house and discovered the bodies in the red-spattered laundry room. Only a small amount of money was recovered. The rest, presumably, floated down the Illinois River.

What prompted the brutal attack and subsequent insanity? One story, which relied on interviews with Tommy's lawyer, suggested that his experiences in Vietnam were to blame. "Like many of our boys in that awful war," the lawyer was quoted as saying, "his life was forever changed by the brutal things he witnessed there."

Pete Terrapin's name appeared only once. In a brief statement, an AP wire story stated that Lt. Pete Terrapin was no longer in charge of the OSBI team investigating the murders.

I closed the folder and replaced it in the file cabinet. Terrapin seemed more of a long shot than ever, and I wondered why Martinez had given me his name.

I almost ran down Heather and Jason when leaving the newspaper parking lot. Heather was at the wheel of a rusted Gremlin, and she waved frantically at me.

"You look like hell," were her first words.

"You stopped me to say that?"

Heather stood by the driver's window of the van; Jason had stayed put in the Gremlin. A stray blast of wind lifted a scrap of paper off the ground and deposited it in the van. I absently tossed it back out the open window.

"Silly," Heather said, patting down her windswept pageboy. "We're organizing a fund-raiser for Charley. Tonight at the Creekside. Can you be there to say a few words?"

"And just what words should I say?"

The acid tone of my voice made Heather back off a step. Her eyes reappraised me. "Are you all right, Viv?"

I looked at my hands on the steering wheel. Dammit, Viv, I told myself, you don't have to be such a bitch. "I'll be there," I said. It seemed safer to change the subject. "What's with the car?" I asked.

"Weirdest thing," Heather said, glad to talk about something else. "Jason's brother brought it by for us yesterday. He said we could borrow it. Then last night we got a call that we thought was from him, from David, that is, saying Jason's mother was in the hospital and we should come right away. So we rushed to the Indian hospital, to Hastings, and no one was there."

Her arms punctuated her words as though she were once again a high school cheerleader. "No David. No Jason's mother. We called his parents' house, and she answered the phone, as sassy as ever. David said he never called us. The whole thing upset Jason, and we ended up spending the night at his mom's."

"That explains why you weren't home when I called."

Heather nodded, not interested enough in my failed call to ask what it had been about or why I was driving Charley's van. As I rushed away to keep my appointment with the wrestling coach, though, I wondered about the sequence of events. Could the phone call to Jason have anything to do with the truck that ran me off the road?

SIXTEEN

Pete Terrapin lived in a neat frame house with a small, fenced yard. Martinez had told me it was next to the cemetery, but I hadn't imagined that the ragged lines of old headstones would encircle Terrapin's property as though the graveyard were a predatory fish with its mouth open wide to devour the house.

I parked the van in front of the house, next to an older model Ford Crown Victoria and wondered how Terrapin managed to drive the car to the highway without shaking it to pieces. The road was deeply rutted and washed out in places.

Through the window, a curtain moved slightly. I had been spotted.

I knocked on the door, and set off a chorus of dogs. The guttural bark of a large dog and the excited yap of two smaller dogs stilled abruptly when a man's deep voice ordered silence. The man who opened the door didn't match the voice. His build was slight, and he was past middle age; his face was a mass of deep crevasses and his hair white. He stood ramrod straight, though, and the expression on his face said he didn't suffer fools gladly.

He waited for me to speak, but my prepared speech stuck in my throat. "Pete Terrapin?"

He nodded impatiently.

"My name is Viv Powers." I paused, and in the silence that lengthened, I saw my salvation.

"Alpha Troop," I said. On the wall behind Terrapin hung a plaque depicting the headhunter decals and crossed sabers of the Alpha Troop of the Ninth Cavalry, the army's elite helicopter unit.

Terrapin's eyes flickered in surprise, but he said nothing.

Somewhere, out of times I thought I had long forgotten, like Bible verses memorized for Sunday School, came my father's lessons. "The Cobra was an awesome fire support platform with its 76 rockets, mini-guns and 40 mm grenade launchers. Did you fly?"

"Scout gunner," he said. "What the hell are you talking about?"

"My father, Sgt. Randolph Gunter Powers, was in Alpha Troop at Tay Ninh, 1970-71. I saw the insignia on your wall."

"Tay Ninh," Terrapin said, his eyes far away. "We thought we were hot shit." His attention returned to me. "If it's about your father, I didn't know him."

"It's not about my father," I said.

A dog whined on the other side of the door, and Terrapin suddenly stood aside and motioned me into his austerely furnished living room.

I sat on a wooden chair next to the woodstove, and he pulled up another opposite me. The dogs, a Doberman pinscher and two small terriers, crowded next to him, their wet eyes devouring me. He told them "go home," and they trotted into a bedroom. Terrapin closed the door behind them.

Standing against the wall next to the front door was a large walnut gun case with glass doors. It held a collection of rifles and shotguns, shiny with bluing. I recognized a folding stock AK-47, identical to my father's souvenir of the war that no one wanted.

"So, Ms. Powers," Terrapin said.

"I need your help," I said. "I'm looking into a crime that occurred eight years ago. You were part of the OSBI team that investigated it. The murder and robbery of James and Sylvia Blackinwater."

His eyes narrowed. "You're a reporter, aren't you? It's about Tommy Hoffing's escape. You're not the first to ask, but you get the prize for best gimmick."

"I'm not here to write a story," I said. "It's personal."

I plunged in and told him about Gil Martin's murder and Charley's arrest. About Gil and Tommy being cousins. That they had a falling out years ago and Gil had feared for his life when Tommy escaped.

When I finished, Terrapin looked at me impassively. "I'm retired," he said. "I don't have access to any information now. I can't help you."

"You were replaced in the middle of the Blackinwater investigation. Why?"

A change came over Terrapin's face. I had managed to jolt him, and to hide his surprise, he went to the window and looked out, his back to me. Beyond him, the wind swayed the tree branches and kicked up dust from the road. The headstones in the cemetery sank into the dead grass.

"I oughtta throw you out," he said. But resignation, not anger, graveled his voice.

I waited for what might come out next. "Ought to" and "going to" were as different as "wish" and "will."

"I like this place," he finally said, indicating the graveyard. "My wife's buried over there. I used to think that when you died, your spirit went on to the next stop — heaven or hell or whatever — and that your body rested in the ground till the trumpet woke it on Judgment Day. When you live so close to the dead as I do, you come to realize that's not so. Maybe my grandmother had it right. She was a full-blood Cherokee, and she used to tell me about the spirit world and how the good and the evil can walk the earth and live among us when they want.

"Sometimes late at night when I'm half shit-faced on Jim Beam, I can hear voices. You might say the wind is just right, and maybe that's it, but I like to think that something's left of the folks buried here."

"What do they say?"

He whirled to face me, as though surprised I was still there. "They don't say anything you or I could understand. Leastwise not till we're one of them."

I weighed the options. Either Pete Terrapin was losing his mind, or he wanted to talk about something but couldn't approach it directly. I gave him the benefit of the doubt and asked a Barbara Walters-type question.

"If the Blackinwaters were buried here," I said, "what do you think they would say?"

"They would say ..." He hesitated. "They would say justice hasn't been served."

I hardly dared breathe the follow-up question. "In what way, Mr. Terrapin?"

"There's no way that boy worked alone. A killer's still out there."

Uttering the words seemed to free him in some way. Terrapin looked me in the eyes and repeated himself. "A killer's still out there."

"Who?"

A look of impatience crossed his lean face. "If I knew that, I'd be at the top of the OSBI pecking order now instead of babysitting this graveyard."

"There wasn't anything in the newspaper reports about a second person."

He sat down again and propped his feet against the stove's warm flank. "There was pressure to wrap up the investigation. We had our killer, and we recovered some of the loot. So my hunch upset the scenario they were playing out, and when I didn't back down, they got rid of me. Early retirement, they called it."

I was disappointed. His certainty was wrapped in a hunch, with no more substance than the voices of the dead he heard at night. "What makes you say Tommy Hoffing didn't act alone?"

Terrapin ticked them off on his fingers. "Three things. The satanic or ritual type carvings on the bodies. My thought is that it was a deliberate red herring. From all indications, Tommy Hoffing had no interest in religion, and he wasn't capable of that sort of inspired misdirection. And then, a certain amount of skill and planning went into the robbery. Everything I know about Tommy Hoffing says he never planned anything in his life. Finally, there was the ropes."

"Ropes?" I was on the edge of my seat.

"Yeah." He looked at me obliquely. "The Blackinwaters were trussed up, tied with the neatest little knots you ever saw. My theory is that it took two men — one to hold a gun on them, the other to tie."

"They were tied up when they were killed?" I heard the incredulity in my voice. The careful method of control didn't seem to jibe with the wanton bludgeoning that followed.

"My theory is that there were two personalities at work. The mastermind and the crazy. Maybe the mastermind never meant for them to die."

"What do you think happened?"

Terrapin tilted back farther in his chair, seeming to bask in my respectful attention. "My guess is Tommy talked too much about the Blackinwaters to someone. They planned a simple robbery: The wall safe was a fire safe, not a burglary safe. So they drilled into the safe door then used a tool, probably a reciprocal saw like a Sawzall, to cut a circle out of the door so they could reach the money. But the Blackinwaters busted in on their party. They tied them up and stashed them in the laundry room. But then something went wrong. Maybe Tommy panicked. Maybe he was just a time bomb waiting to go off."

"Did you investigate his associates at the time?"

"Does a bear shit in the woods?"

"Any good candidates?"

"Tommy Hoffing was a loner. He's the type that after a crime of this type is committed, the neighbors remember him as a quiet man who kept to himself. There wasn't much of anyone in his life except that wife of his."

"What about his cousin, Gil Martin?"

"I questioned him more than once. He was a nervous bastard, but he had an alibi in the shape of a pretty woman. Nothing ever came of it."

"Who was the woman?"

Terrapin frowned. "I can't recall her name. She was a student at the university. I think they had been dating for some time."

"Can I show you a photo?"

I ran out to the van and retrieved the photo I had borrowed from Tapply.

Terrapin studied the faces of Gil, Roz, Tommy and the unidentified woman. "That's her."

"Can you find out her name?"

He thought for a minute. "I'll make a call tonight."

We said our polite goodbyes, and Terrapin walked me to the door. "So. Your father," he said. "He make it back from Tay Ninh?"

"He was too mean to die," I said.

SEVENTEEN

I needed to write the wrestling coach story; I had followed through with the interview earlier, but I wasn't in the mood to write, and I wasn't ready to return to the office. If I ran into Hank, there was no telling when I would get away. The van was pointed south on the Bertha Parker Bypass, and the next exit would take me west to the security of my job.

I often find myself in marginal situations. At some invisible crossroads I turn left when I should have turned right. Or my mouth says okay when my body says no way. "Act in haste, repent at leisure," had been one of my grandmother's favorite sayings. I was a living illustration.

Aphorisms had flown out of grandmother's mouth like verbal flicks of a whip. Yet, I remembered her with fondness — the warm kitchen, her flowered house dress, the smell of hot, soapy dishwater. When I was little, I sat at her enamel-top kitchen table, my legs too short to reach the floor, and picked raisins out of her oatmeal cookies. She fussed at me, but she never made me eat the raisins.

"Act in haste," I said, and I turned the van east, away from the office.

The subdivision at the edge of town featured untended, cookie-cutter houses and stingy lots. The small frame house where Virgil and Gladys Martin lived clearly showed Gil's humble beginnings. A tin roof sheltered a cracked concrete porch that led to the front door. Faded venetian blinds shielded the two narrow windows on either side of the door. A no-frills Ford pickup was parked in the unfenced yard.

A woman with Gil's soft features answered my knock. She was too young to be Gil's mother. Older sister, perhaps.

I told her I had known Gil and wanted to talk to his parents, and she turned away to let me in. I followed her inside, and when Gil's parents, looking shrunken and frail, entered the living room, the sister disappeared into the kitchen.

Gladys invited me to sit on a sofa whose worn arms were covered with crocheted doilies, and Virgil and Gladys sunk into vinyl-covered recliners that obviously were reserved for their use. The walls were decorated with cross-stitched Bible verses and cheap reproductions of religious paintings.

We said the usual things one says in such circumstances. They knew who I was, and they seemed unsurprised I was there. It didn't seem to matter that I was the woman who lived with the man accused of killing their son. Their paper-skinned, lined faces wore identical expressions of numbness.

I showed them the photo of Gil, Roz, Tommy and the woman.

"Her name was Linda, wasn't it, Mother?" Virgil looked at his wife for confirmation.

"Harlot!" Gladys said. Her glasses distorted her eyes.

"Now, Mother," Virgil said, "it's not our place to judge. Maybe that girl's found the Lord by now."

"And maybe those godless boys he lived with will burn in hell." Gladys slumped back in her chair as though her anger had burned the fuse that animated her.

The "godless boys" she referred to must have been Tapply, Allan and Charley. I squirmed uncomfortably, torn between defending them and bolting from this twisted house.

"What was her last name?" I asked.

"Linda Smith," said a voice behind me. Gil's sister folded her arms and leaned against the kitchen door. "Her name was Linda Smith, and she was Gil's girlfriend when he dropped out of college so suddenly."

I tried not to let my disappointment show. Even in a town the size of Tahlequah, there might be more than one Linda Smith; in northeast Oklahoma there could be hundreds. And what if she had married and taken her husband's name?

"Any idea where I could find her?"

This time all three shook their heads.

"Did her family live in town?" I felt like I was extracting water from stones. Not an impossible task, but damn near.

"He only brought her home the once," Virgil said as if he were apologizing. "She didn't say much."

"Do you remember Gil and Tommy Hoffing having a falling out?"

Virgil pointed to the picture with a long, bony finger. "The only fuss I ever knew of was over the sale of that boat."

"They owned the boat jointly?" I studied the photo again. It didn't seem like much of a boat, but then, I wasn't a water person. What did I know?

Gladys smiled gently. "Gil was proud of that boat. He always called it the first of his fleet." Her smile faded. "He never did get another, did he?"

I stood to leave, and Gil's sister walked me to the door. "Don't bother them again," she said in a voice too low for her parents to hear.

As the door closed behind me, I heard Virgil say, "The Lord is testing us, Mother."

Stoics, I fumed, as I drove back toward town. Did God have Gil killed so his parents could pass some kind of test? Did some people exist just so a Supreme Being could make a point?

Thoughts like that could drive a person crazy. I concentrated instead on driving, heading west on Downing Street past the Braum's ice cream store and into the heart of town. The wind had pushed a line of dark clouds overhead, and fat raindrops spattered the dust on my windshield.

The photo sat on the seat next to me. Tommy was on the run, Gil was dead and Linda Smith had disappeared. Only Roz Hoffing could help me now. Abruptly I turned the van around.

By the time I reached the narrow lane leading to the Hoffing house, the rain fell in earnest. It reminded me of the first time I had been here, and I knew I'd never picture the place as anything but gloomy, with water dripping off the dark tree branches.

The battered pickup wasn't parked in front of the house, but that didn't mean Roz and her two boys weren't home. The pickup might be in a forest clearing, waiting for the rain to stop so the boys could load firewood.

I honked the horn two short blasts then shut off the engine. A lone gamehen, its feathers fluffed and head down, perched on the rusty tractor next to the house. If the hound were nearby, it, too, stayed out of the weather.

No one responded to the horn. The house was dark except for a greenish light that flickered out the window by the front door. I walked across the bare yard and up the steps. A feeling of unease stopped my fist before it knocked on the door. Something wasn't right.

From inside the house, came the faint sound of argument, a man and a woman. I edged closer to the door and peered in the window. The flickering glow was from the oversize television, and the argument was between two celluloid figures on the screen. Over the top of the worn sofa, I could see the top of a boy's head. Not enough showed to tell me whether it was Matthew or Junior. I began to think Roz wasn't home.

I knocked on the door. The boy's head dropped, and a small body hit the floor and scooped up the remote control before disappearing. I couldn't see him, but he had to be hiding behind the sofa.

"Matthew. Junior," I shouted through the door. "It's Viv Powers. I need to talk to you."

Someone increased the volume on the television until the voices boomed and drowned out the sound of the rain and my plea.

I tried the knob. The door was locked. The loud TV voices taunted me, distracted me. It was frustrating to be ignored by children. I turned away sharply, planning to go to the back of the house, when I heard the dull thud of metal biting into wood. I knew that sound. A bullet.

I remembered the rifles the boys had carried. Only .22 caliber, but deadly if the bullet struck a vital place on a human body. I had seen only one boy inside. His brother must have gone out the back door and crept up behind me.

I broke and ran for the van. I fumbled the key into the ignition and roared down the narrow, muddy drive. I didn't feel safe again until the van was out of rifle range.

A mile down the road, I pulled to the side and stopped. I shook with anger while a part of me marveled that I could feel so homicidal about two small boys. My rage shifted from them to their mother. Surely they wouldn't dare shoot at a person without her approval. Was she as crazy as her husband?

I imagined myself telling the story to Charley, and slowly my anger gave way to a sense of the absurd. I had survived being run off the highway the night before only to be used for target practice by two small boys.

I started laughing, huge whoops of laughter. I pounded the steering wheel with my hands and stomped on the floorboards. The laughter was driven more by hysteria than humor, but it felt good anyway. I laughed until tears ran down my face, and I gasped for breath. The crafty survivor Viv Powers, stalked by children. What was the world coming to?

By the time my laughter subsided to hiccups, the rain had let up. A hesitant sun poked a hole in the clouds before disappearing again. A robin lit on the forest floor and pecked at the ground. Its red breast was dull, but its appearance cheered me. A hint of coming spring.

It was time to leave this insane place and return to real life. Back to my job. If Hank hadn't fired me yet.

But before I could start the engine, a pickup sped past me, splattering the side of the van with mud. Behind the wheel was a woman with the broad shoulders and ponytail of Roz Hoffing.

"Oh, yes," I breathed. I waited until her vehicle was out of sight, then put the van in gear and followed her.

I wasn't worried about losing her on the gravel road. Hers were the only tire tracks since the rain stopped, and there were few side roads to choose among. For awhile I was content with an occasional glimpse of her pickup, but when we neared the highway, I narrowed the gap enough to see that she turned toward Tahlequah.

I allowed another car to pass before I pulled behind her on the highway. I needn't have worried that Roz would notice my van, however. She seemed intent on her destination, driving recklessly and fast, looking neither right nor left.

When she reached downtown Tahlequah, she drove east a block to Water Street and then turned down a narrow alley and parked. I pulled the van into a parking space on Water where I had a clear view of the pickup. Roz got out, looked up and down the alley as though she didn't want to be seen and then went in a side door.

I tried to remember the order of the shops that fronted Muskogee on that block. A gyro and espresso bar, True Value Hardware, a western wear store, and on the corner, a pawn shop. It had to be the pawn shop Roz entered. She hadn't been carrying anything — at least nothing that wouldn't fit in a pocket. Was she redeeming an item?

I waited while the late afternoon traffic sped by on Water and realized I was hungry. I longed for one of those gyros on the other end of the block. Or a grilled chicken sandwich dripping with barbecue sauce.

After a long time, Roz emerged from the alley door, visibly angry, even from a distance. She hit the side of the pickup with the flat of her hand, and the pickup seemed to shudder. Then she got in, slammed the door and roared down the alley and out of sight.

I didn't try to follow her. A gyro was calling my name, and I had a better idea than tailing Roz Hoffing. I borrowed the phone at the cafe and called a woman who was on retainer by the newspaper.

"Kyra," I said, "I need a favor."

"Don't you always." Kyra's voice was whiskey-soaked and sardonic.

"Credit check on Roz Hoffing." I said the name quietly into the phone so the boy at the counter couldn't hear.

"I don't suppose you'd have anything useful like her social security number." It was a statement.

"Nope." I gave her the address and the husband's name, and she whistled.

"I'll be watching for this story in your rag," she said.

"Until then, let's keep it quiet."

Over the phone, her voice dripped with injury. "Don't I always."

"How long will it take?"

"Depends," Kyra said. "You know the drill. Could be two-three days. Could be weeks."

"Call me when you have something. Anything. Don't call Hank. Don't call Terri or LaRue. Just me."

There was silence. Then: "This job's for pay, right, Viv?"

"You'll get your money."

Before we hung up, I asked Kyra what she knew about the pawn shop I had seen Roz enter.

"All's I hear is the old man who runs it walks on the shady side of the street," she said. "He don't ask too many questions about where your pawn comes from."

I walked down Muskogee Avenue feeling pleased with myself.

My brief euphoria dimmed and my steps slowed as I neared Fay Blackfox's office. I had much to tell Charley's lawyer, but I hated playing the role of supplicant. During our one brief meeting, Blackfox had made me feel like I was begging for Charley's life. I needn't have worried, though. Blackfox wasn't in.

Instead I faced Blackfox's receptionist, a mountainous woman with black braids hanging down her back like vines and an impassive expression on her broad face. When I suggested that she tell me where to find Blackfox, she said, "You need a restraining order against your man? He beating you or the kids?"

I shook my head.

"That's the kinda emergency I bother her with on weekends." She eyed me appraisingly. "What's yours?"

I told her my name and saw a flicker of recognition cross her face.

"You want to leave a note?" she asked. "I'll give it to her first thing Monday."

"Just make an appointment for me first thing Monday." Fay Blackfox was only a stand-in lawyer until Charley's real lawyer returned, I told myself. When Gary Hanson was back in town — that's when things would start happening.

I turned to leave, and the receptionist stopped me. "I have a message for you," she said. "Ms. Blackfox, she said to call you and let you know you're on Mr. Pack's visiting list. I couldn't reach you today, earlier."

Charley. I could see Charley tomorrow. The thought both exhilarated and terrified me.

EIGHTEEN

The affair wasn't black-tie, but Tapply — showing up fashionably late at Charley's fundraiser — wore tails and a top hat. He looked like a young Fred Astaire.

Tapply paused at the door, scanned the crowd, pulled off his white gloves and stuck them in his pocket so the fingers flopped out like rabbit ears.

The Creekside was packed with friends, fans and curiosity seekers — a cross section of Tahlequah society: artists, aging hippies, carpenters, New-Age farmers, students, professors, overeducated and underachieving drunks, Native American activists, and people who defied categorization. Among the many familiar faces were a writer whose new short-story collection had been reviewed in the New York Times and a potter who produced napkin ring sets for the National Public Radio catalog. Local musicians, including the members of Powers That Be who weren't in jail, provided the entertainment. The redheaded Allan Jakes was conspicuously absent. Supporting Mica in her hour of need, no doubt.

The informal jam session was punctuated with pleas from Charley's friends to contribute to his defense fund. I said my few words: thanks for your support, thanks for your generous contributions, it means a lot to Charley and me, blah, blah, blah. Public speaking is not my forte. The large glass jar at the bar choked with green bills and checks. At my request, the money would go directly to Fay Blackfox to pay for the work she had already done.

At the moment Tapply arrived, there was a lull in the action while the musicians refueled with beer. I sat at a table near the stage, feeling an uncomfortable mixture of gratitude and obligation to these people who saw Charley and me as family.

Tapply was alone, and when he saw me watching him, I excused myself from the well-wishers who surrounded me and joined him.

"You're dressed for anywhere but Tahlequah." I brushed an imaginary speck off his jacket.

"I have an announcement to make," he said, "and I want everyone's attention when I make it. Who's the emcee?"

"It's locally organized," I said, "so whoever grabs the microphone is in charge."

Tapply frowned at me as though my answer hadn't met his expectations. I tried again.

"John Franklin knows what's going on," I said, pointing toward Charley's drummer. John's shaggy head towered above the rest of the crowd. "Ask him."

By now, most of the people near Tapply were openly staring at him. A murmur ran through the crowd, and by the time John and Tapply concluded a brief conference and John had escorted Tapply to the stage, the room had fallen silent. A man with a bear would have caused less comment. Top hats and tails probably hadn't been seen in Tahlequah since the last magician performed at the university. But Tapply wore his with an easy confidence.

I watched Tapply as he adjusted the height of the microphone. Tapply's face wasn't like those of most Tahlequah men. His was the smooth face of a businessman and night dweller. The faces of the men around me were rough and weather-worn, lined from years of hard work in the sun and late nights finding warmth in a bottle.

Yet, their silence indicated a certain respect for a man who would wear such a get-up in public. There were no catcalls; no one requested a magic trick.

Tapply leaned into the microphone. "We are gathered here tonight for a common cause," he said in a rich baritone. "We are gathered here in the defense of our friend Charley Pack."

While the crowd listened as though mesmerized, Tapply launched into an impassioned speech about Charley's innocence. He ended with a promise to match whatever amount was raised at the Creekside, and his listeners cheered wildly and once again dug into their wallets and purses to up the ante.

Heather and two other women walked through the crowd with hats, which were soon filled with money. It was getting late, and I wanted to disappear. My head was filled with visions of Charley as martyr, Charley as murderer. Charley as my lover.

I worked my way to the door, but at the threshold, Ray Ballwin blocked the way. Ray was a carpenter who sometimes worked for Charley as a roadie. Tonight, like most nights, he reeked of cheap whiskey. His gray-streaked beard hung down to the ragged top of his T-shirt, which was artfully torn to reveal a new tattoo of the naked figure of a woman. She reclined across his chest, and whenever Ray took a deep breath, like now, her breasts thrust upward.

I tended to avoid Ray after a few one-sided conversations with him about life's cruelties — variations on the familiar lament of riches promised then snatched away. Good fortune gone sour. However, Ray did have good qualities. He was a mellow drunk, which counted for a lot in Tahlequah.

"Damn shame about Charley," Ray said.

I nodded my agreement and tried to maneuver around him.

He anticipated the move, took my arm and went out the door with me. The night air was sharp, and it smelled of wood smoke. The traffic on north Muskogee was light; Friday night was winding down.

I had accomplished one goal and escaped the bar, but now I had a new one: to get rid of Ray.

I shook his hand from my arm. "Walk me to the van," I said. "I'm leaving."

Behind his straggly beard, Ray's face was unreadable. "Damn shame," he said. I wasn't sure if he meant it was a shame Charley was in jail or that I was leaving. I figured he'd had enough to drink that he probably didn't know, either.

"It was that shit Allan Jakes," he said.

"You just lost me."

"Allan killed Gil. I'd bet my life on it."

It was hard to take Ray seriously. I opened the door of the van and slid behind the wheel. "What are you talking about?" I fished the key out of my pocket and put it in the ignition. The van beeped a warning, and I jerked the key back out.

Ray held the van door open and peered in at me. "Allan has that big house in the country north of Tulsa." In the dim light of the street, his pale eyes seemed unfocused.

I shrugged. I had heard that Allan had inherited a gentleman's farm from his father, but I had never seen it.

"Fuck," Ray said. "If I tell you, I'll be next." His voice trembled with a mixture of pride and fear.

I was impatient with this roundabout conversation. Maybe Ray was just working up his courage to hit on me. It wouldn't be the first time he had tried. "Just say it, Ray," I said. "I don't have all night."

He rubbed the bottle in his jacket pocket as though its genie might protect him. "I did some carpentering for him last year. The whole basement of his house is a marijuana garden. Raised beds, grow lights, the works."

My mouth dropped open while my mind raced through the implications. I finally managed some words. "What does that have to do with Gil's murder?"

"I reckon they had a falling out," Ray said.

"You're ahead of me again. Falling out over what?"

"Over the pot."

Talking to Ray was like the eternal labors of Sisyphus. I was pushing a rock up the hill only to see it roll to the bottom again.

"Ray," I said slowly. "What did Gil have to do with Allan's marijuana-growing operation?"

"He only wrote the checks, is all," Ray said. "He used that bar he owned to launder the money. Sweet little operation Allan and him had going."

Later, when I was home, and the fire crackled warmth and Mack curled in my lap and shed cat hair on me as though he'd never deserted me for Heather, I made a list of the goings on at High Spirits. Money laundering, marijuana growing, Mica and Allan's affair, Gil's fear of Tommy. How much did Tapply know, I wondered.

But a darker thought crowded out the others. How much did Charley know, and what did his silence mean?

NINETEEN

Saturday is the traditional go-to-town day in the Midwest. It's the day farmers put on their clean overalls and head for the sale barn; the farm wives don a dress, scrub the children's faces and drive the family car to town to buy the weekly ration of groceries and drygoods. Of course, traditions are dying by the dozen. Now the wives are just as likely to work at the bank or Wal-Mart, and most of the men put in their hours as hired labor during the week and spend evenings and weekends breeding their sows and planting winter wheat.

Still, the Saturday morning streets of Tahlequah were choked with cars, pickups, minivans and sport utility vehicles when I drove through on my way to Tulsa.

I hadn't slept well, and my eyes felt gritty. The light was as subdued as my mood, with huge clabbered-milk clouds floating in the blue whey of sky and hiding the sun. My stomach clenched as I turned the van toward Tulsa and Charley. I felt like I was headed toward a revelation, that when I saw Charley face to face, the truth would suddenly make itself clear.

I tried to concentrate on the highway and not think about what lay at the end of it.

When I drive in Oklahoma in the summer, the vivid wildflowers grab my attention: bright orange butterfly weed, drooping purple coneflowers, yellow sunflowers. On this day, under the dull sky, all I noticed on the road to Tulsa were the trash and dead animals. By the time I reached the place on the McClellan-Kerr bridge where I had been forced off the road, I had counted two dead rabbits, one opossum and one deer.

I slowed to look for signs of my wreck. I noted the use of the possessive. "My" wreck. As though someone could lay claim to such a thing. The mud slick on the highway shoulder clearly showed where the Trooper had careened along a narrow strip of grass before plunging down the embankment.

A sliver of glass reflected light, and while vehicles swept past at 65 miles per hour, I pulled over, opened the door and leaned down to pick it up. A triangular piece of ruby-colored taillight, no larger than a guitar pick. It could have come from the Trooper. It could have been there for years. But the sharpness of its edges made me think it was mine. I dropped it on the seat beside me and went on.

Near Fifth and Denver I parked in front of the library and locked the van. Downtown Tulsa was nearly deserted; only a few stray pedestrians hurried along the sidewalks, coats clutched tightly around them, heads bowed against the chill wind. Even the usually aggressive pigeons were subdued.

Across the concrete plaza, I looked up to the eighth and ninth floors of the gray courthouse as though Charley might be watching for me out a window. The barred windows were blank.

The clenched feeling in my stomach had spread to my chest, and I stopped at the building's entrance to take a deep breath before plunging inside.

I needn't have hurried. A throng — mostly women — crowded the lobby near the bank of elevators. They were queued up to ride the elevator to the visitors' room on the ninth floor.

Visiting hours were from 8 to 11. I checked my watch; it was nearly 10. My heart sank. The moment I had been yearning for and dreading, the moment when I could talk to Charley face to face, might not happen. There were at least four dozen women in front of me, and only an hour to go.

A large black woman who wore the tan uniform of the county sheriff's department sat at a table by the elevators with a clipboard in her hand, checking names against her list. The friends and relatives of prisoners showed their IDs, signed a form and then disappeared into the false brightness of the elevator.

It was nearly 10:45 before my turn came.

In the meantime, I tried to ignore the women around me: some with over-teased hair, rhinestone shirts and cheap shoes; others beaten down, overweight, dowdy. They talked of appeals and lawyers and the kids at home. I wasn't one of them.

When I made it to the woman with the clipboard, she glanced at my driver's license, checked my name off her list and handed me a form to sign. I signed it and handed it back and stepped into the elevator. The elevator stank of perfume. It stopped on the ninth floor, and in a small anteroom, a uniformed man ran a metal detecting wand over each visitor.

I could see through the door into the visiting room. The small and grim space, with dirty walls and a sliding glass door — bullet proof, I assumed — led into the jail proper. There was space for eight visitors: four spots where women stood and four stainless steel stools. Visitors were separated from prisoners by plexiglas windows, no larger than a sheet of note paper. They talked to one another on phones.

My heart sank. I had imagined that I would be able to touch Charley, to feel the electricity that ran through his fingers and to read its meaning.

I watched the routine and realized I would be allowed no more than 10 minutes with Charley. I had so much to tell him, so much I wanted to hear. I tried to organize my thoughts.

Beside me, a woman, her black hair twined with long green curls, wept silently.

The guard motioned me forward, and I walked through the door. Suddenly, each step toward the plexiglas window and stainless steel phone became a battle. More than anything, I wanted to run the other way. The whole thing was too sordid, too undignified, too intense. Too not me.

However, I picked up the phone and peered through the window into Charley's eyes. His startling indigo eyes. He held the receiver to his ear, and when he saw me, he smiled. The smile was genuine and heartfelt, and I felt myself returning it.

"Are you okay?" he said. The sound of his voice through the phone made him seem distant.

"I should be asking you that," I said. "Are they treating you all right?"

He seemed diminished in his orange prison uniform, and his eyes were sunken with fatigue. Even the lines on each side of his mouth were deeper than I remembered. I wanted to touch his face and smooth the lines.

"Well," he said, "it's been a long time since I had so many male roommates."

"Kind of like the old days with the boys at the Farmhouse?"

"The meals, anyway," he said. "Last night 'dinner' was served at 4:30 p.m. Two small squares of breaded fish, a scoop of instant mashed potatoes with congealed gravy, two slices of white bread, black-eyed peas, and one cup of cold coffee in a turquoise-colored plastic cup."

"Yum. Sounds like the summer camp I went to once. Minus the coffee."

Charley's face took on a dreamy look. "You know what I could really go for? A tall stack of buckwheat pancakes, dripping with real butter and maple syrup."

"The minute you're out of here."

"Buckwheat. It's wholesome and hearty. Kinda like sex with you." He leered at me through the plexiglas. It was a half-hearted leer, but I gave him points for trying.

We were having an inane conversation, and the clock was ticking. Somehow this was easier, though, than talking about what mattered. I noticed a band around his wrist, like a patient's hospital I.D.

I held my wrist up and tapped it. "Were you hurt?"

He lifted his arm and studied the yellow bracelet. "It's my lunch ticket," he said into the phone. "I stick my arm through the beanhole, they check my name off, and I get food. We get different colors depending on what we're accused of. Yellow is the color of prestige. Yellow is for murder."

Murder. Suddenly the light patter took on a darker tone. I was afraid to ask, but I had to. "Charley, what happened?"

His manner changed instantly. He looked on either side of him as though someone might be listening. When he looked at me again, his eyes were guarded. "You're going to have to take me on faith, Viv. I'm sorry."

The words hung in the air like bitter smoke.

I fought down the sudden surge of despair and anger and instead filled him in on what I had found out in the past few days: Gil's fear of Tommy, my meetings with Roz Hoffing and Pete Terrapin, Ray's allegations about Allan.

I thought he would be pleased that I was stirring up doubt about his guilt, but to my surprise, he looked angry.

"Just stay out of it," he said. "You're going to make things worse."

"I don't see how they could get any worse."

"They can get worse," he said.

Time was running out; at any moment the guard would force me to make room for the next visitor. Nothing had turned out like I imagined it would. It was unsatisfying, unsettling. I wanted to shake Charley.

"Look," I said, pushing my face next to the glass. "you're not the only person involved here."

The lines deepened on Charley's face. "Don't do this, Viv," he said.

The impasse was profound.

After a moment he asked me to tell Mica and Iris that everything would be all right.

I wasn't ready to give up my anger. "What should I tell myself?"

His long fingers caressed the glass where my cheek touched it. "That you're a survivor."

I stood outside the courthouse, feeling weak and exhausted. A scrap of newspaper blew by in the cold wind, and I followed it back to Charley's van. It wasn't until I climbed in the van that I realized I hadn't even told Charley about being run off the road. It hardly seemed to matter; there was so much we hadn't talked about.

Obedient to Charley's wishes, I went by Mica's house. The huge Victorian looked deserted. No one answered my knock, and when I tried the front door, it was locked.

I stood in the yard and looked up at Iris's windows. Heavy curtains covered them and concealed their secrets. It suddenly worried me that I hadn't seen Iris in the five days since Charley had been arrested. Mica had been evasive when I had asked about her the other night.

Iris. She seemed to both awaken and satisfy Charley's fatherly impulses. He worried about her, teased her, sent her money and badgered her to do well in school.

Now both Mica and Iris were gone. I scribbled a note to them and left it wedged between the front door and the jamb, saying I would be back later.

I drove back through downtown Tulsa on Boston. The graceful spire of the Boston Avenue United Methodist Church faded in my rearview mirror, and the massive bulk of the Bank of Oklahoma Tower, Oklahoma's tallest building, rose in front of me like a beacon. Traffic was light, and most of the downtown shops and restaurants were closed.

I went by Gus Fernandez's office at the Tulsa Dispatch. He worked Saturday mornings and was on his way out. I blocked his way.

"I need a favor," I said.

He groaned. "I'm on my way to the Oilers game. I don't have time for favors." He wore a windbreaker laden with logos in support of Tulsa's ice hockey team.

"It'll just take a minute."

He sighed and turned back into his office. "Make it quick."

"I need a copy of Gil Martin's autopsy report."

"Hasn't been released yet."

He read the disappointment on my face and took pity. "How about the medical examiner's report instead? It's just as good and you don't have to read about how much the deceased's spleen weighed."

Gus left me in the office and returned moments later with a single photocopied sheet. "Tell Hank favors are a two-way street and he's piling up the debt," he said.

I let him think the request had been from Hank and left with the report clutched in my hand.

I grabbed a newspaper from a vendor's stand outside the building, then went down the street to the Middle Path Cafe where I tore into the restaurant's nutty Hot Toddy Bread — a meal in itself — and drank coffee.

While I ate, I studied the sheet Gus Fernandez had given me. It was headed: Report of Investigation by Medical Examiner. It said Gil Martin was 37 years old. His occupation was listed as businessman. The examiner estimated the time of death at 6:30 p.m. Further down on the page, under the heading "Significant observations and injury documentation," the medical examiner had noted, "Body found on floor with rock laying by head."

Probable cause of death: Massive trauma to head.

Manner of death: Homicide.

I tried to imagine Charley with the rock in his hand. Charley smashing the rock into his friend's head. Charley looking behind him to see if anyone else had seen him. Charley running from the room.

The Charley I knew would do none of those things. He was a vegetarian pacifist who defused his demons with meditation.

I crumpled the medical examiner's report into a ball.

I was on my second cup of coffee when I found the story in the Metro section.

Escaped killer suspect in pharmacy murder

A craving for drugs may have been the motive for a recent break-in and murder at a northeast Tulsa pharmacy, Tulsa police say.

Derrick Johnson, a 39-year-old security guard for a Rexall drugstore in the Greenwood area, was beaten to death Tuesday night.

Police are seeking Tommy Hoffing, says a source close to the investigation. Hoffing, who has been called Oklahoma's Charles Manson, escaped a week ago from the forensic psychology unit of Eastern State Hospital. He had been incarcerated there for the past eight years for the bludgeoning murders of James and Sylvia Blackinwater, a wealthy Tahlequah couple.

The pharmacy was ransacked, but the only item missing was a supply of Ativan. The drug is commonly used to sedate patients in mental facilities. The substance is not addictive, according to Nathaniel Myrick, a psychiatrist at Tulsa Regional Hospital.

"If the murderer was an escapee from a mental facility," Myrick said, "he may have been attempting to find drugs and treat himself."

If so, it was a treatment that went badly astray. The victim, who had been on the job for only two weeks, left behind a wife and three children.

A sudden vivid memory of the bloody hand print on the wall of the pharmacy made me fold the newspaper and set my coffee aside. Tommy Hoffing was now the official suspect in the pharmacy murder. If he had killed the man, that placed him in Tulsa the night after Gil was murdered. I added a check mark beside Tommy Hoffing's name to the informal tally I was keeping in my head. The police might favor him for the night watchman's murder, but he was far from the only suspect in Gil Martin's death.

I glanced at my watch. It had been only half an hour since I went by Mica's house — too early to return. But there was a basement greenhouse to investigate . . .

TWENTY

Tapply could have given me directions to Allan Jakes's house, but I didn't know what part, if any, he played in the marijuana-growing operation. Tapply was a hard man to read. Part angel, part devil. So I called Jason at his mother's house. He didn't ask why I wanted to find Allan Jakes, and his voice was blurred and remote as though I had interrupted a post-coital nap. He had been to Allan's once, he said, and the only thing he remembered was that it was on State Highway 11 outside Turley. It was a sprawling white ranch house backed by white outbuildings and surrounded by miles of white wood fence. "We're talkin' white paint out the wazoo," Jason said.

Turley was just north of Tulsa, and Allan's place sounded easy to find. Always the believer in dumb luck, I drove through the urban sprawl of north Tulsa on Highway 75: past the industrial detritus that flanked the tracks of the Atchison, Topeka and Santa Fe Railroad; past the exit for the airport; past the shallow, murky waters of Mohawk Lake. The city suddenly stopped as if an invisible wall stretched across the prairie, and the rolling grasslands took over.

Two miles north of Turley was a place that fit Jason's description. Someone had killed a lot of trees to construct the miles of white fence. Even the long driveway was hemmed with neat, parallel lines. Just to make sure, I checked the name on the mailbox by the white arched entry to the property. Jakes, it read. On closer inspection, the paint was peeling and faded.

A surly sun shone from the sky, dispensing light but not much warmth. And the omnipresent Oklahoma wind blew across the flat land. I could almost guarantee that someone in some Oklahoma bar was blaming the wind on the fact that "Kansas blows and Texas sucks," and then laughing at their cleverness as though it hadn't been said a million times before.

Three handsome bay horses crowded against one another near the white barn, and a rusted tractor was parked in front of the building. Other than the horses, there was no sign of life.

I studied the layout from the highway, realizing that if Allan were home, he'd recognize Charley's van. There was no point in secrecy. With that thought in mind, I drove up to the house and parked.

No one answered the doorbell. I rang again and waited, straining my ears for footsteps, preparing a winning smile for the sight of Allan Jakes's pale, freckled face under his frizzy red hair. I would tell him I had been to see Charley and wanted to update him on the situation. After all, Jakes was the band's manager.

There was no update, but it would do for an excuse.

When I was finally convinced no one was home, I looked around Allan's property as though I were a potential buyer. I walked through the big white barn and admired the old-fashioned corn crib — empty now — and the aging bales of hay in the high-ceilinged loft. The rafters were an ideal place to hang marijuana plants to dry; however, nothing but rusted nails spotted the splintered beams.

On the east end of the barn were the horse stalls. The smell of horse sweat and manure was pleasantly pungent in the dim space. The horses heard me and crowded inside, nickering for a handout. I obligingly dug into the feed and scooped out a measure for each into a long bin. The horses jostled one another with their shoulders and spread the feed with their soft lips. The sweet odor that rose reminded me of the Hot Toddy Bread I'd recently eaten.

I left the barn to check out the other buildings. Behind the house stood a two-car detached garage, badly in need of paint. I peered through the lone, cobwebbed window. The concrete floor was spotted with oil on both sides, but the garage was empty. I wondered if that meant Allan had a hired hand that I would have to be on the lookout for. Allan couldn't be driving two vehicles at once.

The back of the house was sheltered by a long, screened porch. I expected the storm door to be locked, but when I pushed it, it swung open. I hesitated before stepping over the threshold. It didn't make sense that Allan would leave his house unlocked if it held a treasure room of marijuana. Maybe Ray the carpenter had lied.

But the instant I opened the kitchen door and stepped inside, I knew Ray had told the truth. Marijuana has a distinctive odor, somewhat like freshly cut hay, and its heaviness wafted through the overheated rooms.

I listened before I moved farther into the house, preparing my lips to tell lies, arranging my face to show no surprise should I unexpectedly run into Allan. A distant thumping noise made me pause, but the sound wasn't repeated.

I walked through the main level of the house quickly, taking inventory, trying to notice anything that might be important.

Allan's house was filled with what looked to my untrained eyes like valuable antiques. Walnut wardrobes with cherry and ash inlay, a heavy oak dining table and chairs, western-themed oil paintings in intricately carved wooden frames, leather sofas and chairs, Oriental carpets, marble-hearthed fireplaces. The furniture would have fit nicely in Mica's Victorian mansion, but what drew my attention was the neglect.

I didn't know how long ago Allan's parents had died, leaving him the house, but I was willing to bet it hadn't been cleaned since then. In the kitchen, food-crusted china filled with scummy water was stacked so high the dishes looked in danger of toppling. The trash overflowed with fast-food wrappers and pizza boxes. The tile floor was glazed with a layer of grease and ground-in spilled food.

Throughout the house, a heavy pall of dust dulled the furniture, and mud paths scarred the carpet. In the master bedroom, candle stubs stood in gummy piles of melted wax on a table next to the unmade bed. Wilted flowers drooped in a vase. I couldn't imagine Mica sleeping on the grimy sheets with Allan.

The furnace came on with a sound like a sudden rush of wind and reminded me that I wasn't here to judge Allan Jakes's housecleaning skills. I turned toward the stairs leading down to the basement. They were narrow and dark, but light glowed at the bottom.

I walked as quietly as I could, pausing frequently to listen, treading close to the wall so the stairs wouldn't creak. If anyone were in the basement, I'd already given myself away by traipsing through the rooms above. However, I didn't want them to know I was coming downstairs. The power of surprise can be the equivalent of a weapon. Thus saith The Sergeant.

At the bottom, the door stood open, and beyond it I could see rows of raised planting beds, side-by-side. They stretched from wall to wall with narrow, concrete walkways between them and a system of water pipes outlining the shape of the beds. Overhead the grow lights shone like a thousand suns. The small windows were painted black.

The beds were crowded with 4- and 5-foot-tall marijuana plants. Each plant was topped with spiky buds, nearing harvest. The slender, palmate leaves drooped gracefully. The smell was almost enough to make me high.

The gas furnace and washing machine and dryer that stood in one corner added a touch of domesticity. Beside the washing machine was a door secured with a padlock. I took a step toward it, curious about what lay behind the door, but just then I thought I heard a noise above me.

Such an operation wouldn't be left unguarded so that someone like me could just walk in and take notes. There was a fortune in dope in this basement. The realization that Allan Jakes might kill me if he found me here, made me break into a sudden cold sweat. There must be a security system of some kind. Where was Allan? I took one last look at the padlocked door and turned away. It was time to get out.

I tiptoed back up the stairs, turned sharply to the right and ran into someone. In the dark hallway, all I could tell was that it was a man. He had been moving away when I hit him, but he turned quickly and grabbed my shoulders.

We grappled with one another, neither of us speaking, just grunting in the dim light, clawing at each other for an advantage. He was dressed in a heavy coat, and a cap covered his head. I clutched his coat and aimed a punch for his throat, but he turned, and my blow glanced off his shoulder.

I tripped him, and he went down. He swore as he fell. I tried to jump over him in the hallway, planning to run out the door, but he twisted on the floor, snaked out a long arm and grabbed my foot. I fell on my face, and he was on top of me. He forced my arm behind me and bent it until I cried out in pain.

The man was stronger than I. His hands were like iron. Now that he had me at his mercy, he seemed undecided as to what to do next. He swore softly to himself, and I suddenly recognized his voice.

"Tapply!"

He released his hold, and I rolled over.

"Turn the damn light on," I said, rubbing my shoulder.

"Son of a bitch," Tapply said. "What are you doing here?" He reached above him and switched on a light.

We both blinked in the sudden brightness. His face was almost white, and his expression still twisted in the fierceness it must have worn while we fought.

"Playing Nancy Drew," I said. When in doubt, go on the offensive.

"What are you doing here?"

He was ready for the question. "I was thinking about what you said the other night. About Allan having a reason to kill Gil." He pulled a white handkerchief out of his pocket and wiped a trickle of blood from the corner of his mouth. "Jesus, you play for keeps, Viv."

"No point in doing things halfway."

"I was always a fan of the pass/fail system." His voice held a hint of laughter.

"So you were checking out Allan's house for evidence that he murdered Gil?"

"Something like that." Tapply took my arm. "Let's get out of here."

TWENTY-ONE

Tapply's silver MG was hidden on a side road next to a copse of cedar trees, which explained why I hadn't seen it from Allan's house. I pulled the van behind it and switched off the engine.

Tapply sat on the passenger side in fitful silence, playing an invisible keyboard with his long, slender fingers.

"The person who told me about Allan's pot-growing operation didn't lie," I said. The next part was tricky, but I counted on the strength of the offensive. "I also heard that Gil laundered the money through High Spirits."

Tapply's hands gripped one another as if he knew his fingers betrayed his nervousness. "Gil took care of the bar's finances, and our auditor always gave us a clean bill of health."

"Did Gil hire the auditor?"

Tapply's silence was answer enough.

"Look," he finally said. "The business is my life. Don't take it from me."

"All I want to do is find out who killed Gil," I said. "Maybe that will mean Charley can come home, and our lives can go on."

"I'm on your side," Tapply said. "Just give me some time to work things out."

"Work things out? Is that why you broke into Allan's house?"

When Tapply and I had left through Allan's kitchen, Tapply had entered a security code into the burglar alarm that was mounted outside the back door. I hadn't even noticed it when I came in. So much for Nancy Drew.

"How did you know his code?" I now asked.

"He talks in his sleep," Tapply said, with a short laugh.

"You can do better than that."

He turned toward me, his hazel eyes gauging me. "I'll share a little trick with you. You can buy ultraviolet ink at scientific supply stores. You spray it on the doorknob next to the alarm, and the occupant spreads it to the keypad of the burglar alarm when he enters the code. Then the person who wants to enter, me for instance, shines an ultraviolet light on the keypad to determine the numbers in the code."

I was impressed. "Where did you learn to do that?"

Tapply's smile almost disguised his nervousness. "You can buy books about that kind of stuff," he said.

I attacked from a new direction. "What did you really hope to find in Allan's house?"

His eyes glowed wickedly from under his long lashes. "Evidence, my dear."

"And you found?"

"You."

I hit the steering wheel with my palm. "Let's stop playing games for one minute. Allan and Gil were business partners. Something went wrong. A squabble over money. A disagreement over Mica. Allan killed Gil. Can we make that work?"

Tapply looked thoughtful. "Allan and Gil were like a remora and a shark. Allan hitched a ride on Gil. You don't kill your ride. Unless . . ." He was suddenly all business. "Maybe we can make it stick. If Charley will cooperate."

Damn Charley. It always came back to him.

"I saw him this morning," I said. "He told me to butt out."

"But you didn't."

"I can't." Frustration hit me like a granite wall. I was between the proverbial rock and a hard place, between my need to know the truth and my loyalty to Charley. "Loyalty," I said. "What a crock of shit."

"Loyalty." Tapply said the word like an epithet. "Its measure cannot be taken until it's too late to render it meaningful."

He stared out the window at the brooding sky. A black crow flew from the cedar grove. I started to say something, but Tapply's voice interrupted.

"I had a brother," he said. "He was older than me by a dozen years, and my parents worshipped him. They didn't have much, my parents, but they would have sacrificed anything for him. He was an athlete, scholar and musician, and so handsome that girls threw themselves at him." Tapply's voice was hushed, as though he were talking to himself.

"He died the year I was 10," Tapply said. "Drove his car right into a tree. And you would think that the hopes my parents pinned on my brother would have transferred to me. But it didn't work that way. I tried everything, but their loyalty died with him."

"That must have been hard."

"It was good for me. Lessons in life and all that. I learned you have to be loyal to yourself." Tapply looked directly at me. "You can't count on anyone else."

By the time I made it home, it was midafternoon. Charley's and my house perched on a bluff above Spring Creek, and this time of the year, through the bare trees, I could almost see the water below. I turned away from the oversize windows and studied the interior. The house was small, hand-built by Charley and me and our friends. The property was in Charley's name. If I couldn't clear Charley's name, how much longer could I call this place home?

The lower level encompassed one large room organized into office, living and kitchen areas, with a bathroom enclosed along the north wall. The stairs cut through the center of the house, rising to a loft that housed the lone bedroom. The decor was simple, tending toward art created by friends: Terra's reed baskets, Vance's ceramic sculpture, Pam's hand-woven rugs.

It was inevitable that I would compare the cleanliness of Allan Jakes's house with the one in which Charley and I lived. There wasn't much to feel superior about. I threw myself into a cleaning frenzy and mopped, dusted and scrubbed until my lax standards were satisfied.

Finally, I shoveled the ashes out of the Vermont Castings stove and swept up weeks' worth of wood chips and bark that had spilled around its base. Wood heat. Warms you twice, they say. First when you chop the wood and second when you burn it.

After I built a fire in the stove and brewed a pot of coffee, I traded my shoes for fur-lined moccasins and sat in my rocking chair and looked out the window that opened onto the Spring Creek valley. Working had calmed me better than a sedative, and lethargy settled over me like a heavy blanket.

After a long time, four deer — three does and a yearling — emerged among the trees below the house. They pushed aside the leaves with their muzzles, and they seemed to be eating something, acorns perhaps. One by one, they bedded on the ground. Their tawny coats were the same color as the forest floor, and if I looked away, it was an effort to find them again. It was usually the soft white hair inside their ears, pointing toward the slightest sound, that gave them away.

I stifled an urge to go outside and startle them. The scene was too damn peaceful.

Mack emerged from wherever he had been hiding and joined me.

"Life sucks," I told him. I stroked his head, and he leaped into my lap and kneaded me with his paws.

Before Tapply and I left the side road next to Allan's property, we had made an agreement. Tapply knew an accountant who would examine the bar's books to determine whether Gil had used the business to launder drug money. He promised to share the results with me; in turn, I agreed to hold off talking to the police or writing a story for the newspaper.

Once we determined the extent of the bar's involvement, we would decide what to do about Allan Jakes. I wasn't easy with the agreement, but it was Tapply who had access to the records. I also understood that he had an investment to protect, and for him, that would come first. "Be loyal to yourself," he had said.

Before leaving Tulsa, I had stopped by Mica's house again, but the note I had wedged between the door and jamb still ruffled in the breeze like a white flag of surrender.

Now at home by the fire, I dozed off and dreamed of elevators and uniformed guards and someone or something just beyond my desperate reach. I was awakened by a pounding at the door.

It was dark, and it took a moment to remember where I was. I was suddenly wide awake and wary. When you live in the country, far from neighbors, one doesn't simply open the door to the unknown.

On the other hand, the only time I locked the door was when I left the house or went to bed. You would think I would learn.

Just as I switched on the lights, the door burst open and Mica flew through it.

"Where is she?" Mica's eyes were wild, and her expression that of a woman pushed over the edge. She was gasping as though she had run up the hill, and in her hand she waved a gun. Its black barrel caught the light like the head of a striking snake.

I stepped back when I saw the gun.

"You have no right. She's mine." Mica's voice was shrill with hysteria. She gripped the gun as though she knew how to use it.

"Mica, are you on drugs?" I tried to sound calm, but my voice shook. "Put that gun down so we can talk."

"Don't tell me what to do. Don't even try to tell me."

I tried the sympathy routine. "You've been through a lot."

Her pupils were so enlarged that her blue eyes seemed dark. "I want my daughter, damn you."

"I haven't seen her," I said. "Not since. . ." My voice trailed off. I couldn't remember the last time I saw Iris.

But I remembered something else. "She was with you at the High Spirits the night Gil . . ."

Mica wasn't listening, though. "My shaman told me negative energy was coming from this place."

I wanted to ask if her shaman had suggested she bring a gun, but she seemed to have forgotten it was in her hand, and I didn't want to remind her. The short barrel pointed toward the floor. It wasn't trained on me, but it was still a deadly weapon in the hands of an unstable woman.

She raised the gun again and waved it around. "We're going to look around, and if Iris isn't here, you'll tell me where you hid her."

Mica motioned me toward the stairs leading to the loft. I saw an opportunity, and I climbed the stairs, trying not to appear eager.

The pitfall of being your own building contractor is that there's no one else to blame for screw-ups. The builder of the stairs, okay, me, miscalculated the height to the next floor. My error wasn't discovered until the stairs were nearly completed. Rather than start over, I disguised the error by making the final riser two inches shorter than the others. Until Charley and I remembered it, we had stumbled on the final step.

When Mica reached the top, she did exactly as I expected; she faltered and nearly fell forward onto the loft floor. She put her hands out to catch herself, and the gun fell and skittered across the floor.

I scooped it up while she regained her balance.

When she realized she was disarmed, she fell into a heap on the floor and burst into tears.

I wasn't in the mood to comfort her. While she sobbed, I examined the gun.

It was an FN Browning Baby auto pistol, .25 caliber, with a 6-shot magazine, 2-1/8 inch barrel, blued finish with hard rubber stocks. I remembered Gil showing it off one night.

I checked the magazine; it wasn't loaded.

After awhile Mica regained control, and she stood shakily, wiping the tears from her swollen face.

"Do you have bullets for this thing?" I held up the gun.

"No." She stared at the floor.

I handed the gun to her. "Let's start over," I said. "When did you last see Iris?"

Mica took a deep breath. She looked at the gun like it was an unsolvable puzzle and stuck it in her pants pocket. "I wasn't going to hurt you," she said. "I just wanted to get your attention."

"My attention is got. So . . . Iris?"

"The night Charley killed Gil," she said, "Iris and I left High Spirits early. Allan called and told me what had happened. I went back to the bar, and when I came home, she was gone."

"Have you heard from her?" The small shiver of worry I had felt about Iris earlier in the day returned, full-blown now.

"She left a note that said she was going somewhere safe. But she didn't even leave a name or phone number." Mica's shoulders slumped and she began weeping again. "I wasn't too worried. It wasn't the first time she did something like that. And I had other things to deal with."

"So you thought she came here."

"This is where she always wanted to be." The statement was bald and irrefutable. Mica lifted her face, and in the light above the stairs, it looked haggard and old.

"I haven't seen her, Mica."

The sharp odor of alcohol floated through the air. So, I thought, you were able to hold it all inside until you had a few drinks too many. Then you came after me. Nice.

Mica continued her line of thought. "It's always Charley this, Charley that," she said bitterly. "Iris blamed me for leaving him. She blamed me for not being you."

"The point is we need to find her."

"I'm sure you can succeed where I've failed." Mica's resentment boiled over again. "Ms. Perfect. Ms. Competent. Ms. Strong-as-a-horse."

I wanted to slap her, but instead I said, "I'll help you find her. Let's start by making a list of her friends."

We went downstairs. As it turned out, Mica didn't know much about her daughter. Iris hadn't left many clues in her room, either: no diary, no address book, only a school directory, which Mica handed me. None of the names were marked.

Mica listed first names she had heard Iris mention: Lisa, Andrew, Erin, Nina, Jared. None had ever been to their house, but she knew where Nina lived, had met Andrew's mother at a school function. Those were the leads I had.

Saturday evening. Monday I would meet with Charley's lawyer, perhaps learn about Roz Hoffing's finances from Kyra, beg Hank not to fire me, find out what Tapply had learned from his accountant, perhaps learn more about Gil's former girlfriend from Pete Terrapin.

But for now a 13-year-old girl was missing.

TWENTY-TWO

I pieced together enough clues from the school directory to reach Nina's house. Mica sipped hot tea while I talked to Nina's mother. Nina wasn't in, she said reluctantly. Even when I said I was calling on behalf of Iris's mother, she didn't warm to me, as though that were an insufficient recommendation. Her voice was guarded and distant.

"Look," I said. "Iris lost her stepfather this week, and then she disappeared. She may need help."

"Iris has needed help for some time now," Nina's mother said.

"What do you mean?"

"She's a troubled girl," she said. "I don't want her near Nina."

Troubled girl? Iris? When she visited Charley and me, she always seemed happy and well-adjusted — at least as much so as most teenagers. I wondered if she had given some sign that we missed.

"Please," I said, "just give me some more names. I don't know who to ask."

Nina's mother gave me the names and phone numbers of other junior high students who might know Iris. I thanked her and hung up.

Then I turned to Mica. "She said Iris was a troubled girl," I said. "She said she has needed help for some time now."

Mica's eyes didn't meet mine. "She's just like the other girls her age," she said. "She thinks adults stand between her and happiness. It's just hormones. She lies. She sulks. She's departed from her path. I was that way once."

"Departed from her path?"

Mica's face took on the otherworldly look it had worn a few days earlier when she talked about her study group and her shaman. She stroked a gray and white feather that hung from a thong around her neck. "Her animal guide, the dragonfly, would lead her to enlightenment. But she fears the power."

"Does Iris attend your study groups?"

"My shaman sees her need, but she's too young to understand."

I took that to mean no. Perhaps to Iris, her dragonfly pendant was just a pretty piece of jewelry. I was beginning to wonder, though, if Mica's mysticism had blinded her to her daughter's real problems.

I turned back to the phone, but the other people I reached were no more helpful than Nina's mother. The parents I talked to either didn't know Iris or they hadn't seen her recently. When they called their children to the phone, the voices of Iris's friends were hushed, and they didn't volunteer any information.

I marked the final name off the list and turned to Mica. "Write down her class schedule and her teachers' names," I said. "Maybe she confided in a teacher."

Mica looked at me helplessly. "I don't know her schedule."

"What classes is she taking?"

Mica listed the usual: language arts, social studies, science, math. Then she stopped.

I tried to jog her memory. "PE? Spanish? Band? What else did she take?"

"Yearbook," Mica said. "Spanish."

"Teachers' names?"

Mica shook her head helplessly.

According to the school directory, nearly a thousand students attended the school, and most subjects had several teachers. However, only one yearbook teacher was listed. Her name was Audrey Fields.

Her answering machine picked up my call. I left a message saying I was trying to locate Iris and that I would try again later.

"Unless you can provide me with more names," I told Mica, "I've done all that I can right now."

It seemed like far too little.

Mica was on her way out the door before I remembered that I had been searching for her earlier in the day.

"I saw Charley this morning," I said.

She stopped in mid-stride.

"He must have sensed that something was wrong. He asked me to check on you and Iris."

Mica shut the door and leaned against it. "He always was intuitive — for a man," she said. Her earlier hostility had evaporated, and she seemed more like the Mica I knew.

The Mica I had thought I knew.

"He's not doing well," I said. "He's hiding something. Maybe he's trying to protect someone." Until I said the words, I hadn't allowed the thought to surface. *He's trying to protect someone.* Who?

Mica averted her eyes.

"Is that why he's not talking? Is he protecting you?"

Mica hugged herself. "Don't be so melodramatic," she said. "I don't mean that much to him."

"Iris does," I said. I couldn't stop myself from making revelations I didn't want to hear as though some truthsayer had taken over my body.

A look of alarm betrayed Mica's face. "Iris has nothing to hide," she said. Her voice was severe and final.

She has nothing to hide but she's hiding, I thought.

I reached Audrey Fields Sunday morning. The yearbook teacher knew who Iris was, and the concern in her voice sounded genuine.

She said she had something to show me, and we agreed to meet at the school at 1 p.m.

Traffic on the highway to Tulsa was light, the day was sunny, and the forecast promised highs in the mid-50s. I crossed Lake Fort Gibson, where sunlight traced the waves with fire, and a flock of Canada geese skimmed the barren trees. In a matter of weeks, wild plum blossoms would splash the forest with white, and morel mushrooms and wild onions would poke through the rotting carpet of leaves.

I should have been celebrating the coming spring, but my timing was off. I noted the signs of the changing season and then sank back into the dread that hadn't left me since Mica had burst into my living room the night before. I didn't know which worried me more: finding Iris or hearing what she might say.

West Central Middle School was a two-story, red brick building wedged between a complex of bleak public housing and an abandoned field. The first-floor windows were protected with steel mesh. A rusted fence enclosed the asphalt-paved school yard. The basketball goals had chain nets. I had heard that most well-to-do Tulsa parents sent their children to private schools, and now I wondered why Mica and Gil had chosen a school like this for Iris.

Then I wondered why I had never thought about it before. Iris had a life outside the time she spent with Charley and me. It had just been easier not to think about it. To assume a state of well-being. To imagine a normal childhood — whatever that meant.

As promised, Audrey Fields's older model, mustard-colored Volvo was parked on the east side of the building, near a steel door that she had said would be left open for me. I followed her directions to the end of a dimly lit hallway. The lockers that lined the hall were graffiti-scrawled; the tile floor yellow from years of wax buildup.

I entered Fields's classroom expecting more of the same, but it was clean and cheerful, and the walls were covered with posters and samples of students' work. Fields was brisk but welcoming as she rose from the stack of papers she was grading.

"I like a person who's on time," she said, leaning over her desk to shake my hand. She was a big woman, tall and heavy-breasted, wearing gray-permed curls and a flowered dress.

She was soft-spoken but authoritative as she told me about the student population at West Central. "We serve some of the poorest families in the city," she said. She tapped a red pen on the desk as she spoke. "More than 70 percent of our students qualify for free or reduced-price lunches. Half the students will move before the year's out. Our reading and math scores are below the state norm. The building's a mess, and the taxpayers won't vote to raise the levy so we can repair our drinking fountains and paint over the graffiti."

She pointed toward the window. "Did you see the Frosty King across the street?"

I nodded.

"The kids hang out in the parking lot before school and smoke cigarettes and buy drugs."

"What about Iris?"

Fields smiled. "Iris? She's special. A bright student, very talented. I was sorry to hear about her stepfather. That's hard on a kid her age."

"Has she been attending class?"

Fields thumbed through her grade book. "Not since Monday." Her gray eyes filled with concern. "You said she's missing."

"Her mother hasn't seen her since the night her stepfather was killed." I couldn't bring myself to say the word "murdered" or to tell this woman that my lover was the chief suspect.

"Have the police been alerted?"

"She left a note for her mother," I said. "We don't think she's in danger, but we're worried, of course."

I reminded her that she had said on the phone that she had something to show me. She turned away, opened a file drawer and drew out a manila folder. She handed it to me.

"Iris is the lifestyles photo editor for the yearbook," Fields said. "This is the latest assignment she handed in. You can see what I mean when I said she has talent."

The folder was crammed with black-and-white images, but they weren't shot at school. They showed children on the Tulsa streets, day shots, night shots, children on skateboards, children playing makeshift drums on a street corner, children on dirty mattresses in dark rooms, children smoking crack. A girl in a miniskirt leaned in the window of a Lincoln Continental. A boy with pale skin showed off a fresh tattoo of the Grim Reaper.

"Iris. Is she . . ." I wasn't sure what I wanted to ask.

"I've been teaching for 27 years," Fields said, "and I've never had a student produce work of this quality and emotional depth. I see Iris only an hour a day, but we've talked after school from time to time. She stopped coming by these past weeks. I'm worried about her. She seems very mature for her age, but she's just a child nonetheless."

"She has an adult perspective," I said. I looked at the photos again. "This kid." I handed Fields the photo of the boy with the tattoo. "Do you know him?"

"Matt Crenshaw," Fields said. "He started the year here. He's older than Iris, but they were friends. His mother moved recently, and one of the kids told me he was on the street."

"On the street?"

"Homeless." She said the word as though it were normal. "Some of these photos were shot at St. Francis House on 14th. It's a shelter for teenagers. You might find Matt there."

I left Fields marking papers at her desk. I took three things with me: the photo of Matt Crenshaw, directions to the St. Francis House and a growing fear that Iris might need more help than I could offer.

TWENTY-THREE

It was midafternoon when I found St. Francis House. A faded sign and a statue of St. Francis stood in front of it. Clouds had darkened the sky, and in the muted light, the two-story brick building was dark and forbidding as though it were left over from a Dickens novel. Two trees in the front yard had been butchered by an overzealous trimmer, and their stubbed arms framed the open front door.

I hesitated at the door, waiting and listening, not sure of homeless shelter protocol. From inside the dimly lit entry hall, a voice greeted me.

"Come on in. The typhoid epidemic has passed."

"I was pondering whether one should knock on an open door or slip in with the breeze." My eyes adjusted and focused on a man who sat in a wheelchair in the entry hall. His blond hair was pulled back in a ponytail, and his beard was neatly trimmed. He wore a Grateful Dead T-shirt, khakis and Birkenstock sandals with socks.

"Gary Voeder," he said. "I'm chief nut of this nuthouse."

I introduced myself and told him why I was there. While I talked, a group of teenagers, three girls and two boys, walked down the stairs and out the door. Most lit cigarettes when they reached the sidewalk.

"Don't forget, kiddies, doors close at 10," Gary called after them.

One raised a hand in careless acknowledgment, and they disappeared down the street.

Voeder pivoted in his wheelchair to face me again. "Matt Crenshaw is like most of the other kids who live here. Basically good kids who are just trying to survive to adulthood. Either their parents threw them out or said they couldn't control them. Social services stepped in and made sure they had a place to get fed and a safe place to sleep at night. It's not easy being a kid these days."

I showed him a picture of Iris. "Have you seen her?"

He studied the photo then gave it back to me. "I don't think so."

"She's a friend of Matt's, and she may be in trouble."

He looked at his watch. "Matt should be here any minute."

"Where is he now?"

Voeder gave me a look of barely disguised forbearance. "He's at work. The kids who live here either have jobs or go to school. Matt works at the Git 'n' Go down the street. His weekend shift is 7 to 3. I save a plate of Sunday dinner for him."

"Do you think he'll talk to me?"

Voeder gave me the look again. "That's up to him. If you browbeat him or yell at him, I'll throw you out."

I involuntarily glanced at his wheelchair. Of course, he noticed.

"Don't think I couldn't," Voeder said. He flexed his bulging biceps. "I'm in better shape than most people you know."

I promised to behave, and we went to the kitchen to wait for Matt Crenshaw.

He didn't keep us waiting long.

From somewhere in the house a screen door slammed, and a moment later Matt walked into the kitchen. I was positioned behind Voeder, and Matt didn't see me at first, giving me a chance to study him.

He was smaller than I expected from the photo. Slightly built and shorter than average. He peeled off a black leather jacket to reveal pale skin and the Grim Reaper tattoo.

"Hey, man," he said to Voeder, then turned his back to pick up the plate of food from the counter and stick it in the microwave. He punched in the time and started heating the food. His dark hair was long and greasy, and when he swung to face us, the hair hung down over his eyes.

He started to say something, then saw me. He nodded at me pleasantly.

"This is Viv Powers, Matt. She has a few questions for you," Voeder said.

Matt's eyes narrowed, and his body tensed.

"I'm looking for Iris," I said. "She may need help . . ."

Matt pivoted and ran for the back door.

I took off after him.

"Hey," Voeder shouted. But his voice was far behind.

Matt vaulted the back fence and raced down the alley. I was only a few steps behind.

"Matt," I yelled. "I just want to talk."

He glanced over his shoulder and saw I was gaining on him. He grabbed a garbage can and threw it at me.

The can bounced in front of me, scattering a foul mixture of rotting food and damp paper. I slipped on something and nearly fell.

I regained my footing and concentrated on running him down.

Matt had the advantage of youth; my legs were longer. We pounded down the deserted Sunday afternoon sidewalk, through a red light, past brick row houses with tiny yards.

A car pulled up to the curb and a family emerged, dressed in their Sunday best. Dark suits and ties, fussy dresses and London Fog coats. Late church service or a slow dinner at Furr's cafeteria, I thought, as I sped past. They watched us silently with stunned expressions. Mother, father, son and daughter. Matt and I must have appeared to be a prime time thriller bursting through the TV screen to life.

I was gasping for breath, but Matt was slowing. I made one last effort, sprinted until my legs and lungs were burning, reached as far as I could, and grabbed Matt's hair.

He twisted under my grip and yelped with pain. But he stopped.

For a moment, we stood together, bent over, gulping air. My lungs were seared.

"Shit," Matt said. "Let the fuck go of my hair."

"Hell, no," I said. "You'll just start running again."

"I'm gonna call the fuckin' police if you don't let go of me."

I released his hair and grabbed his shirt. "I just want to talk about Iris. Can we just talk for a minute?"

His face wore a sulky look. "You talk, and then we'll see."

We sat on a mildewed bench at a covered bus stop. I no longer re-strained him, but he showed no sign of bolting.

I told him who I was and why I was looking for Iris. He seemed to know about Charley, and at the mention of his name, he relaxed. But when I brought up Mica, he tensed again, and I was afraid he would run.

"You don't like Iris's mother." It was a statement.

"She's bad news."

"What do you mean?" As if I didn't have my own reasons for dislik-ing Mica.

He shot me a suspicious look. "I don't know whose side you're on, but adults side with each other. That's all I know."

"Is she all right? Is Iris safe?"

"How would I know?"

"Would you just ask her to talk to me?"

"What makes you think I can ask her anything?"

I grabbed his shirt again. "Look, you little prick. You don't have the right to make decisions for Iris. Neither do I. All I'm asking from you is to arrange a meeting if that's what Iris wants."

"Jesus." He shook my hand off. "Chill, lady. I'll see what I can do."

I gave him the number at the High Spirits and said I would wait there until I heard from him.

"Let me know today one way or the other," I said, "or I'll find you again. I'm good at that."

TWENTY-FOUR

The High Spirits was open, but only a few people were in the bar. They spoke in subdued voices, and the music played softly. I ordered a beer from a bartender I didn't recognize. I didn't see Tapply and I didn't ask about him.

I sat at the bar, worried that I might miss Matt Crenshaw's call, worried that he wouldn't call and that I would have to make good on my threat. Worried that Iris might burrow in deeper, wherever she was.

Just after seven he called.

"She said she would see you," Matt said. "But you can't bring anyone with you." His voice was cold and angry.

"I won't bring anyone."

"There's a place on Elgin, a club. Be there at 9. We'll be around back in the alley. But no tricks; we'll have friends backing us up."

I wrote down the address and hung up. Nine. I had two hours to kill. I asked the bartender if he knew the address.

"It's a Goth night club," he said.

"Goth?"

He wiped up the beer I had spilled when I took the call. "You know, Gothics. Black clothes, black hair, black makeup. They're into death and body piercing and vampires and stuff like that."

"Great."

The bartender smiled. "Hell, it's not like they're skinheads or Hell's Angels. Just roll with it."

Rolling with it wasn't my style. I drove to the meeting place an hour early. I found it with some difficulty. The street was dark and the club had no sign, only a street number in small figures above the door. It was in a row of dilapidated storefronts that looked mostly deserted.

Traffic was light. I parked the van at the end of the block and looked in the windows of businesses as I walked along the street: a pawnshop with dirty and barred windows, two empty buildings, an insurance office, a small store with a sign offering tarot readings and massages, another empty building and the Goth club.

I tried the door; it was locked. I pressed my ear against the door. Nothing.

"Bastard," I said, picturing Matt Crenshaw.

The opening to the alley was dark and narrow, but it widened to a small lot filled with cars. The lot smelled of mechanic's grease and acetylene torches, and I realized I was behind a garage. The lone security light showed that most of the dozen or so cars were in an advanced state of disrepair. Some had been wrecked, and their twisted shapes were reminders of past terror and pain. Others stood on blocks, their wheels stripped away.

It was like a post-apocalyptic landscape where morning never dawned, and hungry coyotes roamed the dark streets. I realized how alone I was, and I tightened my jacket around me and made a slow 360-degree turn, watching for movement, listening for the tell-tale sound. Nothing.

"Bastard," I said again.

I cautiously made my way to what I judged to be the back door of the Goth club. It, too, was locked and silent, secured with a heavy padlock and thick metal straps.

I retreated to the car lot, found an unlocked car that offered a view of the club door and settled on the torn bench seat to wait. I fiddled with the radio dial and pushed in the cigarette lighter. Nervous habits. In my jacket pocket was a turkey sub I had picked up at a convenience store on my way to the club. I dug it out and chewed it slowly, ignoring the aftertaste of plastic wrap.

The first pair arrived half an hour later. They wore black cloaks, and they trod the alley so quietly that I didn't see them until I heard the shriek of the door opening. The two disappeared inside, quickly followed by another group, all similarly clad in black. The goths were gathering, and it appeared the alley was the entrance of choice.

I watched while more people in black passed through the doorway. By 9 p.m., I guessed the club held about 30 people. I hadn't seen Iris or Matt, but it wasn't likely that I would have recognized their shapes as they passed.

Once I was driving down Muskogee Avenue in Tahlequah when I saw a man on a mountain bike. He was stopped at a red light, and he balanced the bike with one leg casually pushed against the light pole. He wore a black helmet, biker shorts and a gray T-shirt, and his body was lean and muscular. I admired his sexy, confident grace as he waited for the light to change. It wasn't until later that I realized the man was Charley. So why should I expect to recognize Iris's shape in the dark alley?

I gave Matt Crenshaw ten minutes, then I left the car lot and headed for the club. A pale light glowed around the closed door. I approached it slowly, wishing that I, too, were wearing black instead of faded Levis and a gray fleece jacket. I knew I would stand out like a sparrow in a flock of crows.

The door pushed open under my hand, its earlier screeching eased by the constant traffic.

The first person I saw was a tall and willowy woman with parchment-colored skin and long, black hair. Her blank eyes were dark-ringed with liner and she wore black lipstick. Somehow she pulled it off and looked exotic. She pointed at me with a long black fingernail and said, "Richard's mother."

I was vaguely aware of black-garbed figures clustered like oversize vultures around their kill. Music played, slow and menacing. Someone on the stage recited poetry, something about fading to crimson, fading to black.

"I'm looking for someone," I said to the woman. I didn't ask who Richard was.

Before the woman could reply, I saw Matt. He took my arm and pushed me toward the door.

"Not here," he said. "I told you the alley."

"Where's Iris?"

"They won't let her in here. She's too young."

Matt led the way down the alley. I followed him around the corner to where Charley's van was parked. We stopped by the back door.

He nodded toward the van. "I'm going to be right here. If you try to take her away, you'll have to get past me." He let his jacket fall open so I could see a gun tucked in his waistband.

"Shit," I said. "Even the babies have guns these days."

Matt's face wore a mixed expression of determination and pride.

"Look," I said. "I'm her friend. You can relax."

I left him standing by the van and opened the door. In the dim over-head light, I could see a figure huddled in a corner. It was wrapped in one of Charley's wool army blankets.

"Iris?"

She must have been asleep because she jumped when I said her name.

"Is that you, Viv?" she said. Her voice was high-pitched like a little girl's.

I climbed in beside her and hugged her. Her long, blond hair was dirty and tangled and smelled like freshly turned earth. She put her arms around me awkwardly then wriggled out of my embrace.

"I've been worried about you," I said.

She rubbed her eyes. "I think I fell asleep waiting."

I sat beside her. "Iris, are you okay?"

Now that the door was closed, the only light shone from the street through the van windows. Iris was little more than a dark shape. She was larger than I remembered. No longer a child.

"I don't like to make everyone worry," she said. "Tell Mica I'm okay."

"Are you?"

She shifted on the hard metal of the van floor. "I'm kinda hungry."

"Let's go get something to eat."

"N-no. Send Matt for something. A cheese sandwich and a Pepsi. He can get those in the club."

I rolled down a window, handed some money to Matt and told him what Iris wanted. Not that he would take my word for it. He leaned his head in until he could see Iris.

"That right, Iris?" he asked.

"Go ahead," she said. "Viv is pure."

"If I'm so goddammed pure," I said after Matt left, "talk to me. What happened? Why did you run?"

Too many questions at once, but they had been bottled up.

Iris twisted her body like a trapped animal and instead of answering, she said, "Is Charley going to die?"

"Die? Probably not. But he's in a lot of trouble right now."

"What if I killed Gil? They couldn't do anything to me 'cause I'm just a kid."

The question caught me off guard. "Don't even think about it," I said. "The justice system isn't very understanding these days when it comes to juvenile crime."

"But I did it. Really." She was breathless, and her eyes, in the faint light from the street, beseeched me to believe her.

I grabbed her hands in mine. They were cold. "Why would you kill him? Why?"

Iris wrenched away and buried her face in her hands. After a minute she said in a soft voice, "Remember when Mica and Gil got married? I came to stay with you and Charley while they went someplace in Mexico. Remember I was sick, and Charley stayed by my bed all night? He held my head when I got sick and he put cold towels on my forehead. As soon as the sun came up, he found a doctor to see me."

"I remember," I said. Iris was soon well, but the image that stayed with me was Charley in the lamplight, bent over Iris and soothing her all through the long night while she cried.

"When Mica and Gil came to pick me up in Gil's Porsche," Iris said, "I wanted to stay with you guys. Mica was so mad."

"She's not mad now. She's worried."

"*Now* she's worried." Iris's young voice rose with sarcasm.

I turned to face her. "She came to the house last night searching for you. She was nearly out of her mind." I didn't mention the gun she had carried. No need for Iris to know just how desperate her mother had been.

There was a discreet tap on the door. It opened and Matt poked his head in. He handed Iris a paper sack, gave me a look that said I'd better not pull any funny stuff and then withdrew.

She tore into the food. I watched her eat. Her small, sharp teeth made quick work of the sandwich. She reached into the bag, but there was no more food.

"You haven't been eating well," I said.

"I was getting fat."

She was slender as a wraith, like her mother, but where Mica was slight and delicate, Iris was tall and willowy.

"We have to talk now," I told her.

She sighed and crumpled the paper bag until it was a small ball in her hands.

"I'm not going back to her," Iris said.

"We have to talk about that night. The night Gil was murdered." I didn't try to cushion the words, didn't create a gentle euphemism: passed away, went to his eternal rest, met an untimely end, quit this world or any of that other bullshit that we use to shield ourselves from the reality of death.

"I bet you don't know how I got in the van." Iris's teeth flashed white in the dim light.

"No." Until now, I hadn't even thought about it.

"Charley gave me a key last summer when he was teaching me how to drive. I never gave it back. Matt was going to use a crowbar, but I had a key." Iris giggled, suddenly sounding again like the child I had known.

"Iris, we have to talk about something important. You didn't kill anyone. I know you too well. It must be difficult for you to think about that night, but Charley's freedom may be at stake. You don't want anything to happen to Charley, do you?" The last part was cruel, a psychological weapon that I didn't hesitate to use on a young girl. That's how desperate I was.

Iris drew a deep breath, her childish teasing forgotten. "I love Charley. You know I do. That's why I ..."

I waited but she didn't finish her sentence.

"I love Charley, too," I said. "But if I don't know the truth about what happened that night, I can't help him."

"Maybe no one can help him," Iris said.

I ignored her warning. "You were there the night Gil died. You were with Jason and Heather and then you left. What happened next?"

"I went to the bathroom, and on the way back to the studio I passed by the band room — you know where they wait to go on stage?"

"I know."

Iris looked down. "Gil was there. He grabbed me and pulled me in the room. We were fighting, and he yanked off my necklace. You know the dragonfly that Charley gave me. He was such a jerk. I hated him." Her voice, which had started off matter-of-factly recounting the memory, had become shrill.

"So I hit him and I ran away and hid and Charley found me. He was really mad. He said who did this to you? And I told him."

"You hit him." I repeated her words. "Did he fall down?"

She crumpled her paper bag more tightly. "He yelled at me. I thought he was going to . . ." Her voice trailed off.

Gil hadn't been dead when Iris left. My voice seemed unconnected to my body. "What did Charley do?"

"He left and then Mica came and we went home."

"Did he say anything?"

"He said, 'I'm going to kill him,'" Iris said almost inaudibly.

The night took on a deeper shade of darkness, and in the stillness, I thought I could hear my heart beating. We sat in silence and time lost its meaning. Minutes, hours later, a thought rose to the surface.

"What were you and Gil fighting about, Iris?"

"Nothing."

"It must have been something."

"It wasn't. It was stupid." Iris's voice held a note of panic.

"So tell me." I grabbed her wrist, and she twisted from my grasp, and jumped out of the van. I made it out the door in time to see her running figure disappear around the end of the alley.

I would have pursued her, but Matt blocked my way.

"Leave her alone," he said. "You got what you came for."

"I want to take her home," I said, shaking his hand off my arm. "She could get hurt on her own."

"Like she didn't get hurt at home?" Matt's voice mocked me. "Like her old man didn't hurt her?"

I turned to face him. "What are you talking about?"

"You know damned well." In the glow of the streetlight, his dark-rimmed eyes seemed ringed by silver. "Young girl, dirty old man, you know damned well."

And suddenly I did know. It was all too clear. Gil and Iris. Somehow Charley had found out. I finally knew what could push Charley to murder.

TWENTY-FIVE

When I was 6 years old and my sister was no more than a mystery that rounded my mother's stomach, my mother tried to leave my father. I came to realize when I was older that Julia Ward Compton Powers, who was descended from northern gentility on the Ward side, felt she had married beneath herself. After all, Sgt. Randolph Gunter Powers was just an enlisted man with a high school education and a rough and rigid manner.

However, it wasn't her sense of superiority that prompted her decision to leave. It was my father's affair with another man's wife.

At age 6, I didn't understand the outburst of rage on both sides; it wasn't until I was a teenager that I heard about the other woman. All I knew then was that something ugly held our household prisoner, and invisibility was the only safety.

One night their raised voices awakened me. I untangled my legs from the long flannel nightgown that every night tried to strangle me and I crept to the end of the hall. My mother sat in her damask-covered chair, her head bowed. My father, towering threateningly, paced in front of her. Clothing pulled from an open suitcase lay across the floor as though bodies had once filled them before evaporating and leaving behind nothing but their twisted shapes.

"You're helpless without me. Where will you go? How will you live?

Who will protect our children?" His voice was relentless.

I ran back to my room and pulled the covers over my head.

My mother didn't leave, after all, and shortly after that, both my parents began attending the church on the army base at Ft. Leonard Wood where my father was then stationed. The base church proved too tolerant for my mother, and she soon found a fundamentalist congregation that provided her with hellfire and damnation and earned her the name The Saint. At least that is what my sister and I called her.

I remembered that night from the safety of time and the comfort of my bed that stood by the window overlooking Spring Creek. This time no flannel nightgown entangled me; the most I wore in bed anymore was a T-shirt. But I was entangled all the same.

Paralysis. What do you do when you find out your lover is a killer? Your lover's stepdaughter was sexually abused? Your life is unraveling and spinning out of control?

Staying in bed was the best I could come up with. All Monday morning I burrowed deeper under the covers when the phone rang, let the fire in the woodstove grow cold, ignored Mack's plaintive cries for attention.

I felt abandoned by those I depended on. My sister wasn't due back from her trip for another five days. Despite Charley's and my wide network of friends, there was no one I trusted enough to talk to about something so private. Charley was harboring dangerous secrets. Perhaps he had done the only thing he knew to do under the circumstances, and in a way it was courageous. But I resented his leaving me out. As for Charley's and my future, it seemed as murky as the events of the night Gil was murdered.

The part that ate at me, the part that made me despise myself, was that I was more afraid for myself than for Charley. The land we lived on was in his name; he had owned the property before I met him. A small inheritance, he had said, when I once asked how someone who never had any money had managed to buy land. Besides, land in Cherokee County was dirt cheap, no pun intended. Charley and I had built the house, but the land was his.

So I worried that if Charley were convicted of Gil's murder, I would lose this place that meant so much to me, the deep forest where I could wander and regain my sanity, the clear-flowing Spring Creek that soothed my spirit, the little house that hid me from the world.

About mid-morning, someone pounded on the door. I didn't bother to look out the window to see if I recognized the vehicle. This time the doors were locked; I felt secure in my isolation.

I watched a nuthatch land on the red oak outside the window. It clung upside down for a moment then flew away.

I wondered if nuthatches mated for life. It suddenly seemed an important question, and I dug out my Audubon bird guide from the pile of books on the night stand. I was still searching the index for nuthatch when Tapply walked through the bedroom door.

Somehow I wasn't surprised. Tapply was not a man to be denied.

He sauntered across the floor and sat on the edge of the bed. "You're not answering your phone," he said. He wore a soft leather jacket and faded blue jeans. His dark hair was artfully mussed.

I looked at him and then went back to my bird book. I found the entry and silently read from the guide: "Pairs seem to remain together year-round, for the species may be found in twos even in the dead of winter."

Tapply watched me closely. "This is a bad time to lose your focus," he said.

I dropped the book on the floor by the bed. The mating habits of nuthatches seemed inconclusive.

"I talked to Mica this morning," he continued. "She said she saw you last night. She said you weren't making a lot of sense. She said you talked to Iris."

I felt my mouth tightening as though to keep words from coming out. I had gone to see Mica after Iris ran away, but it was none of Tapply's business. Mica had reacted as expected: denial, anger, hysteria. She would have known if Gil messed with her daughter. Why was I doing this to her? Hadn't she been through enough? She tried to be a good mother. And why had I allowed Iris to run again? She finally pushed me out the door. I didn't care. I was leaving anyway.

Tapply was quiet for a moment. He followed my gaze out the window, and his handsome face took on the same brooding look I imagined mine wore. "If Charley killed Gil — if — he had a damned good reason," he said.

Damned good, I agreed silently.

"He hasn't confessed to anything, though," Tapply continued. "Our justice system assumes a man is innocent until proven guilty."

Maybe justice is blind, but truth is a laser, I thought.

"Mica and I had a long talk this morning," Tapply said. He leaned toward me and took my hand to make sure I was paying attention. "She has been afraid all along that Iris killed Gil and Charley was covering up for her."

I felt a dream-like sensation of falling. My voice, when it came, was a raspy whine. "Wait a minute. Last night Iris thought Charley killed Gil. Now Mica thinks Iris did it and Charley's protecting her?" I remembered Iris's confession the night before. It still didn't ring true.

"What if neither was the killer?" Tapply asked. His words were slow and distinct, but his eyes had taken on a sheen of almost unbearable excitement.

"If you came here to play games, leave now."

He ignored my words and squeezed my hand until it hurt. "Just listen for a minute. Who prompted the biggest manhunt this state has seen since the days of Pretty Boy Floyd?"

I jerked my hand away and tightened the covers around me. Tapply was like an animal ready to pounce.

"Tommy Hoffing." He answered his question. "And who did Gil fear in the days before his death? His cousin, Tommy Hoffing." He no longer waited for an answer. "Who do the police believe murdered a security guard in Tulsa the night after Gil was murdered? Tommy Hoffing."

He looked at me expectantly.

"What's your point?" I said.

"Tommy Hoffing could have murdered Gil."

"The police already heard that theory. They didn't buy it."

Tapply's voice was infinitely patient. "That's because they don't have any proof."

"Don't you think they would have found proof if there were any?"

"What if we helped them?"

"What are you talking about?" The future had seemed like a featureless wall; now a small crack opened. Under the blankets, I pulled on a pair of pants. The conversation called for pacing the floor, for expansive hand gestures. The bed was no longer a canvas large enough to contain the ideas that hung in the air.

"Reasonable doubt," Tapply said. "That's all we really need to create."

"You seemed to like Allan Jakes for a suspect the other day."

"Don't you see how much cleaner it is this way?"

"It's obvious. Allan's business dealings might involve your bar; he's Charley's and the band's manager. It's best to leave him out of it." I was looking out the window, and this time a pair of nuthatches landed on the red oak. I took it for a sign.

"Right. No need to point in our direction." Now that we seemed to be in agreement, Tapply visibly relaxed.

I finished dressing and led the way downstairs where I lit a fire and cooked a meal more substantial than I had eaten in a week: whole wheat muffins, two eggs, orange juice and a pot of coffee. Tapply's appetite matched mine. Over coffee, we hatched and discarded ideas.

Tapply said I should go to Roz's house on some pretext and pocket something of Tommy's that could then be planted on the scene.

"You go," I said. "I don't like being shot at by children."

My idea was as quickly rejected. "We need to find Gil's old girlfriend, Linda Smith," I said. "Maybe she can tell us why Gil was afraid of Tommy."

Tapply spilled his coffee, and we were busy wiping it up for a moment.

"You do remember Linda Smith," I said when we were once again settled. "Gil's girlfriend when you guys lived in the Farmhouse."

"Linda Smith," he said. "Vaguely. I can't imagine she would be much help. How did you come up with her name?"

I found my bag by the front door and dug out the framed picture he had allowed me to take from the Clinton Bedroom.

He looked at it for a long time and then handed it back.

"Gil's parents remembered her," I said.

"We'll have to do better than that to stir the police's interest." Tapply said. "That's ancient history."

"Gil and Tommy had a falling out over the boat in the picture," I said. "Something about its sale, Gil's father told me. That's all I know."

"It's something," Tapply said. "But not much."

Neither of us were able to do better, though. Tapply left for Tulsa with the understanding that we would talk again that night.

"Next time you visit," I told him as he was leaving, "wait to come in until someone answers the door."

He winked at me and left.

TWENTY-SIX

The previous Friday I had turned in the interview with the new wrestling coach before the deadline — just barely. I had managed to avoid Hank, but I knew that if I wanted to keep my job, I'd have to grovel and make promises about how much more reliable I would be in the future, family crises notwithstanding.

Tapply's visit had accomplished one visible result: I was up and moving. But as I came closer to the newspaper office, my foot on the van's gas pedal lightened, and I searched for excuses to put off going in. Eventually, though, I ended up in the parking lot of the Tahlequah Daily Tribune.

The afternoon was as unpleasant as expected. Hank used his male wiles — sarcasm, superiority, authority — to put me in my place. As punishment, he assigned the obits to me, and I sat in front of my computer and made phone calls all afternoon, playing the part of the thoroughly chastened employee.

In my usual contrary fashion, I decided to write obits worthy of the New York Times. I'd win Hank's heart back with graceful prose.

I called the funeral homes and asked them to fax their obit information. Cherokee County had three fewer people this week. Two were elderly; the third was a victim of a drunk driver. Phone book in lap, phone headset clamped on my head and two hands on the keyboard, I started calling the surviving family members.

Even after all these years as a reporter, I am sometimes amazed at people's willingness to talk to the press in the midst of tragedy. Hank told me once that it was because they didn't want their loved ones to die without public notice, to disappear as though no one cared.

Sometimes, their openness is as simple as this: No one else will talk to them about their loss. Well-meaning family and friends come by with a covered dish and sit and talk about the weather or the crops or the latest Tulsa Oilers game, anything to distract the bereaved. When all the bereaved really wants to talk about is their memories and their pain.

Inez Ola House, widow of the recently deceased Barney Leon House, age 87, told me that after retiring from Greenleaf Nursery at age 74, Leon had adopted a stray dog that he named Moochie. "Moochie and him just loved their Mountain Dew," she said. After I hung up the phone, I realized I didn't know whether she meant the soft drink or the hills variety.

When I called back, the widow House said, "Lord have mercy, you aren't going to tell that in your paper are you?"

That struck me as funny, and I choked and sputtered to hold in the laughter until we had finished talking.

LaRue Bunch glanced at me uneasily from time to time from the table where she preferred to sit while proofreading. She didn't risk Hank's wrath by talking to me.

Terri Mouse, the other reporter, was at the Cherokee Nation, sniffing around for the latest scandal. It was a quiet afternoon.

At the back of my mind, though, I tried to solve the problem that Tapply had proposed. How could we plant a seed of doubt — a seed large enough to free Charley?

I hadn't even come close to a solution when quitting time neared. Then three calls in quick succession confused matters more.

The first was from Kyra. In her whiskey voice, she told me about Roz Hoffing's finances.

"The bottom line is she doesn't have any."

"What do you mean? How does she live?"

"What I mean," Kyra said impatiently, "is that she doesn't have a bank account, doesn't have credit anywhere. She's a blank slate as far as conventional financial arrangements are concerned. She gets a small government pension because her husband is a disabled vet and she gets some AFDC."

"Aid to Families with Dependent Children," I translated.

"It's not enough to live on," Kyra continued. "The only other thing I could find is that her kids are on reduced-price lunches at school."

"Does she pay income tax?"

"Does Nancy Reagan shit in the woods?"

I told Kyra where to send the bill and hung up.

An image leaped in my mind of the big screen TV in the Hoffing's shabby living room. Where would she get money for something like that? The firewood she and the two boys cut couldn't amount to much income.

I figured there were two people who could answer that question: Roz Hoffing and the owner of the pawn shop on Muskogee. No, make that three: Whoever was paying Roz Hoffing.

Someone had to be supporting her, I reasoned. Roz and her boys weren't living well, but somehow they had enough money to pay for more than food and shelter. Which raised an even more interesting question. What was she being paid for?

I didn't have time to think about it, though, because my phone rang again. This time it was Pete Terrapin.

"You came out to my house Friday asking about Tommy Hoffing," he began, as though I had to be reminded who he was.

"Yes, Mr. Terrapin?"

There was a pause, and when he spoke again, his voice was softer. "You asked about a woman in a photograph," he said. "Gil Martin's girl-friend."

"Linda Smith."

"I guess you're a step ahead of me," he said.

I hastened to reassure him. "Her name is all I have."

"I made some calls after you left. Got her Social Security number from the registrar's office at the university. Had a buddy at OSBI cross match it with vital records."

"And?"

"She's dead. Killed in a one-car accident nearly eight years ago."

I made the obvious connection. "How long after the Blackinwater murders?"

"Four months. There wasn't any evidence it was anything but an accident. Makes you think, though, doesn't it?"

I turned my obits over to Hank, who barely glanced at them before handing me a sheaf of community notes. "These don't make any sense," he said. "Rewrite them and have them on my desk in the morning."

I resisted the temptation to bow.

LaRue had already left, and Hank was on his way out. I waited until the office was empty to call Tapply. I planned to ask him to meet me in Wagoner so we could talk more about our plan to free Charley. Or to discuss whether we should even be discussing such a harebrained scheme.

Before I could dial the number, though, the phone rang in my hand. I jumped.

It was Allan Jakes. He had treated me like a pariah after Charley's arrest as though I, too, were to blame for the death of his marijuana-growing partner.

"I'm calling at Mica's request." His words sounded formal and rehearsed.

"Yes?" I forced my voice to sound neutral.

"I'll be in Tahlequah this evening and she asked me to deliver something to you. Could we meet somewhere?"

I hesitated. Allan Jakes was the last person I wanted to see. And whatever he had to deliver was probably meaningless. From Mica it could be my daily horoscope or a bird feather with special powers. However, he was still Charley's manager. . .

"Creekside," I said, naming the bar where the benefit for Charley's legal defense had been held. "Nine p.m."

"Fine." He hung up.

Sometimes an unrelated event triggers all sorts of thoughts. In this case, as I dialed Tapply's number, I suddenly realized that I had missed my appointment with Charley's lawyer. I hoped Fay Blackfox was the forgiving type because she would be the key in gaining Charley's release if Tapply and I could create reasonable doubt.

At any rate, this wasn't the time to call her. Not until we had a plan.

TWENTY-SEVEN

Tapply and I arranged to meet at the McDonald's in Wagoner, halfway between Tulsa and Tahlequah. No one there was likely to recognize us, and we could talk undisturbed.

I arrived first. It was after 6 p.m., and people crowded the counter. Children cried, parents yelled, teenagers looked bored. I ordered a grilled chicken sandwich and coffee and found a quiet corner from which I could watch the door. I had finished eating by the time Tapply arrived.

His eyes met mine then went to the menu. He studied it as though it were a foreign language. Finally, he ordered French fries and water and joined me.

"Eat here often?" he asked, sliding into the booth opposite me. He nibbled at a fry.

"It's my home away from home," I said. "I see it's one of your haunts, too."

"This and Hardee's," he said. "Once they dominate the world, I'll be free to travel."

Our hearts weren't in the banter, but at least we were able to pretend for a minute that our purpose in being here was nothing more than an all-American night at the fast food joint.

The façade dropped, and we got down to business.

"Know Kelly Joe Jackson?" Tapply asked.

"The guy at the studio, the sound engineer." I wasn't too technical when it came to recording music.

"Right," Tapply said. "I talked to him this afternoon. He remembers seeing a man enter the Clinton bedroom the evening Gil was killed. He didn't think much about it at the time — there's always strangers around a place like ours — and then Kelly Joe saw the guy later out in the parking lot. He appeared to be on foot. Kelly Joe says he just kind of melted into the trees at the edge of the lot."

Tapply was so convincing that it took me a minute to realize that he was trying out a scenario on me.

I played along. "What did the guy look like?"

He leaned toward me. "I think if Kelly Joe had to finger someone in a photo lineup, Tommy Hoffing's picture would jump right out at him."

"Okay, Tapply. What's this guy owe you?"

Tapply batted his eyes in a caricature of innocence. "Owe me? My dear, he's just a concerned citizen trying to do the right thing."

"Sure, and I've been touched by an angel. Have you thought this through? First thing the cops will ask is why hasn't he come forward?"

Tapply smiled. "Well, this is pure coincidence, but Kelly Joe left the studio before Gil's body was discovered, and then he and his girlfriend left town the next morning. Left as soon as the snow was cleared off the roads. He's not the type to read the newspaper, and he didn't even hear about the murder until he got back in town, which just happened to be Sunday. Yesterday. So it took him awhile to put things together. The man he saw. Gil's murder."

I thought about it for awhile. If Kelly Joe was convincing, the police might take a fresh look. I wondered if they had any forensic evidence that directly linked Charley to Gil's murder.

"So just suppose," I said, "the police search High Spirits again. If they don't find any sign Tommy Hoffing was there, and there's no reason they should, then we're back to where we started."

Tapply's eyes glowed. "What makes you think they won't find anything?"

I was in over my head, but couldn't stop. "What will they find?"

"It's better that you don't know all the details," Tapply said. "Just trust in luck and justice."

An elderly couple claimed the booth behind us. I watched as the man sat the tray down and tenderly helped his wife out of her coat and took her arm as she sat down. Her head was a halo of white permed hair; his was bald. They looked like they were in love.

I leaned toward Tapply and lowered my voice. "Why are you sticking your neck out for Charley? What we're proposing here is a felony, maybe several felonies. We're suborning witnesses, obstructing justice, god knows what else." I folded my sandwich wrapper into smaller and smaller squares until I couldn't fold it any more. "What's in it for you, Tapply?"

He looked me in the eyes. "Money. What else? I have thousands of dollars tied up in this CD, and if Charley can't finish recording it and if he can't support it with a tour, then it's all gone."

"Sounds like you've thought it through, but there's still the question of Charley's silence. Why hasn't he said anything to the police? Why didn't he tell them he didn't do it?"

"That part's too easy," Tapply said. "All we have to do is drop a hint that it was a publicity stunt to promote his new CD. The media will buy it; they know musicians are crazy when it comes to creative product."

"And the notoriety of having been charged with murder may sell a few records, right?"

"Couldn't hurt," he said.

"Is that why Allan Jakes is suddenly talking to me again? Did you clue him in today?"

Tapply looked startled. "Allan? I haven't seen him or talked to him recently. Why?"

"He called just before I left to meet you. Said Mica gave him something to deliver to me."

"What was it?"

"How should I know?" I was annoyed by Tapply's questioning. As though he had a right to pry into my private affairs now that we were partners in crime.

Tapply slumped back into his seat. "I was just worried about you. That guy's not to be trusted. I hope he's not coming by your house."

I rolled my eyes. "We're meeting at the Creekside after I leave here. Satisfied?"

"Public place. Much better." Tapply aimed a dazzling smile at me and checked his watch. "Now, back to business."

Something about Tapply and Allan Jakes flitted through my mind, something I needed to ask, but the half-thought disappeared, and Tapply was forging ahead.

"Your role," he said, "is to make sure the media know that the cops have a new lead."

"Christ," I said. "I can't do that."

A shadow of something, anger perhaps, crossed his face. "You have to," he said. "This won't work if the media doesn't get into it."

I had felt earlier that I was in over my head, now I was sinking like a stone. I stood abruptly. "I'm outta here."

Tapply followed me out the door to Charley's van. "Viv," he said softly, seductively, "you have to do this for Charley."

"Have you heard of ethics?" I dug into my pocket for my keys.

"You're a strange woman," Tapply said. "You were ready to lay the blame off on Tommy Hoffing until I asked you to tweak the media. Any then you cry about ethics."

He tapped the van for emphasis. "There are things higher than ethics. There is justice. Gil was a predator. He preyed on someone precious to you. If Charley killed him for that — if — then justice was served. Injustice is locking Charley away for the rest of his life."

I remembered Charley's face through the glass barrier in the jail's waiting room. Exhausted, hopeless, proud. No, he was too good for prison life. He didn't deserve that, no matter what he'd done.

"The other reporter for the Tahlequah Daily Tribune, Terri Mouse, would act on a tip from me." I felt like a traitor. Terri was used to being conned by the politicos at the Cherokee Nation, but she trusted me.

"Good," Tapply said. "Good."

I took my time getting to the Creekside. The night was still young, and I went by John and Corey Franklin's house to pick up Charley's prized Takamine. I opened the case and ran my fingers along the guitar's smooth finish. It gleamed in the lamp light.

John and Corey were full of questions about Charley. Had I come for the guitar because he was coming home? Were there any new developments? As Charley's drummer, John had good reason to be concerned. He was unemployed now, torn between his loyalty to Charley and his need to make a living.

I stifled the impulse to tell them that he might be home soon. "I was just passing by," I said.

My next stop was the Creekside. I sipped a long-neck Bud while I waited for Allan Jakes.

The Happy Hour patrons had long since departed, and the bar was nearly deserted. When Allan hadn't shown up by 9:20, I asked the bartender if she had seen him.

"He was here earlier," she said. "He got a phone call and left."

"He was supposed to meet me here." I had been stood up, an act high on my list of unforgivable sins. I could have been home by now, but Allan had made it sound important that I meet him.

The bartender polished a glass and set it under the counter.

"Was it a man or woman who called?"

"I didn't answer the phone," she said. "But from the way he took off, I'd say the Lord God himself called him home."

TWENTY-EIGHT

I didn't sleep well. Tapply had told me to wait until noon the next day to set my part of the plan in motion, and in my half-dreaming, half-waking state, I rehearsed what I would say to Terri Mouse.

At one point, I got up for a glass of water. I tripped over Charley's guitar case on the way back to bed. I picked it up and took it to bed with me. With my hand on Charley's guitar, I found some comfort until dawn.

As it turned out, I needn't have worried. Tapply's and my plan went better than it had any right to. After Kelly Joe Jackson made his statement to the police, and they showed up at High Spirits for a fresh search of the premises, the media came in droves. I suspected later that Tapply wasn't content with coverage from a small town paper like Tahlequah's and that he took things in hand and called the Tulsa World and KTUL, the local ABC affiliate.

My only regret was lying to Terri Mouse. With Hank's blessing, she took off for Tulsa in her rusty Datsun, camera case in the passenger seat. She came back with the story of the year.

The police did indeed find something in High Spirits, something that placed Tommy Hoffing at the scene. They were close-mouthed about their discovery for two days while they performed tests on it. Terri's years of dealing with the Cherokee Nation, though, had honed her instincts and taught her to cultivate sources. It was she who broke the story.

Behind the bed in the Clinton Bedroom, the same bed I had slept in, the police found a small pocketknife, and on the knife were Tommy Hoffing's fingerprints.

When that story broke, Fay Blackfox obtained an expedited hearing for Charley. Two days later he was free.

In the meantime, I was a wreck. I showed up for work every day, turned in copy as though I were an automaton, and wandered through the house in the dark nights like Banquo's ghost.

I wanted to ask Tapply how Tommy Hoffing's knife had ended up in the Clinton Bedroom, but deep down, I feared what he might say.

The call I hoped for, but the call that didn't come, was from Charley. I knew that Fay Blackfox had told him about the new developments in his case, but he was silent about what he thought. Each night I went home, and each night I lifted the phone to make sure it was connected, but Charley didn't call.

Fay Blackfox called me at the office Friday morning and told me Charley would be released that afternoon. He might need a ride home, she suggested.

I turned in a half-written story to Hank and left. Hank was still flying high from what he was sure would be an award-winning story for Terri Mouse and his newspaper. Newsstand sales were up and he had increased the press run. Tommy sightings were once again at fever pitch. People called in hourly with news and rumors about Tommy Hoffing. Hank actually smiled at me as I left.

The day was sunny and warm, and a fresh breeze blew away the oil refinery smell of Tulsa. In the distance, on the banks of the Arkansas River, the cottonwood trees were leafing out. Ranks of daffodils bloomed in the raised boxes on the courthouse plaza, and the pigeons strutted past the smokers outside the building and pounced on cigarette butts when they fell.

I sat on a bench on the plaza and waited for Charley to be processed out of jail. It took longer than I expected, and I drowsed in the warm sun. Eventually I spotted him at the door, wearing blue jeans and a flannel shirt and carrying a manila envelope in one hand. He shuffled, as though he had grown used to taking small steps, and he looked at the ground as he walked.

I rose to meet him, but before he saw me, before I could reach him, a half dozen reporters with notebooks and cameras descended on him.

"Charley," one shouted, "how does it feel to be a free man?"

Charley's head jerked up, and a quick series of emotions pulsed across his face. He metamorphosed into the loose-jointed, charismatic rock-and-roller and gave them an enigmatic smile.

"Hey, Charley," another reporter said, "what's the first thing you're gonna do?"

By this time, I was at his side. He took my arm and grinned at the reporters. "We're going to Disneyland," he said, flashing a peace sign.

Together we walked quickly to the van and climbed into it, locking the doors. The reporters clamored after us, but the only other thing Charley Pack had to say was, "No comment."

I had been driving the van so long now that it seemed natural for me to take the wheel.

"Disneyland?" I said as I pulled away from the curb.

"Figure of speech," he said.

"Thank God."

We looked at each other. Charley's deep-set indigo eyes, the eyes I had fallen in love with, crinkled, and we laughed.

It would be a long time before we shared another laugh.

As it turned out, the first place Charley wanted to go was to Mica's house. Iris still had not returned home, and he was worried about her. I felt guilty that I hadn't tried to find her again after our rendezvous in Charley's van the previous Sunday night. Somehow she had slipped from my list of emergencies. My concern for her had been replaced by my greater concern for Charley's freedom. A casualty of the conspiracy.

That's not to say that I hadn't thought of her in the past few days, but each time her face appeared in my mind, I told myself that she would be fine. I told myself Matt Crenshaw was protecting her. I had made myself believe it, but now, Charley's worry renewed my own, and I cursed myself for letting her run away that night.

To relieve my anxiety, I told Charley an edited version of everything that had happened since he had been jailed. The distance to Mica's house from the courthouse was short, and the traffic was light. Perhaps I left out a few important points.

The only real concern he showed was when I told him about being run off the road and wrecking the Trooper.

He placed his hand over mine on the steering wheel and squeezed it.

"It's been rough all around, hasn't it?" he said.

Charley didn't volunteer anything about his time in the county jail, and it didn't seem like the time to ask. I pulled into Mica's driveway and cut the engine.

Charley went to the door of the Victorian mansion, but no one was home. We rolled down the van's windows and sat in the driveway, talking about trivial things, friends, food, weather. Mostly, though, we were silent. We sat apart in our own worlds, and if there was a bridge by which to cross the gap between us, I couldn't find the path to it.

I kept sneaking looks at Charley, trying to see if he had changed. Was he really a murderer? Or a victim? Years of practicing meditation had turned his thin face into a mask of serenity; unless caught off-guard, it gave away nothing.

"Let's go home," he said, finally.

I pulled into the street. Just then, though, Mica drove up, and I parked the van again. Charley jumped out of the van and he and Mica met in the driveway in a warm embrace. She wore a long, flowing dress and looked impossibly feminine and fragile.

I felt a stab of jealousy. Charley hadn't greeted me that way.

They were already deep in conversation by the time I joined them.

Mica glanced at me and continued talking. "So we agreed it was for the best, and I took her and her bags over to St. Francis House."

"Iris?" I asked.

They both nodded without looking at me. I remembered the warm atmosphere of the shelter and of the man in the wheelchair. Iris would be in good hands with Gary Voeder watching over her.

"She could stay with me," Charley said.

Me, Charley had said, not *us*.

Mica blinked slowly. "I think she wants to put all this behind her for awhile," she said.

"I have something of hers." Charley lowered his voice. "Her dragon-fly pendant. But it's best that I hang onto it for now. The police think it's mine."

"Was it ... Did Gil ...?" Mica didn't finish her questions, but she asked a new one. "What happened that night, Charley?"

Good question, I thought. But Charley didn't even acknowledge it.

"Iris might think she's putting this behind her," he said, "but I think you need to find her a good therapist."

"Christ!" Mica burst out. "I'm the one who needs the therapist!" Her hands were restless birds, and they fluttered around her. "I'm going through hell. I'm alone. I'm all alone!"

She covered her face with her hands and wept silently.

Charley patted her hair and said soothing things, but he shot me a look that said he didn't know what to do next.

"Call Allan Jakes," I said in a low voice. "Maybe he can come over."

Charley gave me a puzzled look, but before he could say anything, Mica spoke.

"I can't find Allan," she said. "He hasn't been at his house all week. He hasn't come by or called since ..." She stopped to think, and then a change came over her face. The color drained out of it and her self-pity turned to fear and she looked at me accusingly. "Since he saw you the other night."

It took me a minute to realize what she was talking about. "Wait a minute," I said. "We talked on the phone, but he didn't show up."

"Didn't show?" Mica's voice rose in disbelief.

"We arranged to meet at the Creekside in Tahlequah at 9," I said. "Apparently he got there early, got a phone call and left. I never saw him."

"Oh, Jesus. Something happened to him."

I tried to remember every detail of our phone conversation, but it had been brief, nothing more than fixing a meeting place so he could give me something from Mica.

"What did you give him to deliver to me?"

Mica dismissed my question. "It doesn't even seem important now. A book. One of Gil's college books, *Crime and Punishment*. He always kept it on top of his desk. He was reading it the day he was killed. I went in his office for something, and he held it up and laughed in an ugly way and said, 'My downfall'. It seemed stupid to me then, and it seems stupid now."

She looked at me as though everything bad that had happened in the past few weeks was my fault. "And I don't know why I thought you should have it."

"Shouldn't you call the police and report him missing?" Charley said. He was adjusting quickly to his newly won freedom. He leaned back against the stone retaining wall that framed Mica's driveway with his hands in his pockets and legs crossed. He looked as relaxed as if we were discussing which restaurant to have dinner at, and the detachment on his face made me realize that he no longer thought of Allan Jakes as his manager or even perhaps as a friend.

"You know I can't do that." Mica's voice was low and angry. "If the police search his house, he'll have to flee the country. You know what I'm talking about — after all, his drug money is helping finance your music."

TWENTY-NINE

The mood on the drive to Tahlequah could best be described as dismal. I was worried. I had let Tapply use me to frame Tommy Hoffing. Not only that, but I had let the question of finances slide. Was Allan Jakes laundering marijuana money through High Spirits? Tapply had promised to share the audit results with me, but I had heard nothing. If drug money was propping up the bar and recording studio, had anyone besides Allan and Gil known? Gil was dead and Allan had disappeared. The number of people who might be able to answer my questions was dwindling.

I pressed Charley for what he knew, but he remained stubbornly silent, as though the technique that had stood him in good stead while in jail had now become a part of his personality.

"You don't know me," were his final words on the subject, and I seethed the rest of the way home, framing scathing replies and poignant pleas. But I voiced none of them.

Stepping into the house forced us both into the role of actors.

Inside the darkened living room it was quiet, uncomfortably quiet, as though an air of expectation had overwhelmed its earlier, desolate atmosphere. The reason was soon apparent.

At least two dozen people burst from their hiding places and surrounded Charley.

"Surprise! Surprise!"

Jason and Heather unrolled a hand-painted banner that said, "Welcome home, ramblin' man."

John and Corey and other members of Charley's band and entourage pulled tubs of iced beer out of hiding places.

Tapply uncorked champagne.

Smiles and celebration all around. Charley and I went with the flow. What else could we do? For the moment, we were Tahlequah's golden couple, and our friends needed to celebrate what they saw as the triumph of a test of fire and will.

Allan Jakes wasn't present, and even though I asked around, no one had seen him since the night he called me.

The party lasted into the night. John had brought a huge pot of chili, and Heather, who took over my kitchen with easy familiarity, baked a pan of cornbread. The beer flowed freely, and eventually I smelled the sweet odor of marijuana. Drugs were an integral part of the music scene, one that I hadn't thought about much before now — before seeing Allan Jakes's basement garden — other than to note smugly that both Charley and I had outgrown the need to get high.

I watched Charley surreptitiously, though, wondering if I had been wrong about that, too.

At the moment, Charley was in the part of the house we called the office. He cradled the Takamine in his arms and strummed it gently as though he were caressing a child's head.

From where I stood by the bookcase, I could hear what he said.

"I met an old guy in the jail," he told John. "We played music together. We didn't have any instruments, of course, just our hands and mouths and plastic spoons, that sort of thing. Percussion and a cappella. But I learned a lot from him.

"He was in on a 30-day vag charge, and when they let him out, he shook my hand and said he'd look me up when I played in Tulsa. He said I'd be a hell of a musician someday.

"I kinda laughed, and after he left, one of the other guys in the cell turned to me and said, "Man, you been blessed by Sonny Boy Watson."

"Jesus," John said, sounding impressed.

I stepped into the circle of light and joined John and Charley. "Who's Sonny Boy Watson?"

John stroked his beard and looked at me absently. "Just one of Oklahoma's blues legends is all."

"It made me feel small," Charley said, more to John than to me. "I thought about him a lot these past few days, and I realized our music is good, but it's missing something. The music that lasts, that keeps people coming back, doesn't come from the head or even the heart. It comes from the gut. Our music needs more gut."

"What are you sayin', Charley?" John picked up a long-neck Bud and drained it.

"I'm sayin' it's back to the studio for us," Charley said. He sounded like a boy anticipating Christmas. "We're gonna record some of those tracks over again — this time from the gut."

John groaned, but he was an easy-going man. I knew he wouldn't mutiny. But I wondered about Tapply. He was counting on having a finished product to sell while the media remembered who Charley was.

Tapply had been at the edge of the crowd all night. I noticed that he sipped his beer and that, although he accepted joints that were passed to him, he passed them on to the next person without inhaling.

Like me, he was an observer, and when it was time to act, he knew who would support him and who wouldn't. It made him appear decisive and quick-acting, but I had watched him enough these past few days to know that he acted with care and precision. There was little Tapply left to chance.

Just the same, when it came to a man like Charley, Tapply must wonder if he needed to refine his methods. Charley was quicksilver, and the code he followed was complicated and deep.

I didn't think that tonight was the best time for Charley to tell Tapply he wanted to go back into the studio. As far as Tapply knew, most of the recording was complete and nearly ready to master. That was the least of my worries, though, where Tapply was concerned.

Tapply ended a conversation with Jason and Heather, and I slipped beside him as he walked past.

"Let's go outside," I said.

He followed me onto the porch. The night sky was clear, and the pale light from millions of stars traced the outlines of the black hillsides. Tapply leaned against the porch rail, and I sat on the steps. Below us, Spring Creek ran fast, and the first spring peepers sang their high-pitched song.

We listened to the night in silence for a minute, then I said, "You've involved me in something I don't understand, and it worries me. Where did that knife with Tommy Hoffing's fingerprints come from?"

Above me, Tapply's voice was earnest. "I swear I don't know, Viv. As weird as it sounds, I think Tommy was in High Spirits. If not that night, then some other night. Maybe he was laying in wait for Gil. Gil was afraid of him, and apparently with good reason. We were lucky the way that played out."

"That's weak, Tapply," I said. "I'd like to believe there's a pot of gold at the end of the rainbow and four-leaf clovers bring luck and all that other shit. But I can't." By now, I was on my feet facing him. The silence was tense, broken by the sound of an owl's wings as it swooped down to capture prey. The thin scream of a mouse told the rest of the story.

Tapply's face was grim. "If you don't like the answer, Viv, don't ask the question," he said. He turned on his heel and went back inside.

Moments later, he walked down the track beyond the house where our uninvited guests had hidden their cars and trucks, and he was gone.

THIRTY

When I awoke the next morning, I found a note from Charley on the dining table.

"Gone back to work," it said. "You can reach me at High Spirits." He signed the note with the letter C. No words of love or appreciation or hope. Nothing.

I had gone to bed late, but Charley had still been entertaining guests. For all I knew, Charley never did come to bed. I looked out the window. The van was parked out front. Charley must have caught a ride with John or Jason.

The house seemed emptier than ever. Somehow, I had thought when Charley was released from jail he would explain everything and we would rebuild our lives together.

Nothing was working out as I expected.

I sat on the steps in front of the house and let a cool breeze ruffle my hair. The sun slanted through the leafless oaks and lit the white blossoms of a wild plum. A cardinal, plumage bright as blood, landed on the blossoms. High above, wispy mare's tails feathered the blue sky. A feeling more restless than spring fever emptied me of everything but a craving for something unreachable.

It was Saturday, but I went to Tahlequah to the newspaper office. Anything for a distraction.

LaRue Bunch was at her desk when I arrived. Her gray hair was up-swept in a bun, and she wore a dress with a starched collar.

"It's Saturday, for heaven's sake," I said.

She peered at me over the top of her glasses. "End of the month. I'm closing the books."

I was wearing worn Levis and a faded cotton sweater, and it had been her business-like attire I was referring to, but I let it slide. The new subject was more interesting.

"So are we still in business?"

LaRue wasn't about to give away any of Hank's financial secrets, but she couldn't be entirely discreet when the news was so good. "That Hoffing boy keeps running around, we'll all be wearing diamonds," she said.

"I hope Hank's into profit-sharing."

LaRue closed her mouth and turned back to her books.

I wandered to my desk and turned on my computer. I had plenty of work to do, and I chipped away at it for a couple of hours, even though my heart wasn't in it. I was glad the newspaper was doing well, but I knew part of the reason was due to a story I had planted. Hank's success was built on a possible lie. Had Tommy Hoffing been in High Spirits the night Gil Martin was murdered? Thinking about the implications made for a hell of a distraction.

Finally, realizing I was wasting my time at work, I decided to drive to Goat's Bluff along the Illinois River and watch the eagles. They wintered in the rocky crags overlooking the water. I might not find any answers, but maybe there would be some peace.

I stopped by the Git 'n' Go on the east side of town and picked up a bag of peanuts and a Diet Coke. When I came out, I saw Roz Hoffing's pickup parked at the edge of the lot. It was empty.

I hadn't seen her inside the store, and she wasn't in the parking lot. An unpleasant, prickly feeling crept up my back. I opened the door to Charley's van. She was crouched in the passenger side.

"Climb in and drive," she said in a harsh voice. Her weathered face was distorted with fear or excitement.

I hesitated in the open door with the grocery bag in my hand.

"Someone's followin' me," Roz said. Her voice held a note of plead-ing. "We gotta get out of here now."

Her obvious agitation decided me. She wasn't the type of person who was easily rattled. I slipped behind the wheel and started the engine.

"Who's following you?"

"Some guy in a blue pickup."

I checked the traffic around us. At least two blue pickups were in sight. "There's about a thousand blue pickups in this county," I said. "Be more specific."

"It's got a big cowcatcher on the front."

My heart skipped a beat. "A cowcatcher?" I looked again, but both the pickups I could see had ordinary bumpers.

Roz's voice was impatient. "One of them metal contraptions to protect the front of your truck in case you hit a deer or somthin'. He's been on my tail all day. Then I saw you."

I knew what a cowcatcher was. The pickup that had run me off the road had a cowcatcher. But Roz had caught me off guard. Was the man who tried to kill me now after Roz? Was the incident that night more than the act of a drunk or insane driver? "What do you think he wants?"

"How the hell would I know?"

I was headed out of town east toward the river, watching the rearview mirror. "No one's following us," I said. "You don't have to hide."

Roz pushed herself off the floor. She moved with the grace and strength of a large cat. Settling into the seat, she lit a cigarette.

She cracked the window open when she saw me watching her. "Your old man still smoke?"

"Charley doesn't smoke."

"He used to though. Camels unfiltered."

"That must have been before I knew him." Charley a smoker? When I had gone through quitter's hell, he hadn't said anything. Apparently what I didn't know about my lover outweighed what I did know.

"He's a good man. I'm glad he's out of jail. He was decent to Tommy once, and I never forgot it."

"He knew Tommy Hoffing?" We were at the turnoff for Highway 10, which followed the river north. I turned too fast, and the van rocked back and forth. I didn't see a blue pickup.

"All them boys at that shithole they called the Farmhouse knew Tommy. That was where Gil lived while he was in college, you know. I don't know why Tommy hung out there. He was kinda slow, and college boys can be mean." Roz took a long drag on her cigarette and watched the river. "Musta been the booze. I wouldn't have it around the house. He still had nightmares from when he was in Vietnam; booze only made it worse."

"What about Charley? What did he do for Tommy?" I couldn't believe Charley had never mentioned to me that he had once known Tommy Hoffing.

"Whyn't you ask him?"

Roz flicked the still-smoking butt out the window. It bounced on the pavement behind us.

"I'd rather hear it from you." I wasn't about to admit to this woman that Charley and I weren't exactly sharing memories at the moment. It wasn't any of her damn business.

Roz brushed her mousy hair out of her eyes and regarded me intently. "That asshole Gil," she said, "he never would stand up for anyone. Not even his own blood. A guy that used to come around to the Farmhouse, he was from China or somewheres like that, and one of 'em had the bright idea of tellin' Tommy he was a Vietnamese spy. Well, it didn't take much to get Tommy goin'; he would wake me in the night screamin' about this or that. There's a word for it."

"Post-traumatic stress syndrome."

She ignored me. "So Tommy's all worked up about this Vietnamese spy, and he's not sleepin' and he's not eatin.' I find out later that they cook up this scheme to follow the guy way the hell out to Locust Grove. The guy stops and goes into a house, and Gil drops Tommy off and tells him to watch the house while he goes for help." Her voice took on an aggrieved tone. "Gil drove off and left him; he never even meant to go back for him, but your man heard about what was goin' on, and he went up to Locust Grove and found Tommy and brought him home."

"I heard later he gave those boys what for. They didn't play tricks like that again. Not while Charley Pack lived there."

Without even thinking about it, I had been following my original plan — to drive to Goat's Bluff and watch eagles. I glanced at my passenger and decided that while she was in a talkative mood, I should make every effort to keep her that way. Perhaps a scenic view and a shared snack would help move things forward.

I turned onto the Combs Bridge road and we clattered across the bridge — the bridge where Tommy Hoffing had been found curled into a ball next to an empty bag and a few stray bills fluttering in the wind. Below us, the Illinois River ran high and brown with topsoil from the recent rains. Roz looked out the window as though we were on an ordinary outing and she was enjoying the scenery.

The road south was deeply rutted from the winter cycle of freeze and thaw. I negotiated the van through the holes in the road and pulled over where the road widened above the bluff. To the south, the river cut a deep gouge through the limestone, and the barren hills stretched away as far as the eye could see. A pair of eagles soared in the sky, catching the updrafts.

The owner had stretched a five-strand barbed wire fence along the bluff top, and a sign warned trespassers to stay away. Yet, someone had cut the bottom strand of wire.

"What is this place?" Roz said.

"Haven't you ever been to Goat's Bluff?"

"I was raised south of here, I never had much call to come up here.

It's pretty though."

I opened the bag of peanuts and offered them to her. She took a handful and munched on them.

I kept my voice casual. "Are you still getting the checks, Roz? Even though Gil's dead?" It was a guess, but it hit home.

She choked on the peanuts and when she could talk again, she said, "I don't know what you're talkin' about."

"Sure you do, Roz. The big TV in your house. How did you pay for that? How do you keep your boys fed and clothed? How do you pay your gas bill?"

"I gotta get back," she said. "You take me back to my truck." She was angry and her hand was on the door latch, as though she was thinking about opening the door and jumping out.

Apparently she wasn't in the mood to confide. I started the van and found a place to turn it around. "You're in more trouble than you know, Roz. You should talk to me about what's going on. Maybe I can help."

"You shut up!" she said. "You don't know nuthin' about it."

We were back at the Git 'n' Go fifteen minutes later. Roz sat sullenly, wrapped in her thoughts.

I had flipped the turn signal to pull into the parking lot when I saw the blue pickup with the cowcatcher on the front. It was parked beside Roz's pickup.

"Shit," I said.

Roz looked up and saw the truck, too. "Drive on past," she said. "Maybe he hasn't made you."

I knew better, though. The driver's face, hidden in the shade behind the sun visor, turned toward the van, and he pulled into the street behind us.

Adrenaline coursed through my body, and my stomach felt the way it did when I was rock climbing and grabbed for a hold only to feel my hands slipping. Pure terror — even when you know the rope will break your fall.

Roz cursed.

"Have you seen this guy before?"

She shook her head no.

My mind raced through the possibilities. Was he after Roz or me? Or both of us?

There was no hope in out-running him. That much I knew. The van was slower and clumsier than even the top-heavy Trooper had been. It was time to be a fox and outwit the hound. Or, since we were in Oklahoma, time to be raccoon-smart.

THIRTY-ONE

The Saturday afternoon traffic was heavy on Muskogee, and I wedged my way between two cars then turned left onto Waters at the end of a yellow light. The truck was momentarily trapped behind another car.

"You got him!" Roz said. But even as I watched in the rearview mirror, he pulled into the oncoming traffic lane, zipped around an outraged Volvo driver and skidded onto Waters.

"Hang on," I said to Roz.

There was nothing to hang onto, but Roz grabbed her seat belt and fastened it. Her plain face was grim.

"My boys got no one but me to take care of 'em," she said.

From what I had seen, they were more self-reliant than many adults, but this wasn't the time to say so. "We're four blocks from the police department," I said. "You can tell them why this guy's following you."

"No!" The cry was torn from her. "No cops!"

"You'll have to talk to me then," I said. The pickup was gaining on us, and I ignored the stop sign at Downing and swerved onto the busy street. A horn blared.

I was headed in the direction of the county courthouse, which housed the police.

"Don't go there," Roz said, her voice shaking with anger. "I'll tell you what I know."

"We have to ditch this van. It's like driving Moby Dick."

Roz hugged herself and rocked back and forth in the passenger seat. "He'll kill us both," she said. "He's crazy."

"Who is?" I pressed on the gas and shot around the corner of Downing and Muskogee, narrowly missing a woman who had ventured out from behind a utility truck. The woman screamed something at me.

I didn't notice that Roz hadn't answered my question. I was too busy forming a plan and driving. Behind us, the pickup swerved to miss the woman and struck an ancient station wagon, spinning it around.

"We have about one minute," I said. "So listen carefully. My sister lives on Bluff. She's out of town, but her car's in the garage. We're going to circle the block and I'll drop you off behind her house. Here's what you're going to do."

I described the plan, and Roz nodded to show she understood.

I was crossing the narrow bridge on Choctaw that spanned Town Branch when I saw the pickup behind us again, coming up fast.

I pointed out my sister's house to Roz, then took the corner like an Indy driver. I prayed that no children were playing in the street.

"The keys are in the small pocket of my bag," I pointed with my chin toward the leather bag lying on the floor near Roz. She dug around and pulled out a ring of keys.

"Cross me," I said, "and I'll have the police asking you some very pointed questions."

"I'll do what you said," Roz said. Her face wore a look of weary determination.

"One key's for the garage and one's for the Miata," I told her. "Now go!"

I slowed enough for her to leap from the van and roll behind a mass of Japanese yew. The blue pickup made the turn just as I picked up speed again.

I led the way through back streets to the courthouse and drove the van straight into the police department garage under the building. A uniformed cop watched me park the van and ambled over.

"You can't park here, ma'am," he said. He looked like he was too young to shave.

I put on my helpless act. "Isn't this where I renew my license?"

"No, ma'am, that would be at the DMV. They ain't open on Saturday." He unconsciously caressed the gun on his hip.

Out of the corner of my eye, I saw the blue pickup slowly circle the block.

"They don't make it easy for us taxpayers," I said to the police officer.

"No, ma'am." He watched me back the van out of the garage and then turned away.

Outside the police department was a parking lot, and I left the van there. If the man in the blue pickup was watching, perhaps he would conclude that I had dropped Roz off inside. I hoped so.

I went through the courthouse and came out the door that faced the newspaper office. No pickup in sight.

I dashed across the street and let myself in the office. If all had gone as planned, Roz should be in the parking lot behind the newspaper office.

I hurried past a startled LaRue Bunch and out the back door. The small red Miata pulled up, and a smiling Roz reached across and opened the passenger door. The smile transformed her face into someone fun-loving and youthful, more like the Roz in the photo I had borrowed from the Clinton Bedroom at High Spirits.

"This is some car," she said. "I could get used to this."

"Don't enjoy yourself too much," I told her. "I'm driving."

She wiggled into the passenger seat. "So he's gone?"

"For the moment."

"That sure was slick."

"It won't work again," I said. "And he knows where you live, doesn't he?"

The smile faded from her face. "You have to figure he does."

I remembered the guns her sons carried. "That first time I came to your house, you were worried about someone hanging around."

"I guess it musta been him, though we never did see a face. We knew someone was spyin' on us. The dog kept him back."

"Do you have a place to go?"

"My brother's. I took the boys over there this mornin'. He's no account, but beggars can't be choosers."

"For the time being, we're going to put some distance between that blue pickup and us," I said. "He'll be on the lookout."

I put the Miata into gear and drove west. Compared to the Moby Dick handling of the Trooper and the van, the small car was a barracuda, and the way I drove it, the barracuda was on amphetamines.

By the time we reached the bypass on the west side of town, I was satisfied that we had eluded the man in the blue pickup. I headed south, in the direction of the house of Roz's brother, and asked questions on the way.

"Who has been sending you money, Roz?"

Roz was a big woman, but her bulk seemed to shrink into the leather seat of the Miata. "I don't know."

I slowed the car, exasperated. "Are we going to have to go back to the police station?"

"No!" She sat bolt upright. "I'm not lyin' to you, Vivian Powers. I don't know where the money comes from."

By now, we were driving on a gravel road west of the Cherokee Nation Headquarters. The road wound along the side of Stick Ross Mountain. Under the oaks on the steep hillside, small, creamy clusters of Dutchman's Breeches bloomed. The Miata wasn't made for uncivilized surfaces, and I cringed when a rock scraped the bottom of the car. Maggie would never forgive me if something happened to her precious car.

The desperation in Roz's voice made me believe her. "How do you get the money then?"

"I go down to Trusty's once a month, and an envelope is waitin' for me. It has cash inside."

"Trusty's?"

"The pawnshop on Muskogee."

"How much is inside?"

She hesitated, as though trying to decide what I would believe. "Five hundred," she said.

This wasn't the time to quibble over details. "How long has this been going on?"

Roz looked at her hands. They were broad and rough and strong from hard work. "Since Tommy went to Vinita."

"It's hush money, Roz. Why?"

She shrugged expressively. "I've wondered many a night what I don't know that might get me killed someday."

"Gil Martin was murdered nearly two weeks ago. Have you received any money since then?"

Her thick brows furrowed. "There shoulda been some money for me last week, but it didn't come."

"Could Gil be the person who was sending it?"

"I don't know. Maybe."

"Can you think of any reason he would send you money all these years?"

Her hands twisted in her lap. "Maybe Tommy did kill those folks. I think maybe he did. But it wasn't his idea to go there and rob them. Someone else was in on it."

"Gil?"

"Why not? He was in on ever other evil thing Tommy did."

THIRTY-TWO

An old man who lived next door to the post office in Big Cabin, population 271, gave me directions to Frank Darman's place. He pointed me east toward Grand Lake, but Darman didn't live in one of the fancy summer homes that lined the lake. Through the trees, I caught glimpses of the placid blue water. Then the dirt lane turned away from the lake and wound among stunted, leafless trees. The roadbed was soft, and the Miata crept along almost silently until a fallen oak blocked the road. The man had said Darman lived at the end of this road.

The tree trunk was of medium diameter, and I thought I might be able to shove it aside. I parked the car and got out. The forest was silent, too silent. No birds sang, and only the angry chattering of a squirrel broke the peace. The squirrel's anger was directed at something below it.

I strained to see through the heavy underbrush on all sides, but nothing moved.

"Shit," I said.

Before I dropped Roz off at her brother's house, she said something so obvious that I was embarrassed I hadn't thought of it earlier. "That boy that run off with Tommy from Vinita, that Frank Darman, maybe he knows where he was headed to," she said.

The ties between Tommy Hoffing and Gil's murder were like a rubber band that was being pulled tighter and tighter. At any moment the band would snap, and someone would be in the path of its random force.

I had been skeptical when Tapply came up with Tommy's knife in the Clinton Bedroom. It seemed too pat, too convenient. But wasn't life like that sometimes? Now the man who had run me off the road was stalking Roz. What did we have in common besides the tie between Gil and Tommy? It was time to find out why that tie was enough to cause a person to kill.

At least that's what I had been telling myself on the drive from Tahlequah to Big Cabin. A call to the forensic unit of the hospital in Vinita confirmed that Darman had been released and was awaiting trial. Now that I was here in the eerily silent forest, by myself, the situation once again dissolved into chaos. What if Darman was the man who drove the pickup with the cowcatcher? I had told no one I was coming here; it was possible I wouldn't be missed for days. Even though Charley was no longer sleeping in the Tulsa County jail, I had little faith that he would be sleeping in my bed.

A stealthy rustling in the brush. Was there anything in Maggie's car that could be used for a weapon? Or should I just jump in the car and flee?

A reedy voice floated out of the trees. "Folks that come down this road are soon called home to the Lord. Are you ready to meet your Maker?"

"I'm looking for Frank Darman. Tommy Hoffing's wife sent me." The lie sounded awkward and flat, even to my ears. I couldn't see the speaker, and that worried me more than his words.

"Darman answers only to servants of the Lord."

I could place the voice now. It came from above. I looked up and saw a small man crouched in the crook of a massive white oak. Darman.

I wanted to scold him like a misbehaving child who has scampered out of the reach of his mother, but the situation called for diplomacy. "I serve the Master," I said.

"The true Master."

"Right." I hoped he wouldn't quiz me about who that might be.

Darman scrambled down the trunk and stood at the edge of the road. He was small, and he moved with a simian grace. His arms were unnaturally long, which added to the notion that I faced something that wasn't quite human.

His eyes were the murky brown that I remembered seeing when he was bundled into the ambulance. They could have been colored by the sludge that lay at the bottom of the lake.

Darman signaled me to follow him with a jerk of his head. He led the way, swinging his arms back and forth, watching the woods on either side as though he might be attacked at any moment by a creature more fierce or cunning than he.

I should be more careful, I thought. Though what I should be careful of I wasn't sure.

Darman's house, if it could be called a house, lay hidden behind a bend in the road. The structure was little more than a large wooden box with a window and door, hammered together like a child's playhouse. Surrounding it were perhaps two dozen smaller box houses, and to each of the small houses was tied a game cock. When they saw Darman, the cocks began crowing and sparring, wings outstretched, although the ropes that held them by one leg jerked them back to earth.

Darman had said nothing while we walked; now he smiled broadly at his fighting cocks and said, "Ask now the fowls of the air, and they shall tell thee."

"What will they tell me, Frank?"

Darman seemed not to have heard me, though. He opened a plastic bucket, filled a coffee can with corn, and emptied a bit on the ground near each cock. The birds stopped crowing and pecked at the ground.

I remembered the game hens at Roz Hoffing's house. "Tommy Hoffing raised game cocks," I said. Perhaps that was what brought the two men together in the state hospital. Oklahoma was one of the few states in which cockfighting was legal, but betting on the outcome was not. It made for some strange alliances.

"Tommy Hoffing raised game cocks," Darman said, echoing me like a naughty child.

This game I remembered from my childhood. The only way to stop the game was to say nothing. I found a stump and sat on it, trying to look comfortable and carefree.

Darman put away his can and built a fire in a ring of charcoal-smudged rocks. He placed a wire grill on the rocks and centered a black-ened coffee pot over the fire. Then he crouched by the fire in silence and waited. After a few minutes, the coffee foamed over, spitting on the fire, and Darman poured a cup of cold water in the pot to settle the grounds. He used his shirttail for a potholder, filled two tin cups that had been hanging from nails pounded into the side of his house and wordlessly of-fered me one.

The coffee was surprisingly good, scalding hot and strong. I sipped it carefully and tried not to burn my lips on the cup.

Darman stared at me over the top of his cup. His eyes were unread-able — watery, opaque and empty. They reminded me of the first time I saw him. What was it he had said?

I tried the words aloud to test their effect: "Raskolnikov must die."

He blinked once then said with no expression, "Raskolnikov must die."

In my frustration, I forgot how hot the coffee was and burned my tongue. In that instant, diplomacy went out the window. "Yeah, Frank," I said tiredly, "Let's play Simon says. Simon says, Raskolnikov must die."

But Darman's attention had shifted elsewhere. He stared into the fire and said, "No, Tommy says. Tommy says, Raskolnikov must die."

Excitement stirred inside me. "Tommy says? Tommy Hoffing?"

Darman blinked in surprise. He looked at me quickly then looked away again. "Tommy says?" he parroted.

It was a lost cause. I stayed a while longer, but Darman had his guard up, and there were no more slips. But once was enough, I reflected later as I backed the Miata out the narrow road. I was sure the Raskolnikov quote was Tommy Hoffing's, not Darman's, and perhaps it had a special significance to Tommy. Perhaps it even had something to do with his escape. It was time to find a copy of *Crime and Punishment* and to freshen my cloudy memory of Raskolnikov and his crime.

The problem was, where would I find a copy? There may have been a translation of Dostoevsky's masterpiece in my bookshelves, but I was afraid to go home. I feared that the driver of the pickup with the cowcatcher would be waiting for me — perhaps suspecting that I had taken Roz there for protection. That he knew who I was and where I lived I didn't doubt.

There was always the college library, but I had heard recently that it now closed early on Saturday in an effort to save money. The city library was my best bet.

In the end, that's where I went. As an added bonus, the library was next to the courthouse. I could return my sister's Miata and retrieve Charley's van after I went to the library.

The library was quiet. A woman sat on the floor of the children's section with a small child in her lap, looking through books; an old man wearing the long braids of a traditional Cherokee read newspapers. I could see the librarian through the open door in her office, doing something on a computer. I found *Crime and Punishment* quickly — it hadn't been checked out in the past five years according to the record inside the back cover (no barcodes yet in our library). I thumbed through it, still standing in an aisle among the rows of books.

It told the story of the impoverished student Raskolnikov, who murdered an old woman and the woman's sister. I found the scene where Raskolnikov committed the murder and read more slowly. I had studied the book in a Russian lit class when I was in college, and as I read, memories of the story flooded back.

Raskolnikov felt justified in the robbery and murder because he thought he was extraordinary. All great men must from their very nature be criminals in order to get out of the common rut, he believed. In a way, crime was a test of worthiness. Those who failed didn't have the will to succeed.

I wondered whether Gil Martin had studied this book in college and whether he felt that unlike Raskolnikov, he could deal with the guilt and fear that followed a crime. Perhaps Gil had intended only to rob the Blackinwaters with Tommy Hoffing's help, but something had gone terribly wrong.

A theory grows into gut knowledge when it fits all the known facts, and my ideas about what happened eight years ago was rapidly growing out of the realm of theory. Gil's nervous cockiness seemed to point to an underlying fear. And Tommy's escape had seemed to intensify that fear.

A sudden thought struck me. Mica had told me that in the nights before he was murdered, Gil muttered in his sleep about a rash. Could he have been saying instead, Raskolnikov?

However, some of the key elements of my theory were missing. For instance, did Gil and Tommy act alone, or was a third person involved? Did Tommy Hoffing escape in order to punish Gil for making him the patsy?

How did the murder of the security guard at the Tulsa pharmacy fit in? I had a sudden thought: Could someone else be working behind the scenes, trying to set up Tommy once again? How did the other men fit in who lived in the Farmhouse eight years ago? Allan Jakes? Tapply? Charley?

A sound like a groan wrenched out of me. I swung my head around to see if anyone heard, but the mother and child, the old man and the librarian went on with what they were doing as though I wasn't there.

I closed the book and replaced it on the shelf. Raskolnikov was dead. Where was Tommy Hoffing?

THIRTY-THREE

It must have been the red Miata that gave me away. Bobby Martinez, still despondent over my sister's short-lived interest in him, followed me down south Muskogee Avenue. The bar atop his new Crown Victoria flashed red, and I pulled over. I hoped that once he saw I wasn't Maggie, our conversation would be over.

He swaggered up to the car, and I rolled down the window.

"I'm not Maggie," I said.

"You don't fit in that car the way she does," he said.

I was a head taller than my sister, and I felt cramped in the sports car as though a hard bump would put me through the ceiling.

"What do you want, Martinez?"

"I got a front page story for that rag of yours," he said. His fierce black mustache worked up and down while he spoke. "The state boys got a tip earlier this evening that Tommy Hoffing was headed home. They might have him cornered."

"Where did the tip come from?"

"Anonymous phone call," he said impatiently. "You comin' with me or not?"

Martinez followed me to the newspaper office, where I left the Miata in the parking lot and picked up a camera. Then I joined Martinez in his souped up car.

Night had fallen by the time we once again turned south on Muskogee. Martinez refused to answer any of my questions about Tommy. Instead he asked me questions.

"How come you drivin' Maggie's car?"

He already knew about the wrecked Trooper, and I wasn't about to tell him that I had lost another vehicle. When I had left the library to pick up Charley's van, it hadn't been behind the courthouse where I'd parked it earlier that day. I didn't believe that anyone had stolen the van, parked as it was beside the police station. Charley had probably found it there. But how?

"Maggie left me the keys," I said.

"She still at the beach with that foot doctor guy?"

"Lonnie Tritt," I said. "They'll be back Sunday."

Martinez chewed on the ragged end of his mustache, obviously wanting to ask more about his ex-girlfriend's new boyfriend, but his pride won out.

After awhile, he said, "She know you drivin' her car?"

"Shut up, Martinez."

He shut up, and we drove in silence through the ragged tail of south Tahlequah — past Wal-Mart and the shiny new car dealerships to the highway that led to Lake Tenkiller. The lighted farmhouses lay among the folds of the hills like brilliant fireflies. I imagined happy families behind the drawn curtains, eating their carry-out pizza and watching the video they had rented for their Saturday night entertainment.

More likely, though, the families behind those windows were just as dysfunctional in their own ways as Tommy Hoffing's family and as the family I grew up in. There was no such thing as normal.

I glanced at Martinez and at the paunch that was beginning to round his belly. Around his waist he wore a utility belt to which his holster was attached. From where I sat, a corner of the black grips of a 40-caliber Smith and Wesson gleamed from behind Martinez's seatbelt. I knew from earlier conversations that the gun was not the only weapon his belt held. Besides two spare 11-round clips, he had a pair of handcuffs, a baton and pepper spray. I couldn't see it, but I knew the patrol unit also carried a Remington 870 shotgun.

"You ever have to use that Smith and Wesson?"

Martinez looked at me out of the corner of his eyes before his attention returned to the highway.

"Why?"

"Just curious." I had never met Tommy Hoffing, but I felt as though I knew him. I had peeked inside his house, been shot at by his children, survived a wild car chase with his wife. Through those experiences, an image of the man had formed until he was more than a face in a photograph. What would he feel when two dozen armed men hunted him in the dark? Fear? Anger? Would his Houdini-like escape skills once again save him?

Martinez gave me a dark look as though he could read my thoughts. "You know, Powers, this is off the record, but most of the time I cruise around in my mobile office thinkin' about the next stop for coffee and donuts. I hope to God I never have to use my gun."

We rode in silence for a minute, then Martinez snorted. "You're buyin' that, ain't you? I don't even like donuts. Why do you think I got into this line of work if I don't want to use a gun?"

My mouth squeezed shut the way it does sometimes when I want to come back with a snappy retort but have nothing convincing to say. Instead I took a deep breath and let it out slowly.

Martinez, his small rant over, grinned.

I was glad Roz and her sons were at her brother's house, and I hoped they would be spared the knowledge of the manhunt until it was over.

Martinez pulled up beside a dozen other pickups and cars in the yard of the Hoffing place. The house looked rundown and defenseless. In the final illumination of the headlights, I saw the old hound run under the porch, his wiry tail tucked between his back legs. The game hens had disappeared.

Through the barren trees, a fire glowed, and Martinez and I followed the light. The fire was built in the clearing where I had first met Roz and her sons. Two men, rifles held at ready, stood near the blaze while a third dragged brush to feed it. Flames shot tall and hot; sparks exploded in the night sky.

Martinez nodded at one of the men. "Jess," he said.

Jess, a small, pinched man with a deputy's badge pinned to his wool plaid coat, nodded back. The fingers were cut out of his gloves so he wouldn't fumble the trigger of his rifle.

In the dark shadows at the edge of the light, a man held a shotgun while another squatted next to a bloodhound, quietly talking into its floppy ears and pressing a shirt against its nose. They wore FBI windbreakers.

The man with the bloodhound picked up a flashlight and stood, the dog's leash in his left hand. The dog started snuffling the ground. The two men followed the dog in ever-widening circles until they left the light altogether.

The men at the fire watched the FBI trackers in silence until they were out of earshot. Then one pulled a flask out of his pocket and offered it around.

"Reckon they'll find him?" he said.

"That son of a bitch is like swamp gas," said the second man. He took a deep pull off the flask and handed it to Martinez.

Martinez took a swig and passed it to me. The men looked at me as though they just realized a woman was present.

The whiskey left a warm glow in my stomach. I handed the flask to the man next to me then pulled the camera out of its case to give them a clue as to why I was there.

I identified the newspaper I worked for, opened my reporter's notebook and prepared to get background. "What's been happening here tonight?"

The man called Jess shuffled his feet then nodded toward the man who had been feeding the fire. "Calvin's old lady saw Hoffing a few hours ago."

Calvin was short and barrel-chested and his dark, broad face showed traces of Cherokee blood. He walked with a pronounced limp.

Calvin nodded at me. "She was goin' out back of the house to get the wash off the line just before dark. She hollered for me, and I went for the snake-killin' hoe cause that's what I thought it was. Turns out she saw a man stealin' some of our clothes."

"Did you see the man?"

"He run off in the woods before I got out there. She knowed it was him, even though dark was comin' on. Tommy Hoffing's been our neighbor for goin' on 20 years."

"Did you know the Blackinwaters?"

Calvin spat. "I knew 'em."

I put my notebook away, a subtle signal reporters use to encourage people to speak freely. "What were they like?"

The night was quiet; only the snapping of the burning wood broke the silence. The wind shifted, and blew the smoke in my face. I stepped aside, closer to Martinez, and brushed his arm. In the cool night air, it felt right to touch another human being; I wished it were Charley who was beside me. But I pushed the thought aside. Wherever he was, Charley didn't seem to need me right now.

My eyes stung with smoke, so I only heard Calvin as he spoke. "They never did me no bad turn," he said. "Mrs. Blackinwater, she seemed all right. But the old man — some said he'd steal the money out of his dyin' daddy's pockets. He defended folks that shoulda been took out and shot. There wasn't many mourned that man."

"But you can't have a man like Tommy Hoffing runnin' around the country killin' folks," Jess said.

"Even so," Calvin said.

The bottle was passed around again. This time I lifted it to my lips but didn't drink. I didn't want to set myself apart from this group, but at the same time didn't want my mind clouded. The night air crackled with expectation.

Martinez felt it, too. He handed the bottle to the man next to him and said abruptly. "You boys keep the fire warm." Gun in one hand and flashlight in the other, he waded into the brush at the light's edge, following the path the FBI trackers had left.

I started to follow him, but he waved me back, a warning look on his face. Soon, his flickering light disappeared.

I was left behind with the base camp crew — the men who are either too decrepit or too incompetent to be useful in the woods, so they feed the fire and serve as a liaison to civilization. Relay messages, procure supplies, keep the old stories alive.

Perhaps it was The Sergeant, my father, who planted the seeds for the distaste I felt at being lumped with the "left behinds." To hear him tell it, he was always where the action was. He made things happen. He never backed down from a fight. Never, at least, until a Vietcong booby trap blew off the lower half of his right leg.

The men settled around the fire, their rifles at ready, and I silently counted off the minutes.

Jess stared at the fire and spoke to no one in particular. "Did you hear about the teacher over by Westville rolled his truck and got killed?"

Like a Greek chorus, the other two men echoed him.

"Westville."

"A teacher."

"He wasn't wearin' no seat belt. Got throwed out the windshield not 200 yards from his house. Wasn't found 'til next day."

"Seat belt's no guarantee anyway," Calvin said. He wore a Stetson, and his face was hidden in deep shadow. "My cousin Oleta and her husband was on their way home from Indiana — went up to see their daughter — and a piece fell off a semi, went right through the windshield and de- decaptivated Harold. A feller stopped and asked if he could help, but Oleta said it wouldn't do no good. They didn't even call an ambulance."

The men around the fire shook their heads and passed the flask again.

"Be right back," I said to the night air.

Jess nodded absently, but Calvin half rose as if to follow me.

"Gotta pee," I said.

He sank back down in embarrassment, and I was free. Perhaps the women he knew didn't talk that way.

Once out of the light the fire cast, I waited for my eyes to adjust to the darkness. Men's voices murmured in the clearing, but it was quiet in the woods. The crescent moon cast a pale glow that made the trees darker shadows against the black wall of the forest. Once I started moving, rocks and broken branches created an uneven surface that twisted my ankles and made me lurch forward to keep my balance. Limbs whipped my face, and brambles tore at my jeans.

I cursed and backtracked to the trail that led to the Hoffing house. Perhaps I could get in Martinez's car and find a flashlight.

I had no plan, other than following Martinez into the forest. Tonight was the night Tommy Hoffing would be captured or killed. I felt it in my bones, and I wanted to be there when it happened. To find out if Tommy Hoffing had answers to the questions that would not let me rest.

I stumbled back to the vehicles that were parked around the Hoffing's home only to find Martinez's car locked. I checked the others; they, too, were secured against any chance that Tommy Hoffing would double back this way and steal a car.

I sat on the steps of the Hoffing house and listened. The night turned colder and I hugged my jacket around me. Off in the distance, the full-throated warbling of peeper frogs promised that spring was on the way. An owl swooped above me, the rush of air its only sound of passage.

After awhile, the old hound crawled out from under the porch and joined me. His tail thumped on the wooden steps while I petted him.

"You're a sorry sack of shit," I said.

We sat in companionable silence for a moment then his tail suddenly stopped, and his ears pricked toward the direction of the clearing. I couldn't hear anything at first. But in a moment, I heard it, too. The FBI trackers' bloodhound was baying.

THIRTY-FOUR

I stood and looked in the direction of the bloodhound's cry. There was nothing to see, only the dim shadows of trees and hills against the dark sky. But then I saw a twinkling light and another in the distance. They jerked on and off, on and off, like a strobe in the forest, and I realized it was the effect of men with flashlights running through the trees.

The old hound beside me started baying in response to the bloodhound. Its howl was higher pitched than the bloodhound's, and together they sounded like a chorus from the underworld.

Suddenly the hound beside me stopped baying and ran into the woods. The bloodhound was closer now, and its cry held a new level of excitement as though it were closing in on its quarry.

I felt exposed in the open area in front of the Hoffing house. I melted into the outstretched shadows of the trees and waited.

I didn't wait long.

The brush crashed nearby, and I heard the dry, crackling sound as a man ran through last year's leaves. He paused for a minute, and then let out an unearthly cry of fear and frustration. He sounded like the peacock that I had heard once in the trees along the Baron Fork. An animal out of its element.

I crouched under the branches, frozen in pity for the hunted man. That he had murdered two, perhaps three people, seemed beside the point. He was now the hunted. Part of me wanted to reach out to him and help him escape, but I was afraid of the cornered-animal part of him, the part that I was sure would lash out at any human form right now.

The men with flashlights were close enough that I could see their blurred forms behind the light. The bloodhound's excited baying drowned out thought.

Tommy Hoffing ran on into the night, his pursuers closing in. I grabbed my camera and followed. I was too far behind to benefit from their light, and the rocky ground slowed me. For a short time, I was on a trail that followed a ridge top, and it was easier going. But I lost the trail, and the land broke away steeply into a hollow. I half-fell and half-slid to the bottom. Branches scratched my face and tore at my jacket. A creek cut through the hollow; its thin thread of water reflected the pale light. I stepped on a rock in the middle, but it twisted under my foot, and I lurched into the water. The hand I put out to catch myself slid across a wet rock, and its knife edge sliced my palm.

Hardly aware of the pain, I ran on and came to the edge of an open field.

The light was better, and before me, as though it were a tableau, I saw two men running across the field and the bloodhound straining at its leash. Tommy must have already made the shelter of the trees on the other side. A man shouted, "There he is!"

A shotgun blasted, then a volley of shots echoed through the valley.

The bloodhound was suddenly silent. I was dimly aware of other men coming up behind me, and Martinez grabbed my arm.

"You stupid bitch," he said. Any other time, I might have hauled back and slugged him for that, but we both seemed caught in a waking dream. It wasn't Martinez talking; it was adrenaline. It coursed through my body, too, and together we ran to where the circle of lights focused on a still form.

The odor of gunpowder and fear rose like a haze. The night was cold, but I was sweating under my jacket, and the faces of the men around me shone with an oily moisture.

I shook off Martinez's hand and pushed forward until I could see Tommy Hoffing. He lay curled on the ground in a fetal position, his blind eyes half-open, blood pooling under him and running in a scarlet ribbon back toward his house. The Hoffing hound sat on his haunches beside his master, his lips pulled back and teeth bared at anyone who came too close.

Tommy Hoffing was clad in a T-shirt and torn jeans and he wore no socks under his dirty tennis shoes. His hair was long and tangled and greasy.

The FBI men and the deputies spoke in hushed tones as though they were at a funeral.

"He's been tied," one of them said. He turned the dead man's arm over and exposed his wrists, which had red welts across them. "Looks like it was rope."

The hound growled and lunged at the man, and when the man kicked him, the dog ran into the woods.

Martinez stepped forward and took charge. "Givens," he said to a tall, husky man, "you go call the medical examiner. Dr. Wyandotte. Tell him to get out here. Everyone else get back. We've gotta preserve the scene."

Martinez pushed the men back until Tommy Hoffing's body was lying alone at the edge of the field like a pile of debris that a flooding creek had pushed against the trees. The men gathered in knots and waited. They still held their guns ready, as though some new threat might arise out of the darkness.

I put down my camera bag and sat beside it. My hand was sticky with blood from the rock in the creek. With my pocketknife, I cut the end off my T-shirt and bound my hand. The blood soaked through the cotton, like a sin stain that refused to hide. The ground was damp and cold, and the smell of scuffed dirt perfumed the air. After awhile I began shaking.

I closed my eyes and saw the raw welts on Tommy Hoffing's wrists. Someone else had tied the knots, someone who held the knowledge that would bring my theory to life.

I had passed some kind of turning point; my life was on a new course that had been set by Tommy Hoffing and his death. Tommy Hoffing, whom I had never met while alive, now held my future.

Martinez was silent on the ride back to Tahlequah. It was very late, and the stars shone with a brilliant fierceness. There would be heavy frost by morning.

He stopped at the newspaper office to drop me off, and finally spoke. "You're a hell of a poor excuse for a reporter. Wouldn't even take no photos."

I stood, and the camera case bumped against my thigh. The door slammed. Martinez peeled the tires of the Crown Victoria, and a shower of gravel sprayed the side of the building. I watched him drive down the street until the red taillights disappeared.

I let myself into the building and fell asleep on the stained sofa in Hank's office.

THIRTY-FIVE

The cold woke me. It was early; the light outside was gray. I had slept fitfully, and my first thought was of the dreams that had held me captive in the night. I couldn't recall any details, but I knew the dreams had been violent and unhappy, and their residue stayed with me although their substance had melted back into the night.

I let my feet fall over the side of the sofa, levering me up, and I sat for awhile with my head in my hands, feeling hungover, as the details of the night came back. The hound's cry. The shotgun blast and the blood. Tommy Hoffing on the ground.

I wondered if Roz Hoffing and her boys had been notified yet. If this very moment they were mourning the loss of a man who already had been lost to them so long ago.

It should be over, but it wasn't. There were too many unanswered questions. The rope burns on Tommy Hoffing's wrists, for instance, left a hole in what should have been a neatly tied package. And with Tommy Hoffing dead, no one was left to tell what really happened to the Blackinwaters and to Gil Martin. Or was there?

I staggered to the bathroom and splashed water on my face. I kept a toothbrush and toothpaste in my desk, and after brushing my teeth, I ran a comb through my damp hair.

The bandage on my hand, improvised in the dark the night before, was grimy and blood-stained in the morning light. I peeled it off and examined the wound on my hand. It was tender and puckered along the jagged edges. Not serious enough for stitches, though. I administered first aid with aspirin and Bandaids.

It took ten minutes to write a story for Hank. Just the bare facts of Tommy Hoffing's death. Just enough to ensure that I would have a job when I returned. I left a message on his home answering machine telling him where to find it, then I got out of town.

I stopped at Hardee's on the west side of town and got a large coffee and two cinnamon-raisin biscuits, no icing. The coffee lasted all the way to Wagoner.

It was a sunny, crisp morning, and the hills stood out in stark relief against the sapphire sky. The yellowed blades of grass along the highway were weighted with frost, and the sun glinted off them like knives. The day was early, and the highway nearly empty. By the time I got to Tulsa, it was after 8 a.m.

The sun shone off the windows of Mica's house, turning them into blind eyes. I parked the Miata behind her car and knocked on her door. I waited on the porch a long time before she opened it.

She wore a silky lavender robe, and her gypsy hair was wild and unkempt. She held a cup of tea in one hand. The cup was delicate, like her, and I smothered an impulse to knock it from her hand and watch it shatter on the rock steps.

"Tommy Hoffing is dead," I said.

I watched her face. There was no sign of surprise, of relief, of closure.

I pushed her aside and went through the door. "I have to talk to him. Is he here?"

Mica finally spoke. "You should leave." She didn't ask who I meant.

The house hadn't been cleaned, and in the sun's path through the windows, dust motes floated. Ashes from the fireplace in the living room overflowed the grate and spilled onto the rug.

Anger surged through me. "I saw him just after they shot him. He tried to go home, but he didn't make it."

Something crossed Mica's face then. Some semblance of sorrow. "I can't help you, Viv. You don't understand."

"Tell me where Allan Jakes is."

She went toward the back of the house, into the kitchen, and I followed her.

"Just go away," she said. Her voice sounded very tired. She set the cup down then leaned against the counter. "Iris has left me to go live in some kind of halfway house for spoiled children, and now you want to take away the only person who cares about me."

"You're either harboring a vicious killer, or he's in danger because he knows too much."

Her eyes flashed then. "He would never hurt anyone."

I grabbed her shoulders and shook her. "People are dying!"

Touching her was a mistake. Mica's face shut down, as though she had retreated somewhere far inside. Somewhere she used to go when Gil struck her.

I dropped my hands and stepped back. "Either I talk to Allan or I tell the cops about his gardening project in his basement. Just give him that message." I scribbled my office phone number on a scrap of paper and left it by her cup.

As I pulled out of the driveway, her pale face pressed against her living room window, an endangered flower caught in a terrarium.

I parked behind the High Spirits and sat in the car for a long time, staring at Charley's van and Tapply's MG parked side by side.

One spring break when they were roommates at the Farmhouse, Charley once told me, the two had thrown camping and climbing gear into the back of an old VW van and headed to Joshua Tree in California. The high desert monument was peppered with rock monoliths the color of burned biscuits — few higher than 300 feet. It was a climbing mecca, and they shared the campground with other testosterone-pumped youths who boasted about their prowess on the rock and spent the bulk of their time on the ground smoking dope.

But Charley and Tapply had come to climb, and day after day in the gentle March sun they bagged classic routes and fought their way up unnamed rocks.

At some point it became too tame for Tapply. He headed to a sporting goods store in Twentynine Palms, rented two portaledges and handed one to Charley.

"What's this for?" Charley said, unrolling the narrow nylon sheet.

"It's your bed," Tapply said. "Tonight we sleep on the side of the rock."

"Like hell," Charley said.

"Chickenshit."

The winner, Tapply explained, would be the person who anchored his portaledge with the least protection. Although the main anchor would catch the sleeper if the narrow bed fell, the hapless climber would be left dangling in the dark. If the anchor held.

"What he didn't know," said Charley, "is that I had a piece of bombproof protection with me. I hadn't dragged it out before now because we hadn't needed it, so I dropped it in my haul bag when he wasn't looking."

Some of the other climbers had placed bets on one or the other, and as Charley and Tapply took turns leading the way up a fist-sized crack to where they would spend the night, they heard the comments and catcalls from their audience.

"Don't forget to say your prayers!" echoed off the rock walls from below. The sweet smell of marijuana smoke drifted up the crack.

When the fast-dropping desert dusk came, the two set up their aerial camp on a 200-foot high spire above the campground. Tapply placed the main anchor deep in the crack then set up his portaledge off to one side, dangling from a size one cam that he carefully positioned in a smaller crack.

Charley chose a hairline crack near the larger crack, where he used a wired chock the size of a coin to hold his bed. It was nearly dark, but Charley could see Tapply's eyes widen.

"You're buzzard bait, bro," Tapply said.

The two settled in their uncomfortable beds for the night. "I was afraid to breathe," Charley said, "for fear that chock wouldn't hold. As soon as it was full dark, I fished the bigger piece of protection out of my bag. It was a spring-loaded monster cam, and made a little popping noise when it opened. So I very carefully hooked up to webbing to the cam, put it in the wider crack and sneezed when it popped open.

"Tapply goes, 'You still there, man?' It was great. I slept like a baby with that cam holding me up, and when the sun hit me the next morning, I got up, anchored myself to the crack and tossed the cam back in the bag. I didn't tell Tapply until we were on our way home."

"How did he take it?"

"He didn't talk from Phoenix to Albuquerque. Then he started laughing. He learned one thing that day," Charley had told me, his indigo eyes going dark. "I play by my own rules."

I slowly climbed out of my sister's car, reluctant to confront these two difficult men in my life, yet drawn to them by the twin bonds of necessity and habit.

Across River Park to the west, the Arkansas flowed high and dirty, turgid with Kansas snow-melt. The air smelled clean and fresh, and my steps slowed as I entered the musty-odored hallway of High Spirits.

The lights were off in the corridor; a yellow glow spilled from the entrance to the recording studio. As I neared it, I heard Charley's voice. I paused in the doorway. The room floundered in its usual disarray of abandoned musical instruments and ropes of black cable, lifeless under the fluorescent lighting. Charley and Tapply stood next to a table, their backs to me. Between them lay a sheet of paper, and Charley's long forefinger stabbed it.

"The Beatle-esque Powers That Be." Charley read aloud, his voice vibrating with disgust. "Charley Pack, who skewers modern culture like a revitalized John Lennon." He wadded the paper and threw it on the floor. "Your paid hack hasn't even heard my CD. Give it to some real music critics. Let it stand on its merits."

"You're only a man like the rest of us — perhaps more talented — but in debt for your good fortune." Tapply didn't look directly at Charley but seemed to focus his attention on something in the distance.

"Yes. In debt," Charley said savagely. "And you don't intend to let me forget it, do you?"

"I'm speaking as your friend and as a businessman."

A limp stillness fell over the scene.

I stepped through the open door. Both men turned at the same time, like wooden figures on a cuckoo clock. Neither seemed surprised to see me.

"Ah. Your co-conspirator," Charley said, looking at me, but speaking to Tapply.

I ignored his remark and said slowly and plainly: "Tommy Hoffing tried to go home last night, but he didn't make it. He's dead."

Tapply was the first to respond. His face was bland. "Maybe we can get on with our lives now." He picked up the paper Charley had thrown on the floor and dropped it in a metal wastebasket. Then he turned to the mixing board and flipped switches until light spread across its gleaming black surface like lights across a night city.

Charley's expression was unreadable. Lines cut like hatchet marks bracketed his mouth.

"Where were you last night?" I asked them. "The way I see it, someone gave Tommy Hoffing a ride home and then called the cops." The statement was reckless, and the feeling that I had just stepped through a one-way door made my knees weak. There was no turning back now.

Tapply's mouth curved up in amusement. "Well, Nancy Drew, we were both here in the studio until after midnight. If you don't believe me, ask my sound engineer."

"The same guy who saw Tommy Hoffing run away from here the night of Gil's murder?"

"I left early to see a man about a car," Charley said quietly.

Tapply shot him an annoyed look. "You're wearing us down, Viv Powers," he said. "Put us under a bright light, and we'll confess."

"He didn't show." Charley's indigo eyes were changing, the irises darkening to midnight. His wiry body looked forged from iron.

There was no softness in him anymore, I thought. Was there ever?

Charley started to say something else but Tapply's cell phone rang and cut him off. All three of us jumped at the sudden noise, exposing the tension we were trying to hide.

Tapply answered the phone then left the room to talk privately.

Charley and I were left alone. I realized I was wringing my hands. I forced them to be still.

Charley lifted his Takamine from a nearby stand and picked out a tune in a minor key.

"I was there," I said. "They hunted him down with a dog, and then they shot him."

His face was shuttered. "I told you to stay out of this, Viv."

We stood close enough to touch, but we didn't. An invisible but terrible chasm lay between us.

"It's too late," I said. My throat was constricted, and my voice sounded small and weak. "I'm in it."

Somehow in the past few days I had convinced myself that killing Gil Martin to protect Iris was a noble act, but Tommy Hoffing's execution had poured a white, hot light on death. Death is final. It ends any chance for explanation or redemption. It evicts a person from the human species. It isn't right, dammit.

The silence grew between us — too much to say and no way to say it. Charley's hand stilled on the guitar. We looked deeply into each other's eyes and saw strangers there.

"You left yesterday without waking me," I finally said, still talking in that other person's voice. "I thought things would be different when you came home."

Charley touched my hand and said, "Everything has changed." Sadness deepened his indigo eyes.

I felt the calluses on his fingertips, made hard from years of pressing guitar strings against frets.

Then I turned and left without saying goodbye.

THIRTY-SIX

A hard wind scoured the prairie east of Tulsa, twisting dust into miniature tornadoes and gouging trash out of the ditches. Even after the hills of Cherokee County heaved the pavement up and down, the wind continued to press against the Miata. I drove my sister Maggie's car too fast and wished she were here with me to divert me with her sarcasm, her belief that everything had gone to hell in a handbasket long ago, so what was the big deal?

Sunday before noon. All the good people of Oklahoma's Bible Belt were still in church, and the traffic was light. The familiar landmarks passed by in a blur. At the abandoned drive-in movie on the outskirts of Tahlequah, the empty speaker posts bent into the wind like a regiment of old soldiers. On the north side of the highway, the bare fruit trees of a nursery marked parallel rows into infinity.

I returned to the dark and deserted newspaper office and willed Allan Jakes to call the number I had left with Mica.

The odor of ink from the now-silent presses permeated the air. Apparently Hank hadn't felt my account of Tommy Hoffing's death was compelling enough to put out a special issue of the paper. We would go to press again Monday afternoon, and by suppertime, anyone who hadn't already read the story in the Tulsa papers or heard it on radio or TV could read my terse eyewitness account of the fugitive's last moments.

I lay on the grungy couch in Hank's office and wished that like Sleeping Beauty I could fall asleep for a hundred years until something worth waking for — a Prince's kiss or the key to a door into a new universe — broke the spell.

But rest eluded me.

I finally got up and made a pot of coffee. I carried a cup to my desk and sat down to go through the mail toppling from my in-box. The press releases I tossed in the trash, along with the computer catalogs and workshop fliers. A conference on computer-assisted reporting seemed as far removed from my current needs as a frilly pink tutu.

By the time I finished my second cup of coffee, the pile of unwanted paper was demolished, and I moved to the stacks of paper on my desk. Hank had set a folder next to the phone that was neatly labeled "Follow-up."

I opened the folder and glanced through it. It held community calendar events that could be expanded into features; university news releases with Hank's comments punctuating the margins. I snapped it shut and tossed it aside, admitting to myself I wasn't at the office to work. I was here for Allan Jakes's call.

So far the phone had been silent. I picked it up to make sure there was a dial tone. It buzzed maddeningly in my ear. There's nothing more lonely than waiting for a phone call that doesn't come.

My antidote to drowning in a sea of self-pity is to remove myself emotionally by making lists. Put it down objectively in black and white.

I pulled out a stenographers notebook and neatly printed the word "Charley" at the top of a blank page. Then I started my indictment.

Silent when charged with murder.
Didn't want me to investigate.
Fought with Gil the night he was murdered.
Knew Gil sexually abused Iris.
Must have known about Allan Jakes's marijuana business.
Lived at Farmhouse when Tommy Hoffing killed Blackinwaters.
No alibi for last night — could have taken Tommy Hoffing home.

I sat back and studied the list. Each entry by itself could be dismissed, but taken as a whole, they created a pattern of guilt.

I focused on the next to last entry, "Lived at Farmhouse when Tommy Hoffing killed Blackinwaters," and tapped the end of my pen on the paper. It spattered blue buckshot across the page.

Frank Darman had mindlessly parroted Tommy Hoffing. "Raskolnikov must die," he had said. What was the link between the

Blackinwater murders and the current spate of killings? Was Gil Martin "Raskolnikov"? Had Tommy escaped from Vinita with the idea of punishing Gil?

I tore the sheet out of the notebook and wrote at the top of a clean sheet: "Unanswered questions."

One. If Gil Martin and Tommy Hoffing planned the Blackinwater robbery, had they acted alone or had someone else from the Farmhouse been in on it?

Two. What happened to the money that was taken from the Blackinwaters's safe? Did Tommy really throw it in the river?

Three. Was it coincidence that Gil's girlfriend Linda Smith was killed in a car accident shortly after the Blackinwater murders?

Four. Did someone help Tommy Hoffing escape from Vinita?

Frank Darman had been easily recaptured, but in the midst of an Oklahoma winter, Tommy had managed to elude the searchers. In addition, he had apparently traveled from Vinita to Tulsa to Tahlequah — a distance of at least 120 miles and an almost impossible feat for a man in hiding if he were on foot.

Five. How did the murder of the pharmacy guard on Greenwood fit in?

Evidence at the scene implicated Tommy, and the Ativan that was stolen matched the drugs Tommy was sedated with at Vinita. Had someone else killed the guard and planted evidence to implicate Tommy? Why would anyone take such a risk?

Six. How did the man with the cowcatcher pickup fit in? Why did he run me off the road? Why did he follow Roz?

Seven. Who sent money to Roz Hoffing and why?

Eight. How did Tommy's pocketknife get in the High Spirits?

I wanted to believe that by some miracle Tommy had lost it there, but I didn't believe in miracles.

Nine. Where was Allan Jakes and Gil's copy of *Crime and Punishment*?

Ten. Why did Tommy's body have rope marks on the wrists? Had he left one prison only to enter another? Where had he been since his escape from Vinita?

Some of the questions seemed to exonerate Charley. He had been behind bars when the pharmacy guard was murdered and when the pickup forced my wreck; likewise, if someone had planted Tommy Hoffing's knife in the Clinton Bedroom.

But how many people were involved?

I threw the notebook down and stared out the window. The sun had plunged behind a bank of gray clouds, and the wind swayed the young trees in front of the courthouse. The street was deserted.

Perhaps Charley had killed Gil Martin, but I couldn't believe the man I had lived with for eight years had anything to do with the murder of the Blackinwaters. Surely I would have seen some sign of suppressed violence.

But — another thought struck me — what if he somehow found out about Gil's part in the murders? Would Charley have blackmailed Gil?

We never seemed to have any extra money. Anything Charley earned from playing gigs went into buying equipment. He was a sucker for musical instruments, and even though his first love was the guitar (he owned five), he collected exotic instruments: a bodhran from Scotland, a balalaika from Russia, Peruvian flutes, and on and on. And being on the road was costly: gas, motels, food, van maintenance, phone calls.

If he had a pot of money stashed away somewhere, he had managed to hide it from me.

And yet. It was his money that bought the 40 acres we lived on. A small inheritance, he said, and I hadn't questioned him. Now I wondered.

I returned to my desk and picked up the notebook again. The last question on the page jumped out at me: Why did Tommy's body have rope marks on the wrists?

I was so engrossed in my thoughts that I didn't realize someone else was in the room until fists rained on my shoulders, beating a staccato rhythm.

"You fucking car thief," a woman yelled.

I leaped to my feet and twisted around, throwing my arms up to defend my face.

"Maggie!"

My sister glared at me. Her heart-shaped face pulsed with anger, and her short, compact body bounced up and down with unspent energy. One lock of her blond hair stuck out to the side as though an invisible hand pulled it.

I laughed. It had always been my most potent weapon against her. Maggie was the vivacious, beautiful member of the family. I punished her with mockery.

As usual, my laughter fed her anger.

"I mean it, Viv! You stole my car. I called the damn police and got Martinez of all people. He told me you had it." Her blue eyes flashed fire.

"Nice tan," I said, stepping behind the desk to put it between us. "What did you and Lonnie think of Tobago?"

Maggie stamped her foot. "Aren't you listening? Martinez!"

"Yeah. Martinez still has a thing for you."

"I don't want him poking into my business."

"You called him."

"What are you doing with my car?"

Already, Maggie's anger was evaporating. That was one thing I liked about her. She had attitude, but she didn't hang on to it.

So I told her why I had the car, beginning with Charley's arrest. We ended up crosslegged on the striped Mexican rug in Hank's office. The story took a long time to relate, and Maggie listened quietly, eyes wide, breaking in occasionally with a question.

Finally, I leaned back against the couch, spent with the telling. I hadn't realized until now how much I needed to talk about it. A ragged peace soothed the edges of my anger and fear.

"Jesus," Maggie said, lighting a thin brown cigarette. "I can't even leave town a few days without everything going to hell in a handbasket."

"Lucky for you that all your money's invested in handbaskets."

She gave me a look and drew deeply on her cigarette.

We sat in silence for a moment, then she said, "You need to go home and get some clean clothes, feed your poor Mack-cat."

I looked down at myself, not noticing until that moment that my obsession with Tommy Hoffing's death had displaced personal hygiene. My jeans were stained at the knees from a fall in the dark forest, and my T-shirt was torn along the bottom edge where I had carved out a bandage the night before. "What if that jerk with the cowcatcher on the front of his pickup is waiting at the house?"

"Safety in numbers," Maggie said, rising fluidly from the floor. "I'll be your driver and bodyguard."

The thought of my sister protecting me made me laugh. She was a head shorter and 50 pounds lighter than me. Furthermore, as I liked to point out, her long, blood-red fingernails prevented her from doing any real work.

"You can open my mail, too," I said, indicating her nails.

Her eyes narrowed. "I could still swear out a complaint against you."

I hugged her. "I'm glad you're home."

"Damn straight," Maggie said.

THIRTY-SEVEN

The wind had pushed a cold front into town, and last autumn's leaves scattered with each gust. The sky was pewter. I stood in the newspaper office parking lot and shivered in my thin jacket while Maggie minutely examined her car for dents and scratches. Finally satisfied, she muttered, "Humph," and climbed in the driver's side. I settled in beside her, and we headed north.

If Allan Jakes called while I was gone — and I no longer expected him to — he would just have to call back.

I stared out the car window at Cherokee County's austere landscape as if I were seeing it for the first time: faded barns, thin cattle, rocky fields, stunted trees, litter-filled ditches. Telling Maggie about the events of the past two weeks had given me fresh clarity. New shapes emerged, and I knew with a deep-down certainty that I had to see this through to the end. I had to pry answers from the past no matter what the cost. Even if it meant losing this place I had come to care about.

"No one person could have acted alone," I said to Maggie. "It's not humanly possible."

"Duh."

I punched her shoulder.

"Don't savage the driver," she said, turning the Miata into my driveway.

From the outside, the rough-hewn house looked as it always did: a refuge in the forest, a hideaway tucked into the ridges and hollows that wrinkled the north end of Cherokee County. Mack, the gray cat, sat on the front porch and watched us as though we were birds he was stalking.

"Cats are such delightful creatures," Maggie said. She was a dog person, 100 percent.

"At least they don't eat shit, roll in dead animals and get in losing battles with skunks."

"No," she said, opening the door and climbing out, "they only drag half-dead birds into the house, barf hair balls on your carpet, and hold up their tails and walk away when you're starved for affection."

"Cats don't need people; people don't need cats. I like the symmetry."

Maggie snorted. "The Sergeant always said you'd argue with a fence post."

"Would not."

"My point."

Maggie and I approached the house cautiously. Too many people were dying, and I didn't want to be next.

"You stay outside while I check out the house," I instructed Maggie. "If I don't give the all-clear by the time you count to 60, use your cell phone to call the Sheriff's Department."

"Gotcha," she said. She grinned as though we were kids again playing one of The Sergeant's survival games.

Mack darted through the door ahead of me and stationed himself by the refrigerator, mewing piteously. So much for stealth.

I could see most of the house, except for the loft, from where I stood inside the door. No one jumped out at me, and the room smelled of neglect and abandonment. Dust dulled the walnut dining table, and a fine skein of spider webs framed the large window that overlooked Spring Creek.

I quickly peeked in the bathroom and over the railing at the top of the stairs. "All clear," I yelled to Maggie.

She came inside and wrinkled her nose. "This place needs aired out," she said.

"I'll make a note of that." I pulled the bag of cat food out of the refrigerator, where mice can't nibble at it, and filled Mack's bowl.

Maggie and I searched the house, looking for even the smallest of signs that anyone had broken in, but we found nothing. Then I dug out some clean jeans and a sweatshirt, took a shower and bandaged my hand.

While I showered, Maggie found the only ready-to-eat food in the house — peanut butter and crackers — and made herself a snack. She cupped her hand to catch the crumbs.

I followed her example and ate a few crackers and a spoonful of peanut butter, then I threw some clothes in a bag and stuffed the protesting Mack into his cat carrier. Until this was over, Mack and I would stay with Maggie. Public transportation is nonexistent in Cherokee County. Those who don't have a vehicle are dependent on the generosity of others. It was more than the lack of a car, though, that prompted me to ask my sister for shelter. I no longer felt safe in my own house.

For two days, I went to bed early at Maggie's house, ate three meals a day and kept regular office hours. I was waiting for inspiration to strike, but it stubbornly kept its distance. Allan Jakes didn't call. Neither did Mica, Tapply or Charley. Hank was pleased by my new-found devotion to my job. He didn't realize I was just killing time.

I avoided Terri Mouse whenever she came to the office, which wasn't easy with a staff as small as ours. I had abused our friendship to help free Charley from jail. The term journalistic ethics was an oxymoron anyway, I told myself. The TV "news" magazines and all their spawn had hastened the decline. When news becomes entertainment, the temptation to embroider "for the sake of the story" overwhelms the conditioning to stick to the facts. That didn't make it right, the righteous part of me argued. It left a bad taste in my mouth.

Hank told me to write a follow-up on Tommy Hoffing's death.

"Why me?" Silly question, but I was stalling until I could think of a way to put it off. Forever, I hoped.

"You have access to the widow. She trusts you." Hank pulled his soggy cigar out of his mouth and placed it in the special ashtray he kept on his desk for that purpose.

"People are sick of that story." I was picking at a thread on my shirt. It broke, and a button fell off and rolled under my desk. I got on my knees and reached under the desk. Along with the button, I found a notebook. It was the notebook I had been writing in Sunday when Maggie interrupted me. I must have dropped it and somehow kicked it under the desk.

Hank was saying something.

"Huh?"

"The story is due tomorrow." He frowned at me, and his thick eyebrows hunched so fiercely they touched in the middle. "Are you listening?"

"Right. Tomorrow."

Hank shook his head and left.

But I wasn't thinking about Hank's stupid story. I was reading the list. The last question on the sheet jumped out at me: Why did Tommy's body have rope marks on the wrists?

I remembered my conversation with Pete Terrapin — it seemed like years ago — "The Blackinwaters were tied with the neatest little knots you ever saw," he had said while looking out the window at the cemetery that surrounded his house.

Knots. I dialed Pete Terrapin's number, identified myself and said, "What kind of knots?"

He knew what I meant. "They weren't the best knots for the job," he said. "I would have used a combination bowline and slippery half hitch so's I could bear down on it and truss 'em up good."

In the background, I heard the excited yip of his terriers.

I clenched the telephone receiver and said again, "What kind of knots were they tied with?"

"I don't have a name for them." His voice was distant as though it pained him to acknowledge a lapse in the investigation.

"The Sergeant taught me a few knots," I said. "If I could see the crime scene evidence. . ."

Terrapin laughed, but there was no humor in his voice. "Right," he said. "If pigs could fly." He hung up the phone.

"Damn," I said.

LaRue Bunch looked up from the papers she was filing. "Everything all right?" Behind the thick glasses, her eyes radiated concern.

"I'm going to see a man about flying pigs," I said.

As I left the office, LaRue's voice trailed me. "Don't forget the camera."

THIRTY-EIGHT

When Maggie and I were kids, even though she was seven years younger, our parents expected us to play together. Our differences went deeper than the gap in our ages: Maggie was a born mall rat; I preferred outdoor adventure. Yet, when at 16 I obtained my driver's license, The Saint made it clear that the price for borrowing the family stationwagon was to act as Maggie's chauffeur. I ferried my sister and her little friends to the mall and to the dance studio and to phony tea parties where they dressed in their mothers' heels and makeup and jewelry. I made sure Maggie knew my services weren't voluntary.

Maggie seemed to be thinking about those times as she drove the Miata on the winding road that led to Pete Terrapin's house. Her red lips curved in a small smile, and she hummed under her breath.

I didn't want her with me, but she had insisted. And it was her car. I cursed the driver of the cowcatcher truck for making me dependent on other people.

"What a charming place," Maggie said when she saw Terrapin's house and the cemetery surrounding it. "I wonder how old those headstones are."

"Dead people lie under them," I said.

She looked at me. "My, aren't we crabby today."

"Just stay in the car," I said. "He's not going to be easy."

I marched to Terrapin's front door and knocked on it, but no one answered, no dogs barked. His car was in the gravel driveway next to the house; unless someone had picked him up, he couldn't be far away.

I turned back to Maggie's car, but she wasn't there. The car door stood open, and Maggie drifted among the stone monuments in the cemetery.

"No one's home," I said.

"Shush." Maggie put her finger to her lips. "This place is like a church."

I rolled my eyes. It wasn't like Maggie to be reverent, but sometimes she mistook sentiment for deeper feelings. Anything could set her off: the sight of a curly headed girl holding hands with a little boy, clouds that looked like designer fabrics, angels on headstones. I had learned to keep my distance.

At the edge of the cemetery stood a massive black walnut tree, probably one of the few of its size in the county. I hunkered in its lee to find shelter from the bitter wind. Maggie seemed oblivious to the cold. After awhile I found three walnuts the squirrels hadn't buried and started juggling them. When I saw Pete Terrapin and his dogs walking down the road, I let the walnuts drop.

His eyes darted from me to Maggie to the bright red Miata and back to me again. The terriers jumped on me as though they had found an old friend. The doberman stayed at Terrapin's side and looked solemn.

"You've wasted a drive," Terrapin said. His eyes strayed to Maggie.

"My sister admires your graveyard."

"I can't help you."

In the end, though, it was Maggie who crumbled Pete Terrapin's defenses. She joined us, radiating charm and sincerity, with just a trace of tears brightening her eyes, and asked Terrapin to show her around. They went off together, the doberman beside them. The terriers stayed with me and started digging into the soft earth under the walnut tree.

When Maggie and Terrapin returned, his manner was less guarded. It was clear that empathy was the key to Pete Terrapin. I should have realized that after I played the Alpha Troop card when I met him two weeks earlier. Maggie had sensed it immediately. I wondered if he had always been that way or if he had changed after his retirement from the OSBI — or after his wife's death.

Maggie signaled me to keep my mouth shut, in other words to ask no questions and play follow the leader. Terrapin put his dogs in the house, then we piled in our respective cars, and Maggie followed Terrapin's oversize boat down the rutted road and onto the highway toward Tahlequah.

"My name is Alma," Maggie said, once we were on the pavement.

"Very funny. Call me George."

"Don't be slow, Viv. As far as Mr. Terrapin knows, my name is Alma. I found his wife's headstone before he came back from his walk and learned that her name was Alma. Then I introduced myself to him as Alma. When we came to her headstone, I did the little 'Oh-my-God' trick. He went for it."

"You're sick," I said. The gray hills rushed by in the distance.

"I get results," she said, tapping her long nails on the steering wheel.

"So where are we going?"

She looked at me triumphantly. "To see a man about a rope."

The evidence from Tommy Hoffing's murder trial was stored in a brick warehouse in Muskogee, 30 miles south of Tahlequah. Through a door Maggie and I weren't allowed to enter, I caught a glimpse of long rows of metal shelves stacked high with numbered boxes.

A scowl from Terrapin's friend, OSBI agent Fred Taylor, reminded us we were there by a slender thread. Taylor was huge — about six-and-a-half feet tall, 300 pounds — with a billiard ball head and a bowling ball belly. When we had shown up with Terrapin, Taylor refused to let us in the building until after the two men had a long and heated conversation. We were all civilians, Taylor said, and even my press credentials didn't mean squat. He shot a disapproving look in my direction that made it clear he didn't like reporters and then glared at Maggie just for good measure. She lounged against the Miata, doing her best Marilyn Monroe, but Taylor was immune.

Terrapin's voice grew quiet, and I could no longer hear what he said. Taylor ducked his head toward the smaller man — a tete-á-tete between David and Goliath.

A short time later Taylor ushered us into his office, a barren, monk-like room that held little more than a desk and a couple of ladder-back chairs.

"Wait here," he said sullenly.

The three of us stood in silence until Taylor returned with a cardboard box and set it on the desk.

"The rope. Nothin' else," he said. He opened the box, and a fine mist of dust rose in the sterile room. Taylor drew out a plastic bag that held a coil of white cotton rope, the type once used for laundry lines, and held it up for me to see.

"May I?" I held out my hand for the bag, and Taylor handed it to me.

"Don't open it" he ordered.

The trial had been held eight years ago, and a man convicted. Case closed. Perhaps Taylor was less concerned with the purity of the evidence in the bag and more interested in hassling me. His motive didn't really matter. What did matter was the length of rope in the plastic bag.

The bag held two pieces of rope. A brown substance stained the fiber, and a wave of unease hit me when I realized it was dried blood. Blackinwater blood.

I examined the knots through the plastic. Pain, as though a fist clenched my heart, spread under my breastbone. I saw what I had expected to see, yet I wasn't prepared. I had first learned to tie such knots in Eldorado Canyon while I was going to school in Boulder. They were Figure Eights, and rock climbers use them. In fact, Charley had taught me.

The knots were the most persuasive evidence yet that at least one of the occupants of the Farmhouse had been involved in the bludgeoning deaths of the Blackinwaters eight years earlier. It was rock climbing and rock music that had brought the four men together. Presumably they could all tie Figure Eights.

Terrapin watched me; years of interrogating suspects had taught him how to read faces. "What?" he said.

I shook my head helplessly. "I didn't expect the blood," I lied. "Blood makes me sick."

He frowned at me; he knew it wasn't the blood. But I turned and left the room. Let him draw his own conclusions. Let him discover the significance of the knots from someone else.

There is no statute of limitations on murder — or love.

THIRTY-NINE

Cops have a saying: "Believe half of what you see and none of what you hear." I desperately wanted to ignore the evidence, but I had seen it with my own eyes, and even when they were closed, as they were most of the way from Muskogee to Tahlequah, I still saw the symmetrical loops of the Figure Eight.

My despair slowly turned to anger. It was clear that Gil Martin and at least one other resident of the Farmhouse had taken the philosophy of Dostoevsky's Raskolnikov to heart: some men are elected to be above the law. Perhaps they hadn't read the rest of *Crime and Punishment*, in which the impoverished student is driven mad with guilt over his crime.

So who was it? The supremely self-confident Tapply? The secretive Charley? The timid Allan Jakes? Or all three?

Maggie stepped on the gas and passed a slow-moving farm truck. "You haven't said a word since we left Muskogee," she said. "What gives?"

The mutilated body of an opossum lay on the roadside; a red trail traced its last moment on earth. I closed my eyes again. "I was channel surfing on your TV last night and saw something on one of those news magazine shows about the science of beauty. Did you know you can measure beauty? It's all about symmetry. The more symmetrical our features, the more likely we are to be financially successful and to be liked by others. And symmetrical people are even smarter and healthier on average than the symmetrically challenged."

"Jesus," Maggie said, lighting a cigarette, "what did you see back there to set you off like this?"

We were coming into the south end of Tahlequah: the Wal-Mart store, car and trailer sales lots, the stone buildings of a one-time tree nursery, fast-food restaurants. The debris of small-town America.

"Look. Just drop me off at the newspaper office."

"I hate you when you do this," Maggie said. She blew out smoke, and a dingy haze filled the small car.

"I have work to do."

"Yes. Well thanks for the privilege of driving you."

She dumped me at the office and left without saying goodbye. Even her Miata looked pissed off as its red tail flashed around the corner and disappeared from sight.

Hank ambushed me the minute I walked through the door. "How's the story coming?" he asked. His beetle-like eyebrows were drawn together.

I looked at him blankly.

"That's what I thought." Hank's mouth did one of those twisty things that meant he was pissed. "Tommy Hoffing's widow. Your future here is riding on that story." He stalked off to his desk.

I wanted to laugh. My future?

"Charley?" said the man who answered the phone at High Spirits. "He went home last night. You might catch him there."

My heart thudded in my chest. Home. What a deceptive word. I shook my head to clear it. I couldn't afford to let my heart be a part of this. "How about Allan Jakes?" I asked. "Has anyone seen him?"

"Just a minute," the man on the phone said. "I'll ask around." The phone thunked on something hard, the bar probably, as he sat it down. A song by Stevie Ray Vaughan played in the background.

I had a plan, and all three men — Charley, Allan Jakes and Tapply — had to be involved to make it work. I had been sitting at my desk staring into space when it came to me. That in itself should have served as a warning. Good ideas don't occur at desks; they pop into your head while you're exercising or when you're in the shower. Desk ideas are as pedestrian as the dreary rooms in which they are born.

The man picked up the phone again. "No one's seen Allan for days."

"Tapply, then," I said. "Could I just talk to Tapply?"

While my call was being transferred, I reread the note on the paper in front of me. My message to each man would be exactly the same.

"Hey," Tapply said. His voice was like a distant waterfall.

"I know what you did, and I know why you did it," I said, "from the Blackinwaters to Gil Martin."

His voice tried to break in, but I didn't allow any interruption.

"I'm sick of this, and I want out," I continued. "I want enough money to start over somewhere else."

"Have you been smoking Allan's pot?" Tapply said. He sounded bored.

"I need $25,000 by tonight. Six p.m. At the city park in Tahlequah. Meet me at the pay phone next to the swimming pool. Do you understand?"

"I understand your words," he said, "but ..."

I hung up the phone.

I sat at the desk and gathered myself before dialing the number I knew so well — Charley's and my home number.

He picked it up on the third ring. Music played in the background, one of Charley's songs he had been recording for his new CD.

I said the same words to him I had said to Tapply.

"Why are you doing this, Viv," he said. There was a note in his voice I couldn't translate. Anger? Disappointment?

I gently placed the phone in its cradle.

My last call was to Mica. "Allan has half an hour to call me," I said. "If I don't hear from him by then, I'm going to the police. And I know a lot more about him than the little gardening project in his basement."

I gave her my number.

Twenty long minutes later LaRue transferred a call to me. It was Allan Jakes. I gave him the same message I had given Tapply and Charley.

"You're nuts," he yelled. "You have really lost it."

I hung up on him.

I had three hours to kill, so I went to the place where it all began.

The house once known as the Farmhouse is a two-story, wood-frame structure that sits at the edge of town atop the long hill that hems in the west side of Tahlequah. I walked the seven blocks from the office and stopped in the dirt lane in front of the house. The lot was large, and a wall of overgrown brush and spindly trees shielded the building from the neighbors' view. It looked forlorn and abandoned, the paint worn off the wood and the windows broken. A torn baby stroller lay on its side in the front yard, and the concrete walk leading up to the porch was broken. The dead stalks of last year's grass poked through the cracks.

Charley had brought me to the Farmhouse once before — when I first followed him back to Oklahoma. I had thought then, fresh from the yuppie heaven of Boulder, that the old house embodied everything I didn't like about Tahlequah: It was ratty and bleak, and the poverty overwhelmed me. Yet, I stayed. After a time I discovered the town's appeal: People who were surprised by nothing and accepting of everything. Scenery that veered from the sublime (the Spring Creek watershed) to the ridiculous (trash hanging in treetops along the steep mountain roads, "trash trees" in the local vernacular). A measured pace of existence that said we live only once so why rush through it?

People leave Tahlequah, but they always return. And now Charley had brought me with him so that I, too, was captured by this place called Cherokee County.

The first year Charley came to Tahlequah, he had lived on the Northeastern State University campus. He was older than the other students and had recently split up with Mica. He missed Iris and felt guilty about leaving her. He started questioning the decisions he had made and wondered if it were too late to undo them.

Then he met Tapply and Gil. The three formed a band and played gigs at local bars. Charley hadn't started writing yet, or at least his songs weren't deemed worthy of public performance, and the band covered punk rock groups like The Sex Pistols and The Clash. They needed a bass player, and that's where Allan Jakes came in.

"The band was terrible," Charley said, "but everyone who came to see us had such a good time they didn't care that we couldn't play." A few drinking sprees later, they decided to move in together.

They found the old house on the hill. Adopted a couple of cats and a stray hound. Furnished the house with other people's castoffs. The house became the after-hours hot spot for hip college students, where a mixture of alcohol, drugs, sex and heated philosophical discussions ushered in the morning sun.

Tapply mounted plastic climbing holds on the back side of the house, an improvised climbing gym, and the four men tried to outdo one another on the wall. They graduated to real rocks and scaled everything in the area that could be climbed: Goat's Bluff, the cliffs along Lake Tenkiller, the science building on campus.

The end seemed to come quickly. Between music and climbing and partying, there wasn't enough time to study. Charley dropped out and, taking the dog with him, went to Boulder to play in a friend's band. Gil and Tapply opened their bar and recording studio in Tulsa, and Allan tried his luck in Nashville.

That happened eight years ago. After a long silence, Gil and Tapply called Charley, wanting to book his band. Perhaps Gil's new wife, Mica, had something to do with the invitation. I remembered Charley's initial reluctance. But the offer was too good. The band needed the money. Then the recording deal came along, with Allan Jakes thrown in as an afterthought to manage the band's schedule and take care of the endless details that musicians were so lousy at handling themselves.

And now something from the past, something that began in the rundown house in front of me, was rushing to its ugly resolution.

Dusk. The city park was a long, narrow ribbon of grass and trees along Tahlequah's most visible waterway, which was known variously as Branch Creek or Town Branch or Trash Branch. Litter adorned the park grounds — fast food wrappers, empty beer cans and discarded Pampers. But its location had two advantages: It was just down the hill from Maggie's house so I could walk there in my car-less state, and it was sufficiently public to offer protection in case anything went wrong. Not that I would be in any danger. I didn't intend to reveal myself; I just wanted to see who showed up. Then I would decide what to do with that knowledge.

I had told all three men to meet me at 6 p.m., which on a cloudy day this time of year meant it was deep dusk. I arrived an hour early and planned to hide in a row of evergreens along the creek. However, when I scouted the park, a better opportunity offered itself. Next to the rusty dumpster in the center of the park, someone had discarded an appliance box. A drawing on the side showed that it had once held a refrigerator. I glanced around to make sure no one was watching, even though the park was deserted in the cold evening, and folded myself into the box.

The cardboard sheltered me from the wind, and I could see the swimming pool area clearly with the binoculars I had borrowed from Maggie's hall closet. With my pocketknife, I cut an escape hatch in the back of the box, then I settled in to wait.

My legs and back were cramped by 6 p.m., and I propped myself on my elbows and stretched my legs out behind me. Earlier a car had stopped by the dumpster and a man had thrown a trash bag in it. Two joggers had trotted past, but otherwise the park was quiet. A constant stream of traffic flowed above the park on Bluff Avenue, and the Tahlequah rush minute clogged Downing to the north, but the narrow road that cut through the park had little activity.

A light rain began to fall, like fingers tapping gently on my cardboard roof. The wind drove a fine mist inside the box, and the freshly dampened earth sent up an odor of decay.

I had almost given up my vigil when I heard the rumble of a truck engine near the dumpster. I peered out from my dark hole. The pickup, just a few yards from my hiding place, had a cowcatcher on its front bumper. I pushed down the sudden rush of fear and took slow, deep breaths.

The pickup rolled past and cruised the park. At the north end, it turned and came back, its headlights off. I lifted my binoculars, but the driver's head was a black silhouette. When it neared the swimming pool, the pickup veered off the pavement and onto the yellowed grass. Then it thudded into the trunk of a sycamore and stopped.

I watched for movement from the safety of my hiding place. Was this some kind of trick to flush me out? The box commanded a view of most of the park; I was sure I would have seen anyone else who approached on foot or by car. The driver of the pickup and I were alone in the park.

Yet I stayed put.

Each passing minute felt like an hour. I was flooded with a long-forgotten memory. I was hiding behind a stack of boxes in my grandmother's attic and The Sergeant was looking for me. The cavernous space was dark, and The Sergeant's flashlight cast grotesque shadows on the wall.

"Vivian," his soft, persuasive voice said, "Vivian Grace Powers. It's time for us to go home. Your mother and baby sister are waiting in the car."

There was no anger in his voice, but I knew the minute I had shouted to my grandmother that I wanted to stay with her, that I didn't want to go back to the base with The Sergeant, the minute I had ran up the stairs, I knew a harsh penalty would be exacted. Not when he caught me, of course, not in front of my grandmother. No, the payment would come later, after I had time to think about it, after the dread rose to a stifling crescendo.

I shook the memory off and resumed my vigil.

After a long wait the pickup door opened. A man stuck a leg out as though he were going to stand, then he fell face down on the ground. He tried to get up on his knees, as uncoordinated as a marionette whose strings were operated by a drunk, and collapsed again. This time he stayed still.

I didn't recognize the man on the ground. Even though it was evident that something was very wrong, I was reluctant to go near him.

I finally left my shelter and made my way toward him, staying in the shadowy safety of the trees that lined the road. The rain fell harder now and struck my bare head like rice at a wedding. The man lay still as though he were unaware of the cold and the wet. No one else came into the park.

I finally summoned my courage and approached him. I kept thinking that he would suddenly spring to his feet and grab me, and I reached out one shoe and nudged him. He didn't respond, and bolder now, I kneeled beside him to see if he was alive.

His breath came out in ragged, shallow gasps. From the position he was in, I couldn't tell how he had been injured or how badly. But he was unconscious; he needed help.

The man wore a knit cap on his head, a pea jacket, blue jeans and scuffed cowboy boots. He was face down and what little I saw I didn't recognize. But somehow the driver of the cowcatcher truck knew me and he knew Roz Hoffing.

There was a pay phone next to the swimming pool entrance. I used it to call an ambulance.

While I waited for help to arrive, the man moaned and rallied slightly. His eyes opened and focused on me. "I won't kill anyone," he said. "I didn't sign on for that."

I put a hand on his shoulder. "Who sent you?"

But his eyes closed again, and he fell silent.

It wasn't until the sirens wailed into the park that he spoke again.

"Tell Charley," he said.

The ambulance door slid open and two EMTs hurried toward us, carrying heavy, suitcase-like bags.

"Tell Charley what?"

The man's eyes rolled back in his head.

I watched while the ambulance crew stabilized him. When they turned him onto his back to load him on a stretcher, I saw his face clearly. The man's nose had a wire ring.

I swallowed hard. I had seen him once before. The night of Gil Martin's memorial party, he had blocked the door at the High Spirits — the guy with the amulet tattoo and nose ring.

One of the EMTs approached me and asked for information about the man. "I was just walking by and saw him," I said, trying to act the part of the Good Samaritan. The woman took my name and phone number and then the ambulance left.

I was alone in the dark night. Before heading back to Maggie's house, I wrote down the license plate of the cowcatcher truck and peered through the windows. The interior of the truck was as barren as a pilfered tomb.

My plan was a bust. None of my questions were answered. And now I had new questions to worry about.

Tell Charley what? That the guy with the nose ring hadn't signed on to kill anyone?

FORTY

"Not that it's any of your damn business," said Maggie's note, "but Lonnie and I went to Fayetteville to hear some REAL music."

I had returned to Maggie's empty house and found the note fastened to the refrigerator with an Elvis magnet. An almost empty house. Mack followed me forlornly from room to room and cried to go outside.

"Sorry, buddy," I told him. "We'll go home soon. Until then, you're a house cat."

I hoped I was telling the truth. "Home" seemed more and more like an abstract word, an unattainable dream. What had happened to Charley and me?

I stood at the kitchen sink and washed the few dishes I had used to prepare a meal. Mack crouched in the doorway to the dining room, watching me. His ears twitched back and forth, and his attention shifted to something behind me.

I heard a small noise, but before I could react, someone grabbed me roughly from behind and pinned my arms against my sides. I opened my mouth to yell, but my captor let go with one hand and struck me hard across the back.

I gasped for breath and fell to my knees. A heavy body fell on top of me, forcing me all the way to the floor. I twisted and heaved to get out from under, and managed to free one arm. I reached behind me and yanked a handful of hair. A hand clamped a cloth across my mouth.

The cloth smelled sickly sweet. I struggled to get away, but there was a horrible humming in my head and I couldn't breathe. I felt myself weakening; I realized I was going under.

I became vaguely aware of the bumping. I was bumping; my whole body was bumping, flopping up and down and back and forth like a rag doll being shaken by a dog. And all around me an engine growled. I tried to lift my arms to shield myself, but they wouldn't follow my directions.

I opened my eyes, and saw nothing but black. I was covered by something, a blanket perhaps, but my body wouldn't respond when I tried to pull it off. I was tired, so tired, but fear poked hot holes into my head, prodding me to wake up. My brain was expanding with the heat, swelling inside my skull, threatening to explode.

I tried to move my arms again and realized they were tied. Ropes chaffed against my wrists, cut into the tender skin. My legs were bent and cramped; I pushed them out, but there was no place for them to go. I was trapped in the trunk of a car.

I tried to open my mouth to yell, but something held it shut. I thought I might be sick, but I couldn't open my mouth, and I would surely choke on my own vomit. I forced myself to be calm, and after awhile the bumping sensation stopped.

The engine died. I waited in the darkness and heard a door slam. Footsteps approached. A key in the lock, creaking hinges. Rough hands grabbed me and pulled me out of the trunk. When my feet hit the ground, my legs buckled, and I almost fell, but my captor held me tightly.

"Stand!" The voice was low and harsh. I couldn't see the speaker; some kind of hood covered my head.

He shoved me in front of him. My legs wobbled then held, and I stumbled on the rough ground. We seemed to walk forever. The ground was rough and uneven, and I fell every few steps. Each time he jerked me up and pushed me forward again.

I'm going to die, I thought. He's going to kill me and bury my body, and no one will ever find me. I fought down the rising tide of fear and let anger replace it. Get hold of yourself, I scolded. You've got to be ready for any opportunity. I pulled at the ropes that held my wrists, but they were tied tightly.

My head felt clearer now, but it vibrated with pain. I became aware of my surroundings. The branches that whipped and scratched told me I was in a forest. Through the cloth that covered my head, I could smell the rotting vegetation that signaled a body of water.

My ankle twisted on a rock and I went down again.

This time my captor allowed me to stay down. He grunted as he half-lifted, half-dragged me against the rough bark of a tree trunk. I felt a rope being tied around my body and then the sweet smell of chloroform again pressed over my face. I held my breath as long as I could. My lungs screamed for air. I made myself go limp in his hands, and he made a satisfied sound as he released me.

His feet shuffled through the leaves on the forest floor, farther and farther away. I allowed myself to breathe again, and the chloroform that clung to the hood over my head flowed into my lungs. I was dizzy, but I held my breath again and rubbed my head against the tree trunk. The hood shifted slightly. I rubbed it again, and it shifted more. The odor of the chloroform faded, but I continued to work the hood around my head until I felt a drawstring under my chin. With my mouth taped and my hands tied, there was little I could do to remove the hood. That was the least of my problems, though. The immediate threat had walked away, and before he returned, I needed to free myself.

I turned my attention to the rope that held my hands. I could rotate my wrists just enough to feel the knot. I explored it with my fingertips. The rope was small in diameter and had a rough, plastic feel — the kind that is labeled utility rope at the hardware store. Perhaps at a subconscious level, I knew what type of knot it held: a Figure Eight loop, fastened with a slippery half hitch and secured with another half hitch. It's the most reliable of knots and the easiest to release, which may be why few rock climbers bother to learn any others.

I fumbled until I felt the nubby end of the rope. I inched along its length to the half hitch. The sinews of my wrists were stretched to the breaking point, and with a cry of frustration, I dropped the end. I tried again, and again I failed.

I stopped and listened for the sound of the man returning. For any sound. The forest was silent except for the groan of two branches rubbing in the wind. Although I could see nothing, I imagined the night forest and how helpless I must look, tied to a tree with a hood over my head. It was a ghastly picture, and in an effort to dispel it, I renewed my attempts to free myself.

The rope that held me to the tree was loose enough that by twisting, I could rub my wrists against the rough bark. The pain was dulled by the chloroform and adrenaline that rushed through me. I worked to rub the knot against the bark, to force the top loop over the bottom loop. The bark scraped the skin from my wrists and my hands were wet with blood when I felt the knot slip. I reached once again to find the end of the rope and tugged at it. This time, it pulled free, and the rope loosened enough from my wrist that I could pull my hands out of the knot.

I tore the hood off my head and looked around. All was dark in the forest, and barren oaks and hickories crowded round me. In the dimly lit distance, it looked like there was a clearing, but I couldn't be sure. I had no idea where I was.

I started prying at the tape that covered my mouth, but it was duct tape, wrapped all the way around my head, and I couldn't find the end.

I abandoned that problem and started on the rope that held me fast to the tree. My captor had been too sure of the chloroform and his knots were tied carelessly. In a moment I was free. Every impulse told me to run as fast and as far from this place as I could, but it was too late. I heard the crackle of leaves. The man was returning.

I would have to fight or flee, and in my drugged state, he probably had the advantage either way. I ran my hands through the leaves around the tree until I found a rock the size of a baseball. Then I kicked the shoe off my right foot and tore my sock off.

The man was closer. He would be in sight any moment. I pushed the rock into the toe of the sock and wrapped the end of the sock around my hand.

The Sergeant had taught me that the most potent weapon is surprise. The man was no more than a dark shape when he appeared. His eyes were on the ground following the path the flashlight made for him.

I sprang from my crouch, shrieking like some primal cat, and hit him upside the head with my improvised club.

He dropped the flashlight and sank to the ground in slow motion. The light, shining on his red curls, made a halo around his head.

"Allan Jakes," I said.

FORTY-ONE

When I was a child, I played a game with other kids on the base called "Tie up." The object was to tie a person so they couldn't free themselves, and, of course, the tied person's objective was to get free within a certain time limit. Either way, I always won. One day, my friend Georgie Kliethermes said he knew a sure-fire way to tie me so I couldn't get loose. I looked at his pudgy, damp face and said, "So show me."

Behind the base barracks stood a scraggly line of trees that ringed a muddy, stagnant pond. Green scum covered the water, and bubbles rose slowly to the surface and spit out odors of death and decay. It was a place of snakes and biting insects. Within spitting distance of the water, Georgie tied one of my wrists to one tree and the other wrist to another tree, and then he stood back to watch. No matter how I struggled, I couldn't get loose. None of the usual methods applied: using one hand to help the other; stepping over the rope so my hands were in front of me and my teeth could work on the knots. With my hands tied separately and far from one another, I was helpless.

After awhile Georgie waddled away like a bear searching for grubs, while I yelled obscenities. The forest was quiet after he left. I remember the sweat running down my face and my fear as I watched for snakes to slither out of the green water. A long time later Georgie came back with some of the other kids we played with. They all watched silently — with malicious eyes, I thought — until I finally said to Georgie, "Give."

It had been a humiliating experience, but now in the night forest with nothing but the two pieces of rope that Allan Jakes had tied me with, I was grateful for the memory.

Allan lay on the ground, dazed and moaning, and he didn't put up a fight while, with fingers made clumsy by chloroform and cold, I tied one of Allan's wrists and then the other to nearby trees. Sturdy trees.

A white hot anger burned in me, and I pulled the knots tight so the rope wrinkled the skin on his wrists.

Once he was rendered helpless, I pried and pulled at the tape that covered my mouth. It felt like the skin came off my face with it, and my hair tore at the roots when I jerked the tape one final, vicious time. The pain brought tears to my eyes and revived my anger.

I picked up the flashlight Allan had dropped and shone it in his eyes. In the bright light, his blue eyes washed out to pale gray, and he blinked slowly like an owl. His red hair shot out from his head like flames.

"It's not what you think," he said.

My hands were stained with my own blood. I hit him in the ribs with the flashlight, and he yelped with pain.

"You son-of-a-bitch," I said. "I have a monster headache. You better start talking."

"It was all just a prank that got out of hand," Allan said. "That's . . ."

I struck him again with the heavy light, harder this time, and his ribs made a cracking noise.

After he finished screaming, he began crying. "Don't hurt me, Viv," he said in a small voice. "I'm just a pawn, too. Just like you."

I held the flashlight up, ready to hit him again. He had rolled into a fetal position on the ground, with his arms stretched out toward the trees on either side. After awhile, I dropped the flashlight on the ground, and its light flickered and went out. The night suddenly seemed colder, and the wind whipped through my thin shirt. I was sick of violence, sick of lies. I just wanted this to be over. I heard a motor in the distance; Allan heard it, too.

He started talking with a manic frenzy. "I made good money on the pot in my basement. I can share with you, Viv. You can start over some-where — just like you said you wanted. I can get the money tomorrow easy."

The motor sounded nearer.

Allan kept talking. "How much do you want? $25,000? I can double that. I can . . ."

"Shut up," I said. My ears strained to follow the progress of the vehi-cle.

"I don't hold grudges, Viv," he said. "It'll be like nothing ever happened."

"Shut up!"

I kicked him in the ribs again. He cried out and then fell silent.

Headlights stabbed the night. A vehicle bumped over ruts in the forest, its lights alternately blocked by trees and then visible, like a slow-motion strobe light pulsing on a ghostly dance floor. It pulled into the distant clearing and stopped. The headlights remained on, pointing into dark nothingness.

I heard two doors slam, but I was too far away to see anyone. I wadded the hood that had covered my head and stuffed it in Allan's mouth, and then I secured it with his belt. It probably wouldn't stay in place long, but by then, it wouldn't matter. I looked at Allan's coat with longing, but I would have to untie him to remove it, and I couldn't take that chance. He had a knit cap in one pocket, so I pulled it onto my head and told myself I felt warmer already. Then I found my sock with the rock in it and started working my way toward the vehicle.

It was hard to move quietly in the dark forest, and my progress was slow. Roots reached up to trip me; branches whipped my face and arms. My head still pounded from the chloroform, and I knew I wasn't thinking clearly. At one point, I fell on my knees and retched. I felt better with my stomach empty, as though a poison had been released. I wiped my face with my shirttail and went on.

After awhile, I drew close enough to see that the vehicle was a car. The light from its headlights illuminated the forest ahead and showed little of the car itself. It did, however, light Allan's car, which was parked in front of it. I wondered why Allan had bothered to remove me from the trunk and take me into the woods. Perhaps as a final bargaining chip?

Two figures moved in the shadows beside the car that had just arrived. Tall figures. Men. They stood facing each other, their heads inclined as though they were deep in conversation.

I knew who they were. I knew their profiles with the intimacy of a close friend and a lover. Tapply and Charley. Allan Jakes had been expecting someone. I gripped my rock-in-a-sock more tightly and realized what a ridiculous weapon it was.

I crouched behind a bush, feeling sick at heart and trying to consider my next move. My survival instinct screamed at me to run for help, to get away from this place. But I knew that if I ran, I would never feel safe. I would always be watching and waiting. I had to put an end to it here.

One or both of them, Charley or Tapply, had come to finish what Allan had begun.

Something heavy hit me from behind and knocked me over. I stifled a scream and rolled to one side, ready to use my weapon. Something wet touched my face, something that smelled like garbage. The thing whimpered, and I recognized the hound that lived under Roz Hoffing's porch. I knew where I was now — in the forest behind the Hoffing house.

I remembered the first time I had come to see Roz Hoffing. The lane cut east from the house to the bluff above the lake and then ended in a small clearing. Now I was oriented, now I was dealing with something known.

I hugged the dog to me and scratched him behind the ears, whispering to him to be quiet. His tail was like a rope, wagging back and forth furiously. "Good boy. Good boy," I said. I rubbed his belly, and he rolled over.

His presence was oddly comforting. I kept him close and petted him while I tried to decide what to do next. I felt hungover, fuzzy and slow. Ideas swam close to consciousness and then faded.

In the darkness outside the headlights' glare, Charley and Tapply started pushing each other. Charley yelled words I couldn't understand, and then they were at each other's throats, trying to choke one another.

The two men fell apart and then flung themselves at each other like bull elks fighting over a herd of cows. They grunted and cursed, and the only other sound was body striking body. Debris from the forest floor flew up around them, and trees shook as their bodies caromed off.

Tapply landed a hard blow on the side of Charley's face, and he fell back, hitting the ground with a solid thump. Tapply dove on top of him, fists pummeling like a piston, and Charley rolled him over and put him in a headlock. Tapply broke free, and they flew at each other again.

They may have been able to keep it up for hours. They seemed to be evenly matched, and I had been content to watch them from the shadows. However, the hound, which had been by my side, suddenly barked and rushed at the two men.

The twosome became a roiling, twisting threesome, complete with sound effects. Yelps, yells, curses. I had enough. I marched into the melee and hit Tapply on the head with my rock-and-sock weapon.

He fell back, stunned. The hound ran into the woods. The air was rank with the odors of broken earth, sweat and blood. Charley slowly picked himself off the ground, acting like it was the most natural thing in the world for me to suddenly appear, and said, "Why did you do that? Why did you choose me?"

Gestalt psychology holds that not everything we know can be explained by logic. Instead, an organism's response to a situation is a complete and unanalyzable whole rather than a sum of the responses to the specific elements in a situation. In other words, knowledge sometimes strikes us full-blown, but we can't explain the twisted route by which it found us.

"Why did I do that? To save your sorry ass," I said to Charley.

"That's funny," he said, his indigo eyes black in the darkness. "I thought I was saving your sorry ass."

We looked into one another's eyes and Charley started laughing, an exhausted, quiet, don't-wake-up-the-children laugh. After awhile, I joined in and we held each other like we were drowning, exalted and terrified at the same time.

FORTY-TWO

When Tapply stirred, he didn't miss a beat. Sitting on the ground and rubbing the lump on his head, he began spinning his story.

"We were worried about you, Viv."

He started to get to his feet, and I pushed him back down. "Stay there while I think."

His face turned pouty, but he sank back to the ground. "You got it all wrong," he said, sounding like a movie cliché. "Charley and I had a little misunderstanding, but the important thing is that you're safe." He looked around while he talked, and I knew he was trying to figure out a new angle or an escape route. Perhaps he expected Allan to appear and save him.

He was as dangerous as a cornered animal, and if I didn't figure out a way to neutralize him soon, someone would get hurt.

Charley stood off to one side, a distracted look on his face, as though he were composing a song appropriate to the occasion.

"Charley!" I pointed to Tapply's car. "Look in the trunk. See if there's anything in it we can use as a weapon or restraint."

Charley opened the driver's door and popped the trunk open. He emerged a minute later with a handgun. "This work?"

"God, yes."

He handed it to me as though it were a smelly piece of trash that he didn't want to touch. Charley's never been the Ernest Hemingway type: loving firearms and hunting and bonding over a bottle of Jim Beam. That didn't fit his live-and-let-live philosophy. Neither did fighting, for that matter, but he had acquitted himself well tonight.

I felt Tapply watching me while I checked out the gun. It was a Smith and Wesson automatic pistol with an 11-shot magazine, the type favored by the Tulsa police. And it was loaded. The magazine slid into place with a satisfying snap, and I pointed the barrel at Tapply. Now that I definitely had the upper hand, I was beginning to enjoy myself, headache and all.

"I read in the Tulsa paper that the security guard at the Greenwood pharmacy — you know, the guy Tommy Hoffing supposedly killed — carried a gun like this. The cops never found it." I hadn't read any such thing, but it felt good saying it.

Tapply studied the ground as though he saw something interesting there. "And Charley knew just where to find it," he said.

"Hey, man," Charley said.

"Have you heard of triangulation?" I said to Tapply. "You get the story from as many people as possible, and the truth is somewhere in the middle. A kind of Rashomon thing."

"It's my word against his," Tapply said.

"Get up." I motioned with the gun, and Tapply stood. "We'll bring in a third party."

We trooped to where Allan Jakes was tied. Tapply first, me and the gun next, Charley bringing up the rear. Behind a sheltering line of trees, the dog followed us.

Tapply sucked in his breath sharply when he saw Allan. In the darker shadows of the forest, only highlights were visible. Allan's white face, Allan's white hands stretched between the trees, the white ropes holding him in place like an Apache prisoner staked over an ant pile.

"For Christ's sake. Untie him," Tapply said.

"Like hell," I said.

When Charley suddenly spoke, I jumped.

"Gil had her dragonfly necklace in his hand," Charley said. "He was lying on the floor with his head bashed in, and her necklace was in his hand."

No one had to ask who he was talking about. Iris was the daughter Charley never had, and Charley the only father Iris knew. Of course Charley would protect her.

I placed my free hand on his shoulder. "So you put the necklace in your pocket and went to jail to buy her some time. Instead, you were protecting these assholes."

"They've got some really bad karma," Charley said. "I can't believe I didn't see it before now."

"Karma, schmarma," Allan said. "I only did what Tapply told me to.

He threatened me. It was blackmail. He was going to hurt Mica. I didn't know what to do."

"Shut up," Tapply said. He stepped closer to Allan as though he would kick him.

I reasserted my authority by firing the gun in the air. Tapply spun toward me; Allan's eyes widened in terror.

"That was a warning," I said. "Next one hits flesh."

Tapply backed off.

I waved the gun. "Who wants to go first on this question? Who killed Gil?"

Tapply and Allan looked at each other. At the same time, they said, "He did."

"OK. Good. Maybe the bouncer from High Spirits can help with that one."

They both looked at me, startled.

"He's in the Tahlequah hospital right now," I said. "I think he'll pull through."

Something deflated in Tapply at that point. His handsome face closed down; he wasn't trying to impress anybody. He was through talking. He was a fast learner, and from Charley he had learned the power of silence.

FORTY-THREE

Whoever said victory is sweet was an uncomplicated, simple guy. Victory is a cruel two-headed beast. It's like winning the lottery only to find you have a terminal illness.

I had forced the answers I thought I had to have, and now I had a hangover that wouldn't go away. In the days that followed Tapply and Allan's arrest, I went into the office and went through the motions of working: making calls, writing stories, pumping sources. But it all tasted like dust. I hadn't understood the fragility of Charley's and my relationship, and the effect my obsession with truth would have on us. We slept in the same house, but we were strangers.

Tapply's and Allan's story came out in leaks and dribbles — some of it in the form of press releases from the police, some of it from my friend Martinez. Tapply kept his mouth shut and hired a good lawyer, but Allan and the man I once thought of as Cowcatcher, now identified as Vergil "Club" Callahan, were more obliging.

In the weeks before Gil died, Allan said, the two men spent long hours together in the basement of Allan's house, tending their pot, testing it, and telling stories. Maybe guilt was eating Gil and he had to confess to someone. Perhaps he should have found a priest.

The story began eight years ago when Tapply and Gil took a lit class at Northeastern. *Crime and Punishment* became the subject of late night, boozy discussions at the Farmhouse. They could do that wimp Raskolnikov one better: They could commit a perfect crime but not let guilt destroy them. With Tommy Hoffing's help, they robbed the Blackinwaters, a simple plan that went to hell when the attorney and his wife came home early. Tommy Hoffing herded the couple into the laundry room. His job was to guard them while Tapply and Gil cut a circle out of the safe door with the Sawzall. No one would ever know what set Tommy off, but when the safecrackers checked on the sounds they heard coming from the laundry room, a red haze hung in the air, and Tommy was rolled into a fetal position on the floor.

Gil immediately became a babbling idiot, certain death row was his next stop. Tapply cursed for two solid minutes then started improvising like a politician who's been caught in his office with his pants down. It was Tapply's idea to leave Tommy on Combs Bridge with the empty bag, gambling he would stay in that fetal position forever. A few bills snagged here and there in the brush were meant to indicate that the rest had washed downstream in the current of the Illinois.

Tapply and Gil hid the remaining money and a sizable stash of drugs. Then they established an alibi with Linda Smith, Gil's girlfriend, and prayed that if Tommy ever came to his senses he would keep his mouth shut.

The months that followed were tense, but luck was on Tapply's and Gil's side. Tommy was sentenced to the state's facility for the criminally insane in Vinita. Linda Smith died in a car wreck. Months went by, then years. Tapply and Gil went into business together, tied by an irrevocable bond. If one went down, they both did.

Roz Hoffing, in one of her monthly cash envelopes, found a note ordering her to hire a new lawyer for her husband. The bills would be taken care of by her nameless benefactor. Martinez told me the lawyer was under investigation because he also represented Gil.

After a visit to Vinita, the lawyer told Gil that Tommy was getting better, that he was coming out of the deep depression that had held him mute for so long.

Tommy Hoffing became a problem to be solved — along with Gil, who panicked all over again, just as he had eight years ago.

Tapply, in the county jail awaiting trial, kept his silence, but from the evidence, I pieced together a plausible scenario. Tapply helped Tommy escape and killed Gil, intending to place the blame on Tommy and make sure Tommy was killed while trying to evade the police. It might have worked if Charley hadn't entered the Green Room just in time to see Iris's dragonfly pendant clutched in Gil's lifeless hand.

After that it got messy. Tapply was torn. He could parlay his up-and-coming musician's plight into record sales or he could shine the light on Tommy Hoffing and end the fugitive's short run. Maybe he wanted too much.

Unless Tapply talked, we'd never know why the guard at the Greenwood pharmacy was killed. Perhaps the purpose was to establish that Tommy Hoffing was in Tulsa. Perhaps Tapply needed drugs to sedate Tommy. Tell that to Derrick Johnson's widow and three children.

Where had Tommy Hoffing hid during those weeks? When the police searched Allan's house, they found a room in the basement that could have been a prison. The door was secured with a heavy padlock, and in a corner of the windowless room, blankets were jumbled. Police gathered hair samples from the blankets.

When faced with the evidence, Allan broke. He said Tapply brought Tommy by late one night after Tommy's escape and told Allan to find a place for him to stay. One outlaw to another. Allan was afraid of Tommy, but he was more afraid of Tapply. What was he supposed to do?

I remembered the day Tapply and I had grappled in the hallway at Allan Jakes's house. Had he been checking on his prisoner? Had Tommy Hoffing been on the other side of the padlocked door in the basement? It stabbed me with guilt just to think about it.

One thing I was sure of: Roz Hoffing had believed in her husband. I envied her that faith. And I hoped she never discovered the part I played in her husband's death.

She came by to see me at the newspaper office a few days after the funeral.

I rose from my chair and stepped in front of my desk to greet her — as I always do when someone visits — and for the first time, I realized the movement wasn't one of hospitality but was instead an instinctive need to protect myself and my space.

When did that start, I wondered.

"You doing okay?"

Her face was haggard, but she nodded and fingered the pack of cigarettes in her pocket. "Do you mind?"

I found an ashtray in my desk drawer and pushed it toward her. We both sat.

I hadn't spoken to her since the day I dropped her off at her brother's house on Stick Ross Mountain, although I had seen her from a distance at Tommy Hoffing's funeral.

Hank had sent me there to cover the story. I would have gone anyway. Nearly a thousand people jostled for a final glimpse of Oklahoma's notorious killer. Roz sat at the front of the chapel, dressed in a new black dress, her sons on either side. She somehow looked regal.

The circus atmosphere angered me, but by the time I wrote the story for Hank, my anger had mellowed into sorrow. It began with these words: "In life Tommy Hoffing commanded our fear; in death, our respect."

"That was a nice write up you gave Tommy," Roz now said. She glanced around the newspaper office, took a long drag on her cigarette and then slumped into her chair as though she were exhausted.

"Are you back home now?"

She nodded. "The newspapers are done botherin' us. It's peaceful out there."

"That guy who drove the truck with the cowcatcher? Club Callahan? He's been transferred from the hospital to the county jail," I said. "I went to see him the other day."

Roz stirred at this news. "Why did he act so crazy?"

"Maybe he was," I said. "He apologized for running me off the road. Said things got out of hand. Tapply told him to keep an eye on us, and he did with a vengeance. But when Tapply ordered him to come to the park that night and kill me, that was too much. He refused, and Tapply shot him instead. Somehow he made it to the park."

Neither of us seemed to have much to say after that. I played with a pencil. Roz studied her nicotine-stained fingers and finished her cigarette. I figured she had come for a reason, and would reveal it in its own time.

After a long silence, Roz spoke. "A lot of folks come to see Tommy the other day." She watched me closely as she said it.

"It was a nice service."

"One of them TV shows from Hollywood called me up. They want to do a story about Tommy."

"What did you say?" I was only mildly interested in her answer.

"I told 'em you was goin' to write a book. That we were collaborators." Roz stumbled over the word.

"What!"

"Well we could, you know."

"I don't know. I'd have to think about it."

After she left, I turned the card with her phone number on it over and over in my hands while the idea grew on me. A book might be the only way the whole story could ever be told. "The whole story," I mocked myself. As if anyone could ever know the whole story.

Perhaps writing a book would help me dig up more answers. For instance, why had Gil paid Roz all those years? Out of a sense of guilt?

In fact, there was a lot I might never know. Unanswered questions. They nagged at me like something caught in my teeth. Like an itch I couldn't reach.

FORTY-FOUR

I was driving a borrowed older model Nissan these days, hoping that an insurance settlement would help me buy a suitable replacement for the Trooper. As I drove up to Charley's and my house, I saw that his van was parked beside it. In fact, one wheel had flattened a clump of daffodil spears. The squashed daffodils made me realize spring had arrived. Spring, the season of love and renewal, of thunderstorms and tornadoes.

Inside the house, Charley sat on the sofa with his Takamine, picking out notes and singing a song I didn't recognize. His eyes flickered when I came in, but when he saw who it was, he bent to the guitar again.

"She comes and she comes and she goes like the rain," he sang in a soft voice that was unlike his harsher stage voice. I had given up long ago trying to guess whether the "she" in his songs meant me or someone else. That kind of stuff can drive you crazy.

I set a bag of French bread and a bottle of wine on the kitchen counter and then turned to study him. His thinning hair hadn't been cut recently, and it strayed over his ears. A collarbone jutted through the thin fabric of his R.E.M. T-shirt, and I was suddenly overcome with tenderness.

I walked over to him and put a hand over one of his. He stopped playing and looked up at me with his deep indigo eyes.

"Come outside," I said.

Silently, he put the guitar down and followed me down the steps and down the trail to the rock he had once jokingly called Honesty Rock. I wondered if he remembered.

The afternoon was sunny, and a warm breeze fanned the branches above us. Far below, a red squirrel drank from the edge of a deep pool in Spring Creek. The water reflected the blue sky like a tin mirror, wavery and changing.

Charley and I fitted ourselves into the natural bowls of the rock, and we sat while the afternoon turned to dusk, and the breeze died to a whisper.

I was afraid of losing Charley, and I didn't know what to say that could possibly make a difference. In my younger days, I melted men with tears, but that was before I learned that some pain is too deep for tears. Some pain reaches deep down inside you to your most secret, most tender places, and rips you apart. Tears would cheapen that pain.

The whole situation suddenly seemed clear. "We're drowning in physical courage," I said to Charley. "You stayed silent and went to jail rather than betray Iris. I risked my life to learn the truth — even if it meant losing you. What we don't have is moral courage."

"Moral courage?" Charley seemed to taste the words.

"We lack faith. If you had faith in me, you would have told me what was going on and let me be a part of it; if I had faith, I would have known you couldn't be guilty of the things you were accused of, no matter how the evidence stacked up against you."

"It takes moral courage to do the things we did."

"We did them for the wrong reasons, though. We did them because we lacked faith in the people we loved the most."

"That son of a bitch thought he could kill us both," Charley said. "Throw us off the cliff and make it look like a suicide pact. Or, I don't know, maybe a murder-suicide. Then there wouldn't have been anyone left to accuse him of anything except that poor-excuse-for-a-man Allan Jakes."

The light deepened and erased all shadows. Nearby, an owl called.

"I'm learning, though," I said. "About faith. Give me some more time."

There was another long silence.

Finally, Charley took my hands in his. "Time," he said. "Given enough time, there's nothing good sex won't heal."

We looked into each other's eyes then, really looked, past the shallows and into the secret depths to read what lay there. In some odd sense, over the years we had become Siamese twins, twined together by more than flesh and blood.

"You know what we really need?" Charley said. "A big platter of buckwheat pancakes. And I'm just the guy to make them."

I could tell from his voice that it was an effort to say the words of con-ciliation, but the important thing was that he was trying. It made me want to cry.

I swallowed hard. "Hash browns on the side?"

"And scrambled eggs."

We went up the hill hand-in-hand to start the fire.

THE END

ABOUT THE AUTHOR

Letha Albright has worked in newspapers, in a sawmill and as a wilderness guide. Since 1989, she has been the editor of *School & Community*, a magazine for Missouri teachers. She earned an undergraduate degree in psychology in Oklahoma and a master's degree in journalism from the University of Missouri. Albright lives in Columbia, Missouri, with her husband, two children and a cat. In her free time, she climbs rocks and hikes. Albright lived in Cherokee County, Oklahoma, the setting for her novel, for eight years.

Dark Oak 2000 Mystery Contest

Grand Prize Winner will be announced in Fall 2000.

~

Visit our website at www.oaktreebooks.com for information on the winners, guidelines for the upcoming Dark Oak 2001, and details on our other fine books.

~

Oak Tree Press books are available at Barnes & Noble and other fine bookstores, Amazon.com and other internet booksellers, or direct from the publisher.

~

For more information, send SASE to:

Oak Tree Press
915 W. Foothill Blvd. #411
Claremont, CA 91711-3356
909/625-8400 Tel   909/624-3930 Fax